COSEGA
SPHERE

COSEGA
SPHERE

Brandt Legg

LAUGHING RAIN

Cosega Sphere (Book Four of the Cosega Sequence)

Published in the United States of America by Laughing Rain

Cataloging-in-Publication data for this book is available from the Library of Congress.
ISBN-13: 978-1-935070-26-9
ISBN-10: 1-935070-26-6

Cover designed by: Jarowe

PUBLISHER'S NOTE
This book is a work of fiction. Names, characters, places and incidents are products of the author's imagination or are used fictitiously. Any resemblance to actual persons, living or dead, businesses, events or locales is entirely coincidental.

BrandtLegg.com

For Teakki and Ro

one

"They're alive," Taz, a young operative, said to his superior, a man known only as Stellard. As a cool mist rose off the distant Potomac River, the two men quietly considered the implications.

"You're certain?" Stellard asked, eyeing Taz, whom he'd personally selected nearly seven years earlier to lead the search. Seven long years of few leads, countless dead ends, and zero proof that the pair of fugitives they sought, who had officially been declared dead by the US government, were anything but dead.

Taz nodded. "Both of them, alive and well." He traced a finger over the five gold rings on his right hand, imagining a fight. He often jabbed his fists in quick thrusts, as if he *had* to punch something, or someone.

"Then the Eysen . . . it survived, too?" Stellard asked, briskly rubbing his icy hands together. His many layers of clothing offering inadequate protection on the brisk morning, though he was always cold anyway.

"There's no doubt," Taz replied, unzipping his light leather jacket, only a tee shirt beneath. He was never cold. "They *are* alive," he repeated calmly.

From the fourth level of the nine-story parking garage, Stellard looked down on the busy highway. An electrical relay station was visible, spread across the adjoining property. He knew it would be impossible for someone to monitor their conversation. This location topped the Foundation's safe-list for just that reason, yet *this* information, that Ripley Gaines and Gale Asher were alive, was enough to make the impossible suddenly doable. He shivered against the cool air of an early spring Northern Virginia morning and nervously glanced up at the concrete ceiling, reflexively looking for "eyes" and "ears."

Taz knew what the older man was thinking. He could tell the worry Stellard usually displayed had now stretched into fear. "I thought you'd be pleased."

Stellard sighed and squinted his dark eyes out toward the traffic before speaking. "Of course. But you see, as long as we were searching, there was a chance . . . " He sipped from a large paper cup of hot tea and started over. "You see, if the Eysen really had been destroyed, then the world would be safer. So many would be safer."

He mumbled something inaudible, but Taz didn't respond. He didn't understand, but it wasn't his job to understand. He'd been recruited seven years earlier by the Aylantik Foundation to find two dead people. The Foundation, a secretive organization with seemingly unlimited funding, was a private "think-tank" that employed futurists, scientists, engineers, economists, as well as former members of the military and intelligence communities. The brain trust was charged with planning and preparing for the future, a future that they would help shape. However, the Foundation had an even more covert mission within its hidden work—to locate Gaines and Asher.

The pair, Gaines, an archaeologist, and Asher, a reporter, had allegedly been killed by US government agents while trying to escape with an ancient artifact of immense scientific significance. The Foundation needed to be sure they were dead, and more importantly, that the Eysen no longer existed.

Stellard took another look around, then moved closer to Taz. In a raspy whisper, he asked the single most dangerous question he'd ever voiced.

"Do you know where the Eysen is?"

"Yes," Taz mouthed, nodding slowly. "I'm heading there now."

two

"They're coming," Kruse said, voice strained, as the vehicle bounced over a large pothole.

Gale Asher, who'd been on the run for nearly seven years, had never been so terrified. Kruse, a man she trusted with her life, mainly because he'd saved it so many times, looked as close to panicked as she'd ever seen. Gale didn't care about that though. She didn't want to know about panic and problems, she only wanted her daughter to be okay.

The details of the accident were vague. Cira, her and Rip's six-year-old daughter, had been hurt at school and airlifted to the hospital on a neighboring island. It was serious enough that emergency surgery had already begun in order to save her life.

Kruse navigated the rutted dirt roads as fast as he dared. Their armored Range Rover vibrated across the washboard surface, jarring Gale's already shot nerves.

"We have to get you out of the country," Kruse said, concerned, glancing at Gale's distraught face. He'd devoted too many years to keeping the beautiful fugitive alive to risk losing her now.

"As soon as we get Cira," Gale said firmly. "Any word from Rip?"

"He's in the air."

"Coming here?" Gale asked, relieved. Her curly blond ponytail swayed wildly in the dusty air.

"No." Kruse hesitated. "El Perdido."

"What?" Gale shouted. "Why isn't he coming here?"

"Because *they* are coming," Kruse snapped back. "They know where you are."

"How?" she asked, as if hearing it for the first time, finally letting it register that her daughter wasn't just in danger from the surgery she was undergoing, but that there were people on the way who would kill them all.

"The hospital," Kruse responded more evenly. "They took blood."

"But we're in Fiji. We're isolated from the rest of the world, that's why we chose—"

"The hospitals are all linked around the world now," Kruse said, interrupting her. "Ever since Eysen-INU 4.0. It's instant."

Almost everyone on the planet used Eysen-INU or "Information Navigation Units" to communicate, compute, surf the internet, take video and photos, watch movies, and generally do everything. The Eysen-INU was indispensable, virtually replacing phones, cameras, laptops, and desktop computers. The INU design and technology had been modeled after the Eysen artifact, what they now called the "Sphere."

Gale shook her head, staring out the window as a glimpse of the ocean came into view between the trees. "Who's coming?"

"All of them." The tattoo on Kruse's right wrist showed as he swung the wheel around, taking a sharp turn, depicting five bullets penetrating a heart. A new bullet was added each time he killed a person, something he never enjoyed doing, but suddenly it looked very likely that it would be happening again. Kruse, an experienced intelligence operative, who relied on logic and strategy to keep his clients and himself alive, could sense the coming war.

Gale nodded. Of course they were all coming. She hadn't even needed to ask. "How long do we have?"

"Maybe four hours."

"Will Cira be out of surgery by then?"

"If all goes well."

"Then we'll be okay. We can make it," Gale said hopefully. The lush jungle blurring past had once seemed so familiar and safe, but now, like everything, it had become another obstacle.

Kruse didn't think so, but it wasn't the time for that news. Gale Asher was a cool and smart reporter. She'd even developed into quite a scientist since he'd known her, but she was also a mother, and the threat of losing her daughter could turn her into a hysterical, irrational fighter. That was not what he needed at the moment.

However, Gale knew Rip would not have willingly flown away when his daughter was in danger. "Does Rip know Cira is in surgery? Does he know how serious this is?"

Kruse did not answer.

"Does he?" she demanded.

He turned and saw fury flash in her normally magnetic blue eyes. "Gale, it would have been impossible to get him on the plane to El Perdido if he knew about Cira. We told him your cover's been blown and that we're following the 'exit.'"

The exit, a long-in-place and ever-changing plan in case of threat, dictated their moves. Everyone would get out from wherever they were and rendezvous at El Perdido, or, if that were impossible, a list of other "temporarily safe" locations had been memorized.

El Perdido, Spanish for "the Lost," was a remote island far off the Pacific coast of Central America, which had been turned into perhaps the greatest and most comfortable hideout in the world. It was luxurious and beautiful, with every imaginable amenity, and Gale despised it.

Yet their time on the island had saved them from the many groups still searching for them. The world's wealthiest person, Booker Lipton, had funded the island and everything else during their escape and years in hiding. Booker, even more secretive than wealthy, had obtained a reputation as a rogue and dangerous businessman, accused of everything from murder, to treason, to inciting revolution and funding wars. Much of it was true.

Gale, Rip, and their daughter's life were in his hands.

"He's never going to forgive you," she said. "If Cira doesn't make it . . . "

Gale began to cry. She thought of their daughter's bright smile. They'd named her for the Italian word meaning the sun because the sun had been the key to understanding the Cosega Sequence, but it had come to mean so much more as Cira brought light into their lives.

"Cira's going to make it," Kruse growled as Gale wiped away her tears. He also loved Cira. He loved her as much as he'd ever allowed himself to love anyone. "My job is to keep all of you alive. I'm doing my damned job. You have to trust me." He reached across and put his hand on Gale's shoulder. "Times like this, you and Rip are in no frame of mind to decide what to do."

"I know," she said quietly, stifling back tears. She clutched Cira's tiny cloth cat that she'd grabbed on her dash out of the house. Cira slept with it every night, told it her secrets, and used it as a worry doll. "Do we really have four hours?"

"It depends where the agents are." Kruse swerved to avoid a fallen tree. "The NSA doesn't have anyone in Fiji, so they'll borrow someone from the CIA out of Sydney. It's a four-hour flight. The Foundation will have people in LA, that's ten hours, but they could have already been in the air for half an hour or more. Who they have in Hawaii and New Zealand is the real question."

Gale reflected on this. Ever since Rip and she had decided to flee with the Eysen, an impossibly futuristic basketball-sized artifact pulled from an eleven-million-year-old cliff in the mountain forests of Virginia, their lives had been in constant danger. The NSA, FBI, Mossad, and secret Vatican agents had relentlessly pursued them.

Then, seven years ago, they faked their deaths, which had purchased some temporary peace. But when "their" horribly burned bodies, to the point of cremation, could not be conclusively identified, some doubted whether it had really been Gaines and Asher. Because the stakes were so incredibly high, they had continued to be pursued, even in "death."

Rip had called the Sphere "an instrument to view eternity." It showed them events stretching from the origins of the universe into the future, but Gale believed it also held within its core the very essence of existence. In passing, they'd seen cures for cancer and other diseases, plans for astonishing inventions, planets and places too incredible to believe. However, navigating back to where they wanted to go had proved deeply challenging.

Booker had assembled a secret team of science's greatest minds to study the ancient object. One of his companies had managed to partially reverse-engineer the Eysen-Sphere, and had marketed it as the Eysen-INU. Far more than just the ultimate computer, the INU combined and eclipsed every electronic device by decades. He'd sold billions of them, and they continued selling. His power and wealth grew in tandem with the unprecedented sales.

Although the INUs were nowhere as sophisticated as the real object, even though they had so far surpassed any technology the world had seen before — portable and powerful, they did everything, and came preloaded with incredible amounts of information — the Eysen-INU had revolutionized the consumption of information and knowledge. Booker owned one hundred percent of his companies, so the Eysen had taken him from being a common billionaire to becoming the world's first and only trillionaire.

Revelations released from the Eysen had led to the collapse of all the major religions in the world. During the years since the find, and although the Vatican had officially folded, a potent underground movement had emerged in an effort to bring the Catholic Church back to its prior glory. But as dangerous as Gale considered the religious zealots to be, it was the Foundation that scared her the most.

Kruse felt the same way about the Foundation, and at that very moment he was desperately hoping that their intelligence was correct about the Foundation having no agents closer than Los Angeles. The commercial Eysen-INUs marketed by Booker had made the world a smaller place, one in which it was harder to hide. The only advantage they had left was their head start against those coming for them, but Kruse never liked to count on time, because he absolutely knew that time was a funny thing.

three

Taz, wearing his standard black t-shirt, black jeans, leather jacket, and brown construction boots, boarded one of the Foundation's many "new generation" private jets twenty minutes after wrapping the meeting with Stellard. A commercial airliner might take him twenty hours to reach Fiji, but the Foundation pilot could make it there in about twelve.

Still too long, he thought, *but the world is a big place and it takes time to get around. Hopefully the team in the Philippines will get Gaines and Asher long before I reach Fiji.*

A beautiful Foundation "travel executive" brought him a drink. They exchanged smiles, and he remembered an encounter with her six or seven months earlier.

Taz attracted women like a rock star. Maybe it was the green eyes, or the short, shaggy dark hair, or the biceps and his "cut" physique. Taz never gave it too much thought, just took the parties when they came. If asked, he might have chalked it up to the heavy gold rings which adorned his right hand, but most of the women would say it was his intense energy, as if he'd just blasted off the screen as the hero in a "save-the-world" action movie. This time, as he took a few swift punches at the air, he'd have to take a rain check on the private party. There was too much work to do.

He checked the time. His people would reach the hospital in Suva in less than five hours. The girl, Gaines' and Asher's daughter, was still in surgery. No way they could move her that soon. Taz smiled.

Fugitives should not have children, he thought. *Gaines has been the target of the greatest manhunt in history. He's miraculously eluded everyone from the top intelligence agencies for almost seven years. And now he goes and gets himself caught due to a six-year-old's playground accident.*

Taz read the report on his Eysen-INU. The little girl had been playing, and somehow a game the children called "ribbon tag" became bloody after one child had sneaked in a pair of scissors to cut the ribbons. After a chase and tangle, Gaines' daughter fell, the open scissors penetrating her eyes.

Every parent's nightmare, he thought, *but much more for Gaines and Asher. Even if their daughter doesn't lose her sight, she's going to lose her parents.*

Another update came in. The NSA and CIA were sending units to Fiji, including a crew from Sydney, Australia—three hours out. *Damn, they'll beat us! That's going to complicate things.*

He scanned the maps. Nothing closer than Manila. *No wonder they chose Fiji. There's nothing close enough to threaten them.*

He messaged Stellard. They could try to bribe someone in the hospital, or the local police, but doing that long distance was almost impossible. They could work contacts within the US government, but the prize was too great and could not be shared. That also ruled out the Mossad, who were, most likely, also on their way. The final option Taz suggested made Stellard's mouth go dry. It was too great a risk.

"What happens if the NSA gets them?" Taz asked, defending his proposal. "Or the Israelis?"

"We've looked for these two for more than seven years and you want to just let them go?" Stellard said, adjusting the temperature of the space heater near his feet. "We may not ever find them again."

"I'm *not* saying let them go," he said, his rings clicking along the side of the INU. One of them was set with a small round sapphire representing his prey—Gaines and the Sphere. "But our only play here might be to tip them off, get them to trust us, use the satellites, and track them. There are only so many ways to escape a small island surrounded by thousands of miles of ocean."

Stellard understood the stakes far better than Taz did, and knew that the Foundation had enough power that it might be able to pry the fantastical artifact away from the CIA, or even the NSA, but that would be an unacceptably long shot. On the other hand, if Gaines and Asher escaped and Taz followed their every movement, then the Foundation might be able to get the fugitives to cooperate. They'd had seven years to study the Eysen-Sphere; surely that kind of knowledge would save the Foundation's own scientists an enormous amount of time. Time the Foundation desperately needed as the deadline for launching the ultra-secret future-altering plan known as the Phoenix Initiative was looming. Delays caused by uncertainties in the computer models for the complex operations had been frustrating the Foundation's leadership for months, and after the Phoenix Initiative, the risks would be even greater. Flawless leadership would be required to guide the world through its greatest transformation since the dawn of modern man.

"What about Booker?" Stellard asked, then mumbled something Taz couldn't hear.

Taz stared back at his superior's image, projected from his Eysen-INU. It was a fair question. Booker was not to be underestimated. He also had the resources to track Gaines, and then there were the BLAXERs, the small army he employed, a force that far exceeded the number and skill level of the Foundation's agents. Additionally, Booker had every advantage due to the enormous wealth at his disposal, much of it derived from Eysen, Inc., his privately held company, which had a market cap of $1.8 trillion. His other holdings were difficult to evaluate, but most estimates pegged them somewhere between $100 and $300 billion. The Foundation had considerable funding behind it, but nothing close to that level.

"If he doesn't know we're converging on Fiji—" Taz began.

"Don't be a fool," Stellard interrupted. "Booker knew before you did."

"He can't win them all."

"I can't think of any he's lost."

"Then he's due," Taz persisted. "It doesn't matter. We don't have many options here. You decide. Let the CIA get him, or follow them. Which is riskier?"

"Which is *smarter*?" Stellard tended toward caution, while his protégée more often played with the devil.

If there had been time, Stellard feared the Eysen enough that he would have used the Foundation's contacts within the US military to bomb Fiji into oblivion. An operation like that would take weeks to put into place though, and the obvious fallout would make that kind of bold strike impossible until they were closer to the Phoenix launch date. Still, nothing less than the future of the human race depended on either capturing or killing Ripley Gaines.

four

Booker Lipton set down his five-nut herbal smoothie, answered his scrambled phone, and listened while Rip Gaines blasted a string of obscenities.

"Are you through?" Booker asked calmly, only after Rip paused to breathe.

"Are you going to authorize my return to Fiji?" Rip shouted.

"No way, Rip. That would be suicide, and you know it."

"Cira and Gale are there!" Rip insisted breathlessly. "I'm not going to leave them to get captured, while I run away. My daughter, Booker, my *daughter*!"

Rip thought back to the time the Sphere had shown him his death. By then he'd been used to the Sphere's giving exact weather forecasts months in advance, including earthquakes and other natural disasters. He'd routinely seen world events such as worker's strikes, plane crashes, fires, elections, and other seemingly minor events, long before they happened. The problem was, he didn't know how to control it. He couldn't get back to the places where he saw those events, or to the point that had given details of his death. But while there, he'd had a choice.

Did he *want* to know how? Did Gale want to know her date? Cira's?

Gale had declined, thinking it would weigh on her too much, and both decided they could not bear knowing Cira's. In the end, Rip didn't want to know the cause of his death, but he'd noted the date and memorized it, right down to the exact second of his final breath. Now he wished he'd found out Gale and Cira's dates as well. Then he would at least know . . .

It wasn't safe to take out the Sphere while on the run, but as soon as they reached El Perdido, he decided he would immediately go deep into the swirling universe of the Eysen.

"Kruse and Harmer are with them in Fiji," Booker said. "You know they'll get them out safely."

"What was the security breach?" Rip asked. They hadn't told him about Cira's accident. The BLAX agents accompanying him to Hawaii had only said that there had been a major breach and he could not go home.

"We don't know exactly," Booker lied, "but Foundation and CIA agents are en route."

"I need to talk to Gale."

In the years since the discovery of the Eysen-Sphere, Rip had occasionally felt as if he lived in another world, another time, or perhaps what could be more accurately described as another dimension. Gale had managed to keep him grounded, but she also walked on the fringes of reality when exploring the Sphere. Cira, more than just a daughter, had been their anchor to the present day. Without her joyful presence, they certainly would have been consumed by the depths of the ancient Sphere long ago.

"You know it's not safe to contact Gale now. We're in an exit. No communications."

The constantly rehearsed evacuation plans and the numerous contingencies to deal with imminent dangers and blown covers were collectively known as "exit." The procedures had been memorized, the steps meticulously designed. Their lives were at risk, and only by perfectly following every procedure of the exit could they hope to survive. Rip understood.

"Damn it, Booker, if you're lying . . . If Cira and Gale are not safe and waiting for me when I get to the rendezvous, I'll never forgive you. I'll shut down the Eysen, and I swear . . . "

Rip owed everything to Booker, and definitely the last seven years of his life, but he also knew that the trillionaire lied easily, and that he would mislead anyone whenever necessary to achieve his goals.

Rip finally voiced his greatest concern.

"Are they still alive?"

"I assure you that Gale and Cira are very much alive. We're taking care of them. Just get to the rendezvous and everything will be all right."

"No, it won't. They know we were in Fiji. The NSA will track everything in and out of there for the last year. They'll trace me to Honolulu, and they'll run down every boat or plane leaving Fiji from yesterday on until they catch us." Rip's voice shook with anger and fear. "The NSA will probably be at the rendezvous before I get there."

"Get ahold of yourself, Rip. I've kept you safe for seven years. There is a plan in place, just follow the damned procedures."

Rip thought about Booker's priorities; the Eysen-Sphere, the greater good. Sacrifices could be made.

"You'll sacrifice Gale, or Cira, if need be, to protect the Sphere," Rip said.

"I don't deny that," Booker replied. "You know what's at stake. But I don't have to. Trust me and we'll get through this."

Rip remained silent, realizing no other options existed. Even if he *could* get away from his BLAX escorts, he didn't have any money, not that that mattered. The NSA, CIA, Mossad, or the Foundation would pick him up in a matter of minutes if he broke cover.

However, there was one possible escape route. During their years in Fiji, he'd had to go to Hawaii a number of times. Although Booker paid to have a decent lab built in their island house, the real Eysen research was done at the University of Hawaii. Booker had funded a major archaeology department as a cover and to facilitate Rip's continued work on the Sphere. He'd covertly brought a group of the brightest scientists in the world — contractually sworn to secrecy and subject to AX monitoring — to help analyze the Sphere, utilizing the most sophisticated equipment available, some of it actually derived from plans contained within the Sphere itself. Booker also had a team at the university using data obtained during those sessions to further electronically dissect the original Eysen in order to continue to improve the mass-produced INU models, which had recently been reduced to the size of a softball.

Rip thought about donning the elaborate feature-altering disguise he used to get in and out of Honolulu. *If I can somehow get back to Hawaii, I've got contacts there that I can trust. Someone will help me. Maybe there's a way . . .*

But there were too many ifs, too many unknowns.

How will I even find Gale and Cira now that they're on the move? No, I better stick to the plan. Booker will get them to the rendezvous, or else I'll shut down the Sphere.

"I discovered a long time ago that it's usually not a good idea to trust people who say 'trust me,'" Rip finally said. "But I also know that trusting you has always been the right path."

Booker thanked him. After the call, the trillionaire immediately pulled up a screen and checked on Rip's daughter, who was still in surgery. Cira could easily die, but even if she lived, the price would most likely be permanent blindness. Rip would hate Booker for keeping that from him, but before he could tackle that unpleasantness, he still had to save her.

Booker's AX and BLAX armies already had dozens of personnel in Fiji, plus Harmer and Kruse were on the scene. Every minute that passed meant teams of agents from at least four different adversaries were getting closer to converging on the hospital. Without the opportunity to arrest either Ripley Gaines or Gale Asher, they would all want their daughter. How was he going to prevent them from taking a helpless six-year-old?

The tragic timing of the accident, which forced them to run again, could not have been worse. Rip, now completely distracted by the fate of Cira and Gale, had already been facing down a ticking time bomb, the Foundation's Phoenix Initiative. Unlocking the Sphere meant more than discovering the wonders of the universe or fantastic technological advances, it held the fate of all of civilization.

In the years since the discovery, Rip and Gale, along with Booker's corps of top scientists, had been racing to prevent the future shown in the Eysen-Sphere and prophesized by an earlier Sphere-holder known as Clastier. What originally seemed like ample time had quickly closed in on them as the Sphere proved mind-bogglingly vast, as in containing *all* of time and space, and had been growing increasingly more unpredictable. "It's impossible to tame," Rip often said.

They had cracked enough of the Cosega Sequence — the Sphere's computer-like boot-up process — that they understood basic navigation and much of what they saw. However, the Sphere's complexities seemed to grow constantly, always outstripping their capacity to master it.

"Something is missing in the Sequence. Another way of looking at it, or another layer," Rip had said years earlier when he presided over the first secret meeting with Booker's scientists. He and the others had become convinced that if they could uncover more about the origins of the Cosegans and the Sphere, they could find that missing key.

The Sphere's stunning views of the world had convinced the scientists that the future, and humanity's existence, were doomed unless they could discover how to use its power to change the planet's destiny.

The pressure weighed on everyone involved. Two of the scientists had already committed suicide in the face of overwhelming odds at stopping it — a chain of events, already underway, which would lead to the culmination of the three *Death Divinations*: A super plague that would kill billions, irreversible climate destabilization, and World War III.

five

Gale grabbed her pack as they dashed from the Range Rover toward the waiting chopper. Everything she needed was in there. She'd been prepared to run, they all had, and in some way she'd been running every second since they discovered the Eysen-Sphere.

Kruse climbed into the small helicopter after Gale. It would fly them to the hospital in the capital city of Suva, on the island of Viti Levu. Fiji was made up of hundreds of small islands, on one of which Gale, Rip, and Cira had been living for almost five years. Cira had been airlifted with Harmer from the school playground almost ninety minutes earlier.

For the first year after Gale and Rip "died," they bounced around the world in a dizzying whirl of travel where they almost never slept in the same place for more than one night. The tension, the constant fear of being caught, and the race to dig deeper into the Eysen's secrets set a grueling and unsustainable pace. Finally, when Gale became pregnant, Booker moved them to El Perdido.

At first it was a wonderful reprieve, but other than a small staff, along with Kruse, Harmer, and a few other AX agents, they were alone. Gale came to see the isolated island as a prison. She wanted Cira to grow up with other children, and after convincing Booker, they selected Fiji. Its remote location made it a natural choice, and was big enough to get lost in, yet small enough to be safe.

They'd been happy there. Cira had thrived in her small English school. Gale had even started to occasionally feel normal, as normal as one could feel while looking into the Sphere every day. They watched, miraculously, as if a portion of the universe had been a high definition look at both the origin and end of the world.

Now they would have to return to El Perdido . . . if they made it out of Fiji in time.

How could she not have seen this coming in the Sphere? They'd been so focused on trying to understand who the creators of the original Eysen had been, the ones they called the Cosegans. Rip and Gale believed if they found answers to what they called the five Cosega mysteries within the Sphere, they could possibly uncover the key to stopping the Divinations:

1. *What is the Sphere?*
2. *Who were the Cosegans?*
3. *Where did they come from?*
4. *Why did they leave the Sphere?*
5. *What happened to them?*

After successfully decoding what Rip called the "first layer" of the Cosega Sequence, they had spent years exploring its endless views and information. Even after all that though, they still could not comprehend the enormity of the Sphere, nor imagine a fraction of what it could do.

Gale's mind had become cluttered with what she referred to as "exSpheriences," some of the most haunting of which were her talks with dead people. At times the conversations threatened her sanity, but many gave her peace. Through the Sphere she had found forgiveness from Fisher and Tuke, two men who had died after innocently helping them escape. She and Rip had also encountered Topper, an old family friend killed by Vatican agents, "out on the plane," as they called the part of the Sphere where they found the dead.

Gale didn't call them dead anymore. She preferred "departed," since they seemed to have only left Earth but still existed somewhere. So far Gale had not encountered the Stadler brothers, two more friends lost to the fight to save the Sphere, but she'd had several long talks with Larsen.

Larsen had been Rip's closest friend, and technically the one who really found the Sphere. He and Gale had also dated for a brief period before she met Rip. Gale recalled the first time, after Larsen's death, when she had encountered her old friend inside the Sphere. He had appeared as a projection from the Eysen-Sphere, and although Gale believed in life after death, she had seen him shot to death by a Vatican agent only a few feet away from her in the old Las Trampas church in New Mexico only months earlier, so the initial jolt left her stunned.

"I wondered if I'd see you and Rip again," were Larsen's first words.

Gale gasped, and then just stared.

"Don't be so surprised," Larsen continued. "You should know by now that the Eysen contains everything."

"Rip's asleep," Gale had said. "Should I wake him?"

"Next time. He'd only be jealous." Larsen smiled. "Rip thinks he's an archaeologist, but one day he'll realize that he's just wandering in the dark, limited by the physical."

"Where are you? What's it like?"

"I'm not sure how to answer that. The earthly plane is like a pinpoint in the universe. I'm everywhere, as well as being there, just not physically. And Gale, it's good. I can see and feel everything. I explore time. It's beyond anything I could even make you understand."

Larsen swirled around and split into billions of points of light.

"I am able to appear as you remember me by connecting our auras at a subatomic level, the makeup of human form as occupied by the energetic particles far smaller than what physicists call quarks and leptons. I mean *infinitely* tinier."

His voice filled with excitement, but still came out as a loud whisper. Gale couldn't decide if it was a dream.

"The soul is real, and it consists of trillions of universes within each of us. It's a circle both within us, and what we are within."

And then he was gone.

Her thoughts went back to Rip and what they still had to do. ExSpheriences were one thing, but somehow they needed to find the missing layer of the Cosega Sequence and answer the five Cosegan mysteries.

Recent discoveries by Rip and the team in Hawaii might bring them much closer to all of it, as well as the solution for stopping the Death Divinations. Rip had made his latest trip to confirm the new theories which might finally grant them full access to the ultimate power contained within the Sphere.

It holds everything ever, Gale thought. *Surely it can save my daughter, too.*

−O−

Harmer, a cigarette held tightly in her lips, met them on the helipad. The stocky woman, who looked older than her age of thirty-nine, was like a second mother to Cira. A special bond had formed as she escorted her to and from school every day.

Always on guard, always knowing there were threats that could destroy them in a blink, Harmer had never figured the incident would be a kid with scissors on the playground. Gale could see the pain in her eyes as Harmer relayed everything that had happened and then stamped out her cigarette.

Kruse checked the sky again as they ducked inside the modern, one-story building. He knew time was working against them. While they probably still had a couple of hours, there could easily be a surprise at any moment.

He eyed everyone they passed. Anyone could be an agent, a leak, a mistake. He could feel it all crashing in on them. They were wasting time. They needed to get Gale out of there. The only thing working in their favor was that all the enemies coming toward them would attempt to take Gale alive because they needed the Eysen. Otherwise, the hospital would have already been leveled by a cruise missile or a drone strike.

"I don't understand," Gale was saying to Harmer as Kruse tuned back into their conversation.

"They will not let you into the operating room," Harmer replied as she led them quickly through the maze of hospital corridors, all of them looking identical.

"I'll wear a mask. Other than school, she's never been away from me. I'm her *mother*! They aren't going to do surgery without me in the room."

"No exceptions," Harmer said calmly.

They corralled Gale into the surgical waiting room, a large open area adjacent to an outdoor garden, filled with fake plants and old magazines. Harmer left to try and hunt down the doctor who had first seen Cira, but returned smelling of fresh nicotine ten minutes later without success. "We're lucky, Gale. The surgeon is a good one, trained in Australia and an eye specialist."

"But you said the admitting physician told you that Cira could lose her vision."

"Cira was a mess when she first came in. They had tried to clean her up in the chopper, but she was screaming so much it was hard enough to stabilize her. By the time they finally got her sedated, we were here."

"Oh, my poor little girl," Gale gasped.

"The doctor was giving the worst case, but the surgeon believes there's a good chance he can save her vision in at least one eye. Possibly both."

Gale thought of the time the Sphere had shown the inside of a flower as it grew and bloomed – the pulsing energy, the colors, the passion of nature. Later they saw what amounted to a time-lapse internal view of an oak tree growing from an acorn to a hundred year old giant. The Sphere had shown them nine months inside a woman's womb, even the creation of planets and stars. Gale knew nature had the power to heal anything. She pictured those events in the Sphere and silently begged for her daughter's eyes.

Another excruciatingly slow hour dragged by. Kruse spent most of the time on the roof, watching for trouble, listening to Booker's updates through a receiver fitted into his ear. The US government had mobilized a team of Navy SEALs. Their escape window was closing – fifty-seven minutes.

"Get her out of there!" Booker warned.

"She won't leave Cira," Kruse said.

"Once the SEALs get them, Gale will be confined to an offshore military prison and they'll use Cira to make her talk."

"I know, but she won't listen to reason."

"Then drug her," Booker ordered. "Just get her *out* of there."

Kruse returned to the waiting area at the same time the surgeon appeared. He was younger than Gale had expected, still in faded green scrubs, a surgical mask pulled down on his neck.

"Cira is okay," he said. "The procedure went well."

Gale let out a long breath. "Her vision?" she asked.

"Too soon to tell for sure. It'll be a few days before we can test that, but I'm extremely optimistic."

Gale closed her eyes, saying a silent prayer of thanks. "I don't know what to say. I'm so grateful for what you've done."

He nodded, smiling slightly. "You can go back and see her now, but she'll be under the anesthesia for at least another hour or so."

Gale looked at Harmer, who had tears in her eyes, and then back at the surgeon. "We want to take her home right away."

The surgeon looked confused, as if he hadn't heard her correctly. "Right away?"

"We want to take her home. . . *now*."

"What?" the surgeon said, suddenly irritated. "That's out of the question. She can't be moved for at least forty-eight hours, and she'll need to remain here for a minimum of two weeks. Maybe you don't realize exactly what she's been through. Any movement would dramatically increase her chances for blindness."

Gale looked back at Harmer, and then followed Harmer's glance to Kruse.

"Doctor, could I speak with you alone for a moment?" Kruse asked.

"Come on, Gale. Let's go see Cira," Harmer urged, ushering her away.

The scene wasn't as bad as Gale had imagined, but it was still difficult to bear. Cira's entire head was bandaged down to the tip of her nose. Her limp little body, hooked up to monitors and an IV, appeared tiny and lifeless. Gale took her hand and kneeled next to the bed until Harmer found a chair for her. She tucked Earth, the little cloth cat, in the sheets next to Cira. Harmer, knowing Cira's attachment to the animal, smiled.

A few minutes later Kruse came in and met Harmer's eyes. Kruse had already notified Harmer of the plan in her earpiece. "Gale, we're just about out of time. We have to leave Cira here for a few days, but Harmer will stay behind and bring her to you as soon as the doctor says she can move."

"I'm not leaving her," Gale declared with the conviction of a wounded tigress as she turned back to her daughter.

"Gale, I won't let anything happen to her," Harmer said. "I promise."

"You'll be dead, Harmer," Gale said without even turning around. "At least they won't kill me. They'll keep Cira and me as bait for Rip, but at least we'll be alive and together."

"What makes you think they won't move her?" Kruse asked.

"Because. I. Won't. Let. Them!"

Harmer grabbed her from behind as Kruse jabbed a needle into Gale's upper arm. After about twenty seconds of struggling, Gale slumped onto her daughter's bed. Eight minutes later, Kruse and a still unconscious Gale were on a helicopter heading to a small airstrip on the far side of the island. Booker had alerted him that Suva's Nausori Airport had just been shut down and all flights grounded. The Americans were on the way.

six

Stellard, part of the original group that had started the Aylantik Foundation, looked like a distinguished banker. His hair was graying at the temples of a square and sturdy face, etched with lines formed from serious deliberations. He was in charge of stopping problems before they became problems.

He'd long worried about Gaines and the Sphere. If they still existed, they could ruin *everything*, as in life as they knew it. Those thoughts kept him up nights, that made him constantly cold. He knew that if they could just launch the Phoenix Initiative, he would finally be warm.

More than anything, he believed in the organization's mission to save humanity. *The world is such a mess*, he thought as he stared at the giant globe which occupied a dark corner of his spacious office. The lighted globe, the size of an automobile and amazing in its detailed depictions of the Earth's geography, had been custom-made for him. It spun slowly by way of some brilliant mechanism he didn't understand, but the data it displayed—numbers of births, deaths, total population, airline flights, currency fluctuations, disease rates, wars, all manner of data—was something he definitely could comprehend. Through the Eysen-INU interface on his desk he could isolate and manipulate the date. A digital countdown clock on the wall above the globe displayed the number 364.

"It's fitting that three months before the Phoenix Initiative commences, we finally locate Gaines," he muttered to himself as he cleared some of the "clutter" from the globe. He shook his head, took a moment to try to warm his icy fingers, and then pushed the button.

The airline flights, represented by streams of clustered lines streaking across the world, made the planet appear scarred, and the pulsating population points reminded him of impact craters on the moon. With the globe clear, except for the final filter, the borders, which he kept in place, he marveled at the beauty of the planet. Another command entered into his Eysen-INU made the giant globe spin until Fiji was displayed front and center.

"We won't get there in time," he whispered to himself. "Where will they go?"

The phone buzzed, jarring him away from his thoughts. It could only be one person. His assistant had implicit instructions to block everyone else.

"Stellard," the familiar voice that always sounded like a college quarterback giving a locker room interview began on the other end of the secure line. "We're ahead of you, but it'll be only with military assets that we get them."

The voice belonged to Jeff Wattington, the Foundation's highest-ranking undercover contact within the US government. Stellard wasn't surprised. The CIA, NSA, and FBI had kept a small but well-funded group continuously searching for Gaines, Asher, and, more importantly, the original Eysen-Sphere, just in case any of them had survived. Just in case the blown chopper had been what they now knew it to be, an elaborate cover-up.

Immediately after the morning meeting with Taz, Stellard had sent a control number that would let Wattington know to call in. It had been a couple of years since the two men had communicated, but Stellard expected daily exchanges now. Now that the sky had fallen.

"How high?" Stellard asked, wanting to know how far up the chain of command the crisis had risen.

"It's a joint CIA/NSA operation," Wattington answered. "The President will be briefed only if and when they locate the Sphere."

"We may have to remind the President that she owes her position to the Foundation."

"This is not even on her radar yet. She wasn't in office when Gaines found the Sphere." Wattington paused, as if reading something. "She was an uninformed US Senator from California then."

"What about her connections to Booker?"

"As you know, Booker has influence, but with the history, specifically his corporate army engaging NSA operatives in Mexico and the southwest . . . " Wattington paused. "We may not be able to prove he was behind the killing of all those federal agents, but it's made everyone wary of getting too close to the rogue tycoon. And now that it's clear he was involved with the cover-up—"

"He's a snake," Stellard interrupted. "And clearly he's received more than just blueprints for the Eysen-INU from the Sphere. Who knows what Gaines has been feeding him for the last seven years!"

"Yes, it's extremely unnerving to the power structure."

Stellard nodded silently as he reached into his pocket for a hand-warmer. He knew that the power structure Wattington was referring to wasn't the current administration in Washington, or even a specific government from any other country. The real power structure was comprised of the wealthy elite who operated behind the scenes, the "string-pullers." Many belonged to the Foundation, some of them among its founders. They'd all seen what a relatively small amount of information from the Eysen-Sphere had done to the world's once great and mighty religions. It *ended* them. The fear within the US intelligence community lie in a single question.

What *else* did Booker have? What did he *know*? Although, after seven years without any new revelations, other than producing ever-smaller and faster commercial Eysen-INUs, Stellard had started to believe that the Eysen-Sphere might really have been destroyed.

Until today.

The Foundation had an even greater reason to worry about Booker and his Sphere. He would know the future. Not just the one originally "scripted" one, but the one the Foundation had carefully designed. He would know how to stop it. He was surely already trying to do just that.

"That's why we've never ended the search," Stellard said, shivering. "Booker without the Eysen-Sphere is a formidable foe, but with the Sphere he's the devil."

"On that, the Foundation and the US government agree," Wattington said.

"What else can you tell me about the government's pursuit?"

"We've got SEALs targeting Fiji right now."

"Damn," Stellard said.

The Foundation's tentacles reached far into the corridors of Washington, including the Pentagon. Its influence, a product of the collected wealth of its members, knew almost no bounds, but the special ops were controlled by General Guster Gunnison, who described himself accurately as a "stone-cold patriot." He believed America was the rightful world leader, and he opposed anyone or anything that might impose on her sovereignty, including, and especially, organizations such as the United Nations, the International Monetary Fund, and the Foundation.

"Is anyone closer?" Stellard asked, frustrated, looking at another pop-up window of the weather, noting a cold front.

"Negative. Fiji is down in that dusty corner of the world where nothing ever happens."

"So what's the plan if the SEALs get Gaines, or . . . the Sphere?" he asked, nearly choking on the final word.

"Not much has changed in seven years," Wattington replied. "There are factions within the government that work for others, and some of them, such as the Foundation, can be quite persuasive, but it would be my guess that if the SEALs get it, especially with Gunnison in charge, it would get fast tracked to HITE."

HITE, short for Hidden Information and Technology Exchange, was a super-secret government entity so classified that most US presidents did not usually learn about it unless they got a second term in office. HITE had been established after World War II to handle captured Nazi secrets, technology, and even metaphysical data and artifacts. If a UFO of extraterrestrial origin really did crash in Roswell, New Mexico, during the summer of 1947, HITE would have wound up with the wreckage and whatever it may have contained.

The name was a bit of a misnomer because the hidden technology and/or information were never exchanged. Instead, a select committee made up of top US intelligence leaders with security clearances much higher than the President of the United States decided who, where, when, and *if* the information would be released. HITE was the ultimate strategic advantage because its members could ignite huge shifts in power and wealth by introduction of new technologies, be it nuclear weapons, computers, satellites, pharmaceuticals, etc.

In this case, however, the Eysen-Sphere was more than just technology. It was a view into the future. HITE would have the power, along with whomever they decided to share it with, to destroy the Phoenix Initiative, and with it, the Foundation.

Stellard had to find a way to get to Gaines first. He had to stop Gunnison. "What are the options?" he asked, trying to mask the desperation in his voice while grasping a hot cup of coffee with both hands as if it was keeping him alive.

"I don't see any."

"Damn it, Wattington, there are *always* options. You're on the inside. We have you there for a reason."

"Gunnison is untouchable. Anything I could do is way too risky."

"Risky? *Risky*! Doing *nothing* is risky!"

"I'm not just talking about possibly losing my job. It could mean prison, even the death penalty."

"You'll be protected."

"Will I? If the Foundation is powerful enough to protect me from charges of treason and espionage, then they should be powerful enough not to need me." He chuckled nervously and rubbed a hand over the stubble on his face.

"Do you have the ability to stop the SEALs?"

"It would require everyone we have inside . . . We might be able to slow them, maybe an hour."

"Do it."

"You want to risk the entire operation, possibly blow cover for twenty-two Foundation moles, to gain one single hour, which won't even be enough? That's crazy."

"If HITE gets the Eysen-Sphere, then we won't need the operation anymore. The Foundation will be done."

seven

Now closer to fifty than forty, Rip's appearance had hardly changed in the years since discovering the Eysen. He sported the same rugged good looks, same shaggy, unkempt hair, same stubbly face, always a few days between shaves, and maybe a few more laugh lines, but otherwise, not much had changed. Gale, too, had hardly aged, in spite of having had a child and the stress of living on the run. They joked that perhaps the Eysen was the fountain of youth, and on some days he believed it.

But on this day, if he'd passed a mirror, he would have thought death was near, not knowing whether Gale and Cira were going to survive the next few hours.

He glanced around El Perdido as if Gale and Cira would be there. Unlike Gale, Rip had loved the island. It had felt safe, and it was. Booker had programmed some elaborate glitch into the satellite mapping and monitoring systems that one of his companies sold to governments around the world, thereby rendering the tiny speck of land invisible. He'd even installed specific buoys miles out into the waters to keep ships from getting too close. There were also the techniques learned from the Sphere that could slightly alter reality, or at least the perception of it. The government had named the method Eysen Anomaly Matter Interference, or "EAMI," but to them it was just a theory, a way of explaining the unexplainable.

Booker accumulated islands like others collected stamps, and he counted on the vastness of the ocean to hide his many secrets. El Perdido, like most of his hundreds of other islands, made use of the latest technology available to ensure varying degrees of privacy. Even before the Sphere and its treasure trove of new-tech, Booker's companies were on the leading edge of aerospace, high-tech weapons, surveillance equipment, and computers. He supplied most of his enemies, including the US government, but his connection to those firms was masked behind layers of paper and false identities.

Rip made his way up to the skyroom, a tower rising four stories above the main house, its twelve-by-twelve-foot room surrounded by the lush canopy of twisting trees, pruned just enough to allow wide panoramic views of El Perdido and the ocean. The digital binoculars gave him even more coverage. He'd be able to see them approach most easily from there.

As the sun set, he thought about the time difference. It was already late afternoon the next day in Fiji.

"Where are they?" he wondered out loud as he took the Eysen-Sphere out of his custom pack. Long gone were the days of wrapping the Sphere in an old shirt and stuffing it into a regular backpack while dodging government and Vatican agents. A sophisticated pack had been made to Rip's specifications; bulletproof, shockproof, waterproof, and trackable, exclusively by Booker. The case also had several other features to help protect the Sphere and its caretaker, including fingerprint ID, sleeping gas, electro-charge stun capability, and a short-range flame thrower.

The Eysen glowed gold and red. Rip had spent nearly every single day for seven years studying the artifact, but it still seemed incomprehensible to him. In many ways, the original Eysen-Sphere remained as much a mystery as it was the first day it fell from its stone casings in the mountains of Virginia, and yet so much had happened since then.

He'd recently confessed to Booker that the great Sphere had led him to the edges of sanity. "I have found understanding of the world that has crushed my intellect, and knowledge that has erased my intelligence." The

Eysen-Sphere was much more than the computer they first believed it to be. It was indeed the most powerful object that had been discovered in the Solar System.

Rip's Eysen-INU lit up, not the basketball-sized original, which they often called the Sphere now, but the softball-sized commercial Eysen-INU. His hopes rose, thinking Gale might have found a way to contact him, but he saw immediately that it was Huang. After Gale or Booker, Huang was the one he would have most wanted to hear from at that moment.

Huang, a Chinese genius, lived in Hong Kong. Booker had hired him away from the largest Chinese Internet company when he was twenty-four. Now forty, he'd proven himself invaluable on many occasions. He knew more about technology on nano and quantum levels than almost anyone alive. Huang had also been a major influence on Booker's development of Universe Quantum Physics, or UQP. From the earliest days, after Gale and Rip had "died," Huang had been their connection to the outside scientific community, and had personally recruited many of the Hawaiian crew of scientists from all over the world. More than that though, Huang was a friend.

"Huang, do you know what's going on?"

"I know you're in exit. And you're not with Gale and Cira."

"Gale's second biggest fear has always been that we would be separated during an exit," Rip said, wincing as if his own words stabbed at a raw wound. "Like any parent, her greatest fear was that something would happen to Cira."

"Double whammy, and I know she has a tough time relying on Booker."

"They got off on a bad foot."

"Yes, but the Sphere has proven that in spite of all of Booker's flaws and crimes, he is a *good* man. He could have seized the Eysen for his own selfish means at any time."

"Gale thinks he's already done that. She believes he's put the Sphere and all of us at risk when he decided to manufacture a consumer version of the Eysen-INU, not to mention what other tech he's pulled from our work."

"Sure, Booker is crazy, but we all know what's coming. He needs a gigantic war chest for the battle against the Foundation . . . and others."

"I know. I owe everything to Booker," Rip admitted, "and I believe him when he says he's spent the past twenty years getting in a better position to try and stop the future, or at least change it, but he takes lots of risks."

"Talking about risks, just think of the coming catastrophe . . ." Huang's voice trailed off in sadness. "What if we can't stop it?"

The question had haunted Rip for years, ever since they discovered what the future held, a sickening apocalypse. He didn't always agree with the trillionaire's tactics, but imagining a world without Booker meant there would be no chance to avoid the billions of deaths and the brutal misery that would follow.

A world without Booker was more than possible. Many people wanted him dead. Fortunately, Booker had perfected the art of "being invisible." He was so good at it that there were often rumors of his death, many likely perpetuated by the man himself. Gale, Rip, and Booker had that in common. In order to save the world, they had to "leave" it.

"We're closer than ever to stopping it," Rip assured him. "Did you read the most recent report from Hawaii?"

"Yes, it blew my mind!" Huang said. "That makes the timing of this breach even worse."

"It is, and Booker's got me back in isolation," Rip said, knowing Huang knew exactly where he meant. Huang had long been the only other person with knowledge of Gale and Rip's movements. In case something happened to Booker, it would be up to Huang to continue to safeguard them. "Can you find out anything about Gale and Cira?"

"I'm on it. I'll tell you as soon as I get something," Huang promised. "In the meantime, what else do you need?"

"What was the breach?"

"Don't know, but I've been working on that, too."
Booker, knowing Huang would tell Rip about Cira, had
purposely kept the news from him. Huang knew the
tycoon could be deceptive when necessary. "We'll find it."

"Booker may not know, or he may not want us to
know," Rip said.

Huang started working his bank of Eysen-INUs,
looking for answers. Booker had secret "back-doors" into
many of the systems of intel and communications that the
governments of the world, including their militaries, law
enforcement, and intelligence agencies, relied upon.

"Something woke up the world all at once," Huang
explained. "NSA, the Foundation, CIA, FBI, DHS, Mossad,
I even see some activity from former members of the
Vatican Secret Service . . . Every enemy is coming for you.
They all want the only thing that can save you, the
Sphere."

"The Sphere is the only thing that can save us all."

eight

Gale came to slowly, groggily. "Where are we?" she finally asked in a slightly slurred voice, then began panicking as she looked around. "Where is Cira?"

"She's with Harmer back at the hospital."

Gale's confused look changed to one of seething rage. "Damn you, Kruse! You betrayed me. How could you? I'm her *mother*!" Adrenaline overcame the effects of the narcotics in her system and she kicked and hit him repeatedly.

He deflected her blows until she finally weakened. Her head throbbed in a woozy fog. Like in a nightmare when being chased and one's legs didn't work, she couldn't find the way back to clarity, to find her daughter, to save Cira.

"I'm sorry Gale, but this was the best way to protect you both," Kruse said, rubbing his leg where she had landed her hardest kicks on his shin.

"This wasn't your damned choice to make," she said, glaring back at him, shocked by the betrayal.

"I wish there had been another way," he said.

"There was. Let me stay with my daughter. Now get ahold of Booker so I can tell him how much I hate him."

"They were *his* orders, Gale. Talking to him won't do any good."

"Oh, I know it was him. That old businessman doesn't care about anyone who doesn't have his face on money." She spat the word "businessman" as if it was an obscenity.

"But Booker does care about the Sphere, and he may think it belongs to him, but it's ours! Rip and I have given up our lives for it, and we can make it go dark if anything happens to Cira."

Gale had never really trusted Booker, going back to her days as a business reporter for *The Wall Street Journal*, when she covered many of his business exploits. Booker routinely took over companies, sliced them up, cutting jobs, shuttering factories, and sometimes worse. She'd never seen anyone with such a relentless need to accumulate wealth.

Long before she knew him personally, Gale had written in an article, *"Booker pursues money and power as if he wants to buy the entire world, as if he needs to own it all."* Then there were the criminal investigations. Booker didn't seem to think laws applied to him, and certainly not the ones that pertained to insider trading, or anything having to do with the Securities and Exchange Commission, the Federal Trade Commission, or the anti-trust regulations in the US or Europe.

She thought of Rip. *He's defended Booker all along, but he won't now, not once he finds out Booker ordered me drugged and abducted while leaving our daughter at the mercy of the monsters who've hunted and tried to kill us even since before Cira was born.*

Rip often talked of Booker's "good side," how allegedly he'd anonymously sent hundreds of thousands of poor kids to college, saved thousands of homes from foreclosure, single-handedly funded countless humanitarian charities, built water projects and schools across Africa, Central and South America, and poor regions of Asia. Gale had always had a hard time believing it, and after the events of today, she would no longer try to reconcile the two opposing views of the world's wealthiest man.

"I mean it," she repeated. "If I lose my daughter, he will lose the Sphere!"

Kruse nodded. He, like Gale, knew she meant what she said, but they both also knew that without Booker,

Gale and Rip would be dead because of choices the two of them had made years before.

"Kruse, you let me talk to him!"

"I'm not going to waste time trying to reach him," Kruse said. "Even if he *would* talk to you, it won't do any good right now. Booker knows how you feel. He knows at this very moment that you probably want to kill him, but *you* know that he's already doing everything he can to protect Cira."

Gale nodded. She did believe that Booker would try to save Cira, but she doubted it was his top priority. Suffocating in helplessness, she pulled her knees to her chest as a terrifying wash of anxiety burned inside her, causing physical pain. The thought of Cira alone was debilitating. The idea that agents from some adversarial agency were about to storm her room was more than she could bear. It took her breath away.

"How?" she asked, hardly able to get the syllable out between gasps. "How . . . is he . . . going to . . . protect her?"

Another AX agent on the plane signaled Kruse before he could answer her.

"Now, listen to me carefully Gale. This plane is about to crash into the ocean," Kruse said. "If you want to survive this and see Cira again, then you must do exactly what I say."

"Crash! What are you talking about?"

"In order to live, you're going to have to die again."

She heard the pilot radio in a distress call. Another agent quickly assisted Gale into a special underwater air-suit, which had only recently been invented from Cosegan technology gleaned from the Eysen-Sphere.

"I don't understand," Gale protested again, confused and scared.

"There isn't much time. You'll be tethered to me, but should we get separated, there's a tracking device built into your suit. Any of us can find you." He pointed to the two other agents and the pilot. "It's SPAM equipped, Slight Propulsion Assisted Movement."

The plane started a rapid descent.

"Wait!" Gale shouted as they finished suiting her up. Her stomach wasn't keeping up with their sudden loss of altitude.

"I'll explain on the other side," Kruse said.

"What?" she shrieked.

"Just brace for the impact!"

"Head between your legs," an agent yelled, shoving her neck forward.

"As soon as we're under, we're going out that door." Kruse pointed. "That door," he repeated.

It was the last thing she heard before the crash.

nine

Harmer paid off the surgeon, a doctor, two nurses, three orderlies, and a security guard. Each was given thousands of dollars to do what they all might have done for free; protect the little girl so she might see again. Harmer had explained that Cira's parents were whistle-blowers, similar to Edward Snowden — it was true enough— and that they had to flee, but because their daughter could not be moved, the CIA, NSA, or US military would take custody of the girl. Harmer told them the urgency of the overzealous US authorities meant that Cira would most likely be moved before it was safe.

"It's too great a risk," Harmer explained. "This precious six-year-old little girl shouldn't have to be made blind because her parents got into trouble."

After receiving a substantial pile of cash, the surgeon reluctantly agreed to the scheme and officially discharged Cira. All data would now show her no longer at the hospital. Then a nurse and an orderly carefully and slowly moved Cira's bed from the ICU. Her new quarters, a small private room, would be quickly remodeled.

The heart of Harmer's elaborate plan got underway when a rushed delivery of construction materials arrived from a nearby home center. A contractor, related to one of the nurses, slapped up a false wall and then mounted white shelving boards. The construction was completed in a miraculously short time. Harmer stood back and stared at the former entrance to Cira's room, which now led to a small storage closet.

If they're looking closely they might notice, but if we're lucky, they'll miss us, she thought.

A nurse and the orderlies swiftly stocked the new storage closet with medical supplies. Cira's room would now only be accessible from a twenty-by-forty-two-inch concealed door cut into the new sheetrock. The secret entrance was located at the far end of the closet, hidden by a rack of hanging uniforms. Harmer had rearranged the garments three times.

"This is a lot of trouble for nothing," one of Harmer's paid-off-nurses said. "When the agents find out the girl has been discharged, why would they still bother to look for her?"

"Oh, they'll look."

"But it's a big hospital. Will they search every room?"

"Every room and every closet," Harmer said, worrying as she checked the appearance of the storage closet again. As a final defense, Harmer would be in the room with Cira, and planned to take hostage the first agent who found his way into the secret hiding place. At least that way she could force a standoff that could buy Cira more time until help might reach them.

Once she was convinced nothing more could be done, Harmer, a nurse, and an orderly moved into Cira's room. The other paid-off-nurse and two extra orderlies were on stand-by. The paid-off-security guard would be Harmer's eyes and ears throughout the rest of the hospital.

Harmer reported the scheme to her boss across a scrambled line.

"It's a weak and dangerous plan," Booker said, sipping on a green tea, acai, and seaweed smoothie.

"There's no alternative. Cira can't be moved," Harmer replied in a strained voice.

Booker, frustrated, could not think of another option. He admired Harmer for her dedication to him and to the mission, for her loyalty to Gaines and Asher, and for putting herself in such jeopardy, but he knew her efforts were mostly, if not entirely, for Cira. Harmer loved the child.

"Any of those orderlies or nurses could crack as soon as the big guns show up," Booker warned.

"I know," Harmer said tensely. "Again, no choice."

Booker checked the time. It wouldn't be long now. "I'll have people ready and waiting to get you and the girl out as soon as you say."

"Let's hope it gets to that," Harmer agreed, knowing they would have to survive hidden in the hospital for at least a week before any kind of evacuation could be attempted. Harmer had made up her mind that it would be safer for Cira to risk capture than trying to move her too soon. If the worst happened, she'd have to count on someone in the chain of command taking pity on the child and allowing her to remain in the hospital until her eyes healed properly. "If not, maybe they'll let her stay here."

"Not likely. They cannot risk the other patients," Booker replied. "The NSA knows there are at least half a dozen groups that would attack the building in an effort to capture Gale and Rip's daughter, and most of them wouldn't give a damn if she's blind or not. They want the Eysen, and would gamble that Rip would trade anything to get his daughter back."

"I know."

Harmer thought of the odds. The NSA and CIA were formidable opponents, but Booker had contacts and plants within their high walls. However, the Foundation was the greatest enemy. They, too, had people planted throughout the US government like a cancer, and although Booker was the wealthiest person in the world, he was also not very popular among the world's elite. The next one hundred and nine richest people on Earth were part of the Foundation, and about seventy percent of the three hundred billionaires below them were also either direct members, or affiliated in some way with the Foundation.

They had enough combined money and network to oppose Booker.

The fight had been building for years. Booker and the Foundation had opposing visions for the future. Because of the Sphere, Gale and Rip were caught in the middle, and now their daughter had become the latest pawn and youngest victim.

The problem, Harmer thought, *is that both Booker and the Foundation think they can save the world while believing the other is going to destroy it. They can't both be right.*

At that moment, Harmer didn't care about the power struggles of the rich. Her only concern was saving Cira's eyesight. "We never should have let them come to Fiji."

"They insisted," Booker sighed. "Gale was tired of the isolation and wanted Cira raised in a more normal setting."

"I remember, but you could have said no."

"They knew the risks."

Harmer looked down at the sweet little girl, bandaged and sedated. She reached for her tiny hand and held it. "How is Gale?"

"So far, so good," Booker replied. "But the pilot just sent a distress signal, so I'm holding my breath."

twelve

Wattington and his twenty-one fellow moles were part of the greatest infiltration of US intelligence in history. The men and women, all working on behalf of the Foundation, had lived and acted as perfect NSA and CIA employees for seven years. The Foundation had dozens of other operatives in the Department of Homeland Security, the FBI, and various military intelligence agencies. There were also hundreds more in other US governmental agencies. More of their private spies worked around the globe. The Foundation had been using their cash to conduct a slow, deliberate, and complete *coup d'état* of every country in the world.

The NSA had the lead on the Eysen-Sphere matter, and the CIA had the closest ties to the Hidden Information and Technology Exchange. In fact, historically, the CIA had sent more "inventory" to HITE than any other agency.

Stellard and his bosses had been clear; they would rather risk all out war than see HITE get the Sphere, and Wattington had been inside the CIA long enough to know with certainty that the world had evolved into a more dangerous place. Gone were the days of a simple country versus country war. Terrorists weren't even the real threat. Their strikes were used by the elites to manipulate the masses. It was all a dangerous game. Corporations had private armies, their own espionage networks, and money had corrupted every government. If money couldn't buy someone, manipulation would be applied.

Whereas the NSA was the main eavesdropper, the CIA was the meddler, starter of wars, toppler of regimes, pusher of drugs, spreader of epidemics, maker of "kings," and general confusers of truth. The Foundation used its contacts to muddy things so that the only clear path belonged to them.

"Like crooks learn to be criminals in jail, spies learn to be conspirators in the CIA," Stellard liked to say when he was planning for the future. But on this day the future was in doubt, and all his time was spent trying to control the past.

It began to look like he was going to get a break. Wattington had, through an incredibly intricate and perilous series of moves, managed to delay General Gunnison and the SEALs. At least for the time being, his maneuvers would go undetected. Stellard tried to shake off the inner cold that even his extra-thick long johns couldn't protect him from.

That piece of good news only got Stellard and the Foundation halfway to where they needed to be, namely Fiji, and specifically in the same room or vehicle with Gaines and Asher. During the two hours since the most wanted dead people since Jimmy Hoffa had been discovered alive, the Foundation had been attempting the impossible. However, the Foundation was controlled by some of the wealthiest people on Earth, therefore, doing the impossible was almost always possible.

"We have someone on the ground. They'll be at the hospital in minutes," Stellard explained to Taz over an encrypted text as soon as word came from Wattington.

"How? Who?" Taz said, slipping a golden ring of a snake consuming itself on and off his finger. The nervous habit surfaced whenever he multitasked. At the same time, he communicated with Stellard, he scanned recent satellite images of Fiji, checked locations of several Foundation units, and reviewed data on Booker's secret army.

"Sugar was the sweet solution," Stellard texted back. Turns out that sugar was Fiji's most important export, as well as a major employer in the island nation. As luck would have it, a Foundation member had acquired the formerly state-owned sugar mill monopoly a few years earlier, during a privatizing period forced by World Bank debt restructuring. This gave Stellard what he needed — contacts and influence in Fiji. It was rough and dirty, but they now had local police on the Foundation "payroll," ready to do his bidding.

Stellard conveyed the plan to Taz, and was optimistic that not only would they be first on the scene, but they might even be able to track Gaines and Asher. When they hit the hospital, local police would also converge on the girl's school, where they expected to learn the address where the fugitives had been residing. Police had orders to empty the place and hold the evidence for Taz.

Stellard stayed connected as Taz contacted the locals and assumed command. After some back and forth, he was able to direct things from the plane. His Eysen-INU could accommodate as many calls as needed, and would mute automatically as he alternated between conversations.

The officers assigned to the school reported that the little girl's name was Cira Bradley, and that they had an address. At the hospital the news wasn't so good. The girl had been discharged, but they were interviewing her doctor.

"Search the building," Taz ordered. "Talk to anyone who might have had contact with her parents. How long ago was she released?"

"Sir, we're working on it," an officer shot back in accented English. "Trying to unseal medical records isn't standard procedure here. Especially in a pediatric situation."

Taz thought of the stakes, knowing that for the forces that were heading to Fiji, unsealing medical records would be like opening a candy wrapper. Fiji was about to be invaded. If Gaines wasn't found, the sovereign nation would essentially be occupied. But the country consisted of more than three hundred islands. Gaines could be anywhere.

"Damn it, where did they go!?" he yelled in the open line.

"Easy, Taz," Stellard said as the other lines muted. "These locals are our only chance to beat the others."

"They're gone! No one will find anything," Taz said. "Don't you see? If they didn't know we were coming, they would never have risked moving a six-year-old girl fresh out of eye surgery!"

"Yes. Of course Booker Lipton would have had a well practiced evacuation plan in place, but as wealthy and powerful as he is, the man is still constrained by the laws of time and physics. They could only be so far. They haven't had much time since the surgery. Gaines could be two blocks away holed up in some cheap motel right now."

"Then we need access to the current satellite feeds. We've got to trace them out of here before the NSA does."

"Wattington is working on that."

"I'm sure he is, but we need it *now*."

"Sir, we're in the residence," an officer said in a thick accent from one of the other lines.

"Is it occupied?" Taz asked, already knowing the answer.

"Not presently," the officer responded. "Small place. We haven't sorted through every shadow, but there don't appear to be many hiding places."

"Can you get me visuals?"

"One of the men is working on it, but we don't have the full crew yet. We rushed here in the chopper, you know."

Taz did know. They were busy trying to get every chopper they could find into the air to search for these ghosts. "How do they do it?" he asked Stellard. "You've read the files. From the time they took the artifact from that cliff in Virginia, half the world was after them, and yet there were almost no confirmed sightings. And Dixon

Barbeau, the one man who actually *did* capture Gaines, we now know was in on their escape."

"They got lucky," Stellard said.

"No one is that lucky . . . no one."

"We've got some people going to have a chat with Barbeau now," Stellard replied. "He's no longer with the Bureau, but still seems to be involved in investigation work. We're not sure who's paying him, but it might still be a government agency, or . . . Booker Lipton."

"Why am I not surprised? Damn it, I wish I were on the ground." Taz twisted the gold ring on his middle finger, a Mayan scull, and turned his attention back to the former residence of Gaines and Asher, now also known as Rick and Terry Bradley.

Images began streaming from his Eysen-INU. He could see a cup of tea on the kitchen table, still half full, a plate of nori rolls beside it. "They left in a hurry, obviously to get to the hospital. They didn't take the time to sterilize the place," Taz said out loud, though he was mostly talking to himself. "We may find something helpful here."

twelve

Huang knew the connection was scrambled nine different ways and routed across the globe like a crazed ping-pong ball. The call was safe. Still, he double-checked the encryption codes before telling Rip the bad news. Only hours had passed since they last spoke, but to Rip it felt as if it had been years.

"I don't want to tell you this," Huang said reluctantly.

"Gale?" Rip asked, trying not to panic.

"Cira. She's alive, okay, but . . . "

"What?"

"There was an accident on the playground. Her eyes were cut with scissors."

Rip's whole body tightened, his mouth went dry, thinking of his sweet angel suffering, bleeding, her eyes. Her *eyes*! "No, oh please no!"

"She had an operation. May need more, but they think she will see again."

Rip's fears and desperate worry swelled into confusion and anger. "Does Booker know?" Rip demanded, then answered his own question before continuing his rant. "Of course he knows. If you know, he knows. What's his problem? I know what he's doing! He knew I'd never come here without them." Rip pounded his hand on the table and glanced out the windows at the water — nothing but water for a million miles. "Can you get Gale on the phone? Can you connect me to their room?"

"I can try, but it would not be safe for them."

"Wait . . . Cira's accident was the breach, wasn't it? The hospital link . . . The NSA is heading to Fiji! Everyone is heading to Fiji! Are they out? How much time will they have to get out? Are they on the move . . . damn it, can they even move Cira yet?"

"You need to talk to Booker."

"You bet I need to talk to him. I need to do *more* than talk to him. Damn, damn, damn!" Rip pulled up the emergency section of his Eysen-INU, but the connection didn't go through. It was the first time he'd been unable to reach Booker since they went into hiding after their "deaths." Rip wasn't sure if Booker was just avoiding him or if something horrible had happened. "Huang, get me in touch with Gale or Booker, *please*."

"I'll try."

Rip could only wait until Huang worked his magic, but as the minutes since their call ended began adding up, he realized he was not completely powerless. Although trapped on the remote and beautiful island of El Perdido — or "El Prison," as Gale had always called it — Rip possessed the most powerful object known to man.

"To hold all the stars in your hands," Rip whispered to himself as he held the Eysen-Sphere in the sun, then gently set it down above the Odeon Chip on a teakwood table. A moment later it levitated and images projected out.

Each session was always like his first: the indescribable wonders, the lights, the magical floating Sphere shining out visions of the universe, Earth, humanity's past . . . and the blurry future. He stood yet again in awe, as if dancing in a dream, surrounded by clouds and stars in a gentle rain of colors.

They had learned so much, but the most important questions concerning the eleven-million-year-old treasure still remained unanswered. Rip had dubbed the people who created the Eysen the Cosegans, named for his once controversial Cosega theory. Cosega, an old Indian word meaning "before the beginning," turned out to be an incredibly accurate choice.

Rip's hypothesis hadn't gone back far enough before the beginning; he was off by more than ten million years. No one with any kind of decent reputation within the scientific community, other than Rip, dared to entertain the notion that intelligent humans had existed for more than the last 100,000 years. Even Rip, who believed a sophisticated society on par with ours might have risen and fallen in prehistory, hadn't dared to dream that they'd achieved such an advanced degree of knowledge and technology — far beyond what humans enjoy in the present day — until he held the Eysen.

Still, after all the years spent studying it, he second-guessed everything, especially the choices that resulted in the deaths of those who helped to protect it, particularly Larsen, his closest friend. Lately what he'd been most unsure about was the decision to hide it. Enough information from their early research had been released, causing the world's religions to collapse, but the world went on, seemingly missing the significance.

What if they had let it *all* out? It had become a constant debate among Rip, Gale and Booker. Every commercial Eysen-INU that Booker sold came preloaded with actual data from the original Eysen-Sphere, complete with the new history, new science, and more, but humanity still drifted rapidly toward a perilous future. A future made more immediate because of Cira, who would have to endure what was coming. Yet now even that was in doubt.

He stared at the Eysen-Sphere, mesmerized anew, as it floated in the air. "Like a wizard's crystal ball . . . What are you truly capable of?" Rip asked out loud. "You contain the history of the universe, all human knowledge, and you grant glimpses into the future . . . " He paced around the Eysen-Sphere, thinking of it somehow as something different, something more than he'd ever considered before. "Can you be used as a weapon? A time machine?" He laughed at his absurdity. "Can you save my little girl?"

During their seven year quest into the Sphere, they'd found so much, yet frustratingly little in the way of practical understanding. What was it for? Why had it survived? Who were the Cosegans, really?

"Crying Man, are you there? What about the other ghosts who dwell inside this ancient orb?"

Rip called the man who had silently guided them through the turmoil and vastness of their early days of exploration into the Sphere. Back then, Crying Man had been an almost daily presence. Then, inexplicably, he had all but disappeared five years earlier. They'd only seen him twice since, and not once for more than three years. Rip's instincts told him that the Sphere might be the only way to save his loved ones. He and Gale had devoted their lives to its study, and, by default, Cira's life too.

"It's time to give back, Crying Man," he said, his tone more pleading than demanding. "Please, my daughter is only six. She's never done anything wrong in her life, she only knows the innocence and beauty of the world."

As a single tear slid down Rip's cheek, incredibly, Crying Man appeared in life-sized form, fully projected out from the ancient Eysen-Sphere. He stood opposite Rip, the Sphere between them. His stern expression, contrasted by smiling eyes, gave him the aura of a parent upset with a child over some minor mishap.

Last time he'd seen him, Crying Man had had long hair. Now his head appeared completely shaved beneath a white hood of light, flowing, silk-like cloth. It matched his long robe, which was tied with a sash that seemed to be made of a thin, green, glowing, neon-like-light. His robe ruffled around him as if in a steady breeze, although the air in the skyroom was still.

Rip stood transfixed, part of him shocked at the appearance of a man he'd just called across eleven million years, and part of him not at all surprised. He wanted to ask, "Where have you been? What took you so long?" but instead he smiled, as if seeing a long lost old friend, and said, "Thank you."

twelve

Gale woke with a start, quickly taking in the cramped metal cabin, and decided she was on a ship. Cira flashed into her mind.

A uniformed woman sitting next to her smiled. "Welcome back," the woman said. "Let me just check your eyes." She shone a light and then moved it away. "Good. How do you feel?"

"Where's my daughter?"

"I have no information about that," the woman said. "I need to check your vitals."

"My head hurts," Gale said. "Where's Kruse?"

"Yes, you suffered a contusion during impact, but there's no concussion." She held out her hand. "Take these."

Gale eyed the pills suspiciously.

"They're just aspirin," the woman said, checking the digital readout as a blood pressure cuff deflated.

Gale figured if they wanted to drug, her they would have done it while she was unconscious. She sat up and took the pills. "Kruse?" she repeated, suddenly worried he might not have survived.

"He'll be along in a few minutes. He's checked in on you regularly."

"How long have I been out? Where are we?"

"You've been onboard about forty minutes. We're on one of Booker's subs." There was a knock at the door. "Come in," the woman called.

Kruse peaked in and grinned as soon as he saw Gale sitting up with open eyes. The woman got up and squeezed past him, Kruse taking the now vacant seat.

"So you're fine?" he asked.

"Hardly. My daughter might be blind, might be in custody, or worse, she's all alone. I've been kidnapped by my bodyguard, and apparently I'm somewhere under the ocean on a private submarine. Booker has his own sub?"

"Six of them," Kruse said. "He rotates them in and out of the area."

"Why?"

"Just in case."

"In case of *what*?"

"For just such an event as this," Kruse said, as if it ought to be obvious. "To evacuate you, Rip, Cira."

"Well, he missed a couple of us."

"Look, Gale, cut me a break here. I'm doing my job. Don't shoot the messenger."

"Shoot the messenger? You *drugged* me! You could have refused the order."

Kruse nodded. "I saw no other solution."

"The NSA is going to find us."

"I don't think so," Kruse said. "Not today. It's a good plan. The crash was planned. They'll find just enough wreckage to know it was real. They can check the satellites, but they'll see no boats or planes nearby."

"Won't they think of a rescue sub?"

"Even if they do, it will be dismissed because how could there be one in the area? Too coincidental."

"But it was here."

"They don't know that."

"He's had subs here all these years?" she asked, skeptical, but very impressed.

"We have contingency plans upon plans for every eventuality, and—"

"You didn't have one for Cira."

"No one expected a severe playground accident. That was a regrettable mistake, but Harmer is with her.

Resources are being brought to bear. We'll keep her safe,
Gale. I promise."

"I hate you."

"I know."

She looked at Kruse, a man she had previously trusted
and come to love like a brother. She didn't really hate him,
in spite of his betrayal, because obviously he'd been doing
what he thought would best to protect them. He was a
surrogate for a man she did despise though, and until she
could scream at Booker, she could find no forgiveness, or
even kindness, for Kruse.

"They will think you and Cira died in the crash,"
Kruse continued. "This is the most remote ocean on Earth.
People are lost here, no bodies found, just fragments of the
wreckage. There's security footage of you leaving the
hospital with Cira and getting into the plane. We took a
dummy, roughly the same size as Cira, its head fully
bandaged, IV attached to its arm."

"So they won't know she's still at the hospital?"

"No," Kruse said, smiling proudly.

"But they'll check the records. They'll talk to the
doctor."

"All handled."

"Money?"

"Naturally."

"But they'll search."

"She's in a secret room. They won't find her. Harmer is
right there with her. They'll believe she's gone. Escaped
with you on the plane."

"They won't believe another crash, another death.
We've used up that trick."

"That's why they will, because no one would be crazy
enough to do it again. Even if they don't, you know this is
all about buying time."

"And time is a funny thing."

Kruse nodded.

"But what about Rip?" Gale asked. "They'll look for
Rip."

"Rip is already at El Perdido."

She closed her eyes at the thought of returning there, then opened them and stared directly into Kruse's hard face. "If anything bad happens to Cira, I will kill you."

"If anything bad happens to her, I'll let you."

Forty-four

Once the security guard got Harmer's Eysen-INU tapped into the hospital's surveillance camera network, Harmer relaxed a little. Now at least she could see for herself what was happening. She wished she could smoke one more cigarette before the action started, but it was not to be.

Sooner than expected, people came looking for Cira and her parents. Harmer watched with a combination of relief and confusion as police filled the hospital. They swarmed and quickly covered all the exits. It didn't take long for the man-in-charge to discover that Cira had already been discharged.

Harmer could see him speaking into his Eysen-phone, a smaller, oval-shaped object about the size of a traditional cell phone. The phone linked to a person's Eysen-INU over the internet, and was about the only accessory needed. Many people just kept their Eysen-INUs with them all the time and didn't bother with a separate phone. One day, Booker's company, Eysen, Inc., predicted they would be able to make Eysen-INUs as small as marbles.

Harmer's remote hope that the police might quickly leave was dashed. Obviously, whomever the man-in-charge spoke to on the phone had ordered a search.

Still, the regular cops would be less likely to find Cira's hiding place than the CIA, the NSA, or the military. As Harmer counted more than twenty officers, it became obvious this wasn't just a local operation. Clearly one of the "big guns" had enlisted the police, but which one? The inflated numbers of the police meant serious trouble, and Harmer started to consider options for escaping. Even if they weren't initially discovered, the police could just hold the facility until their paymasters arrived. It might help to know who was coming first.

Harmer reviewed their enemies. US Intelligence, the Israeli Mossad, the Foundation, and Scarlet, a fragmented group of former Vatican Cardinals who declared that the Eysen-Sphere had been a fraud meant only to destroy organized religions, particularly the Catholic Church. She figured it was the US government that was the most likely to have had the assets — CIA, NSA, DIA, the military, etc. — and networks in place near enough to pose the biggest threat. However, *any* of the others could have found a way to influence the local police.

Harmer eyed the video feed of the hallway they were on as two police officers checked each room. They were four doors away from the phony supply closet which concealed their room. The nurse and orderly watched nervously as Harmer readied her weapon. The orderly was particularly jittery. He was one of only five people in the building who knew the girl had not really been discharged, and with so many cops, any of them could crack. He wondered why so many police had come to arrest the six-year-old's parents. Who were they really?

"They're going to find us," he blurted.

"No," Harmer whispered firmly.

"The wall isn't even properly finished," the orderly said, pointing to the backside of the sheetrock.

"*Quiet,*" Harmer hissed.

The police were now two doors away. Harmer looked at the wall. It was true that if they spent too much time in the supply closet, even more than a cursory glance, they would likely notice something — untaped seams in the sheetrock, no paint, the tiny panel at the end, not even a correct mix of supplies — and all it would take was a few minutes before Harmer would be dead and Cira in custody. She knew there was no way to defend the room.

A wing and a prayer, Harmer thought to herself. Counting steps, she momentarily met eyes with the nurse. With a slight look at the faux wall, then at Cira, and finally back to the nurse, Harmer conveyed a list of instructions in half a second. The nurse nodded and asked the orderly to help move Cira's bed to the corner. The three of them would be safest there when Harmer engaged the police.

Two police officers entered the room next to Cira's. Unfortunately, there was no camera in there. Patient rooms were not part of the hospital visual monitoring system. Harmer had noted that the cops were spending an average of about ninety seconds in each room. She looked at the time on her Eysen-INU, and waited.

The nurse and the orderly were barely breathing, but Harmer worried that at any second the orderly would shout out. She never should have brought him in there, but maybe it was better than having him out there on the loose. Harmer could feel the tension coming from him, but didn't dare turn around. She didn't want to do anything to disturb the desperate hush, which seemed to be the only thing holding the room together. The nurse, "a cool customer," had muted all of Cira's monitors. Perhaps her stoic presence could also somehow keep the orderly calm.

Ninety seconds had passed and Harmer felt the dampness on her trigger. She was sweating, not typical for her. The camera on Harmer's Eysen-INU was on. Thousands of miles away, Booker silently watched the wall with the rest of them. Frustrated, he switched his gaze between screens showing the situation around the world – Gale's plane over the Indian Ocean, Rip on El Perdido, various AX teams, and tracking any number of mobilized groups in pursuit of them all. Not since the days following Gale and Rip's death had their mission been in this much jeopardy.

Booker communicated with an AX team already in the air over Fiji. They were ready to parachute down and take the hospital by force and evacuate Cira, but that was not an option Booker wanted to use. Even if they *could* get the six-year-old safely out of the building, she would most likely permanently lose her eyesight, and they would still need to escape Fiji undetected. That was not a promising scenario since the NSA now had the island nation under every form of scrutiny. They would know when a butterfly landed on a new flower, or which seagull caught the most fish. Still, if the police, or anyone else, discovered Cira's room, AX would go in. They would have to try, if for no other reason that to be able to show Gale and Rip that Booker had tried to save their daughter.

Two and a half minutes. The police were staying in the room too long. Harmer's mind raced. Were they in there preparing an assault? Had the patient seen something while they were constructing the wall? Harmer clearly remembered closing all nearby doors while the work on Cira's room was being done. *The patient couldn't have seen, so what the hell is taking so long?*

Three minutes.

They must know! Harmer heard the orderly sigh behind her, almost more of a wince. *Damn it, he's not going to last much longer.* Suddenly, two more officers entered the hallway. *What's this?* Harmer took a deep breath and scanned the rest of the cameras, looking for any other signs of an impending build up to an attack.

Three minutes, twenty seconds. Booker saw the new cops and relayed a command to the AX agents in the air. "Be ready on my signal."

fourteen

Taz and Stellard had discovered enough about Gaines and his Sphere that the entire Foundation was on high alert. All of its many assets — money, connections, control, power — were being mobilized, but the Foundation's most powerful tool — a young, brainy woman and the object she studied — were secreted away in a highly secure, yet unassuming office park in northern California.

Savina, thin, beautiful, and brilliant, commanded the attention of everyone who shared the same room as her. It didn't matter if it was filled with men, women, scientists, billionaires, or dogs. With long brown hair, dropping below her shoulders, and an affinity for wearing blue jeans and striped tee-shirts, she looked eighteen instead of thirty. The Foundation had paid a lot of money to retain her.

As one of the brightest physicists in the world, she'd been extremely sought after. No one would have guessed by her parents — her mother a librarian, father a plumber — that she would turn into a child prodigy, but even in her crib, as she counted and organized toys, the signs were obvious. Savina was reading by two, and at four she'd devoured a couple of years' worth of *National Geographic* magazines from the family bookshelf. When her mother gave her some advanced math and science books, the spark really ignited.

Savina looked into the smooth, highly-polished dark ball in front of her, and waited as it cycled through the Sequence. Watching it always made her smile, not because of the remarkably impossible show it displayed, she was long over the dazzle of that, rather her smugness came from the advantage she had over her adversary. Savina now knew there was another Eysen-Sphere on Earth, but the newly no-longer-dead Dr. Ripley Gaines, she believed, did not know another Eysen-Sphere remained.

Each day for nearly five years she'd begun her studies of the ancient object watching the Sequence, trying to decode the universal depths of knowledge contained within its infiniteness. Every one of those days had been an adventure, expanding her already genius mind.

As recently as two weeks ago she'd requested a larger staff, but as always the Judge said no. "The Judge," as she called the wealthy man who'd hired, and inspired, her out of grad school, was not truly a judge, at least not in the legal sense. His philosophy of what the world ought to be had changed her life, and in turn, she had changed his. With this new information that the other Eysen had not been destroyed, she was certain he'd give her the staff she needed.

The Judge's denial of her request had nothing to do with cost. He'd given her everything else she'd ever wanted. The facility in which she studied the Eysen-Sphere was among the most advanced in the world. No, it was a matter of security. Savina and her two assistants had been vetted, investigated, and triple-checked in every manner available. Unbeknownst to them, he also kept them under around-the-clock surveillance, monitoring their phone, email, mail, Internet, and their physical locations and actions.

Savina would not have been surprised if she'd known, nor would she have cared. She knew the future was at stake — everything — and she believed the Judge knew what was right. If anything, her work had proved his prophetic genius even more. The future she'd seen inside the Sphere showed a potentially humanity-ending plague emerging soon. The views changed radically when the Phoenix

Initiative was added to the equation, and the closer they came to the launch, the higher the survival rate became.

"Hello, Dr. Ripley Gaines," she said into the Sphere as her two male assistants looked surprised.

"He's alive?" one of them asked.

"Apparently," she replied, adjusting her large tortoise shell eyeglasses. "And we're going to track him down."

"Is that possible?" the assistant asked. "I mean to *find* him *inside* the Sphere?"

"Remember the research? The Eysens can connect to other Eysens."

"Yes, I remember the *theory* based upon the time, centuries ago, when there were multiple Eysens still floating around out there . . . no pun intended," he said, glancing at the Eysen-Sphere levitating above the table. "But we looked, and we found nothing. Maybe Gaines is alive but the Eysen didn't survive?"

"Possible, but doubtful," Savina replied in such an assured manner that her pronouncement seemed indisputable. She'd been homeschooled, finished high school level at age twelve, and graduated from MIT at sixteen. Next was Harvard, and in between then and the Sphere, she'd worked at a number of universities, research labs, CERN, including time at the Large Hadron Collider, and even NASA.

"So why didn't we find it?"

"We didn't try hard enough," she said absently as she peered into the center of the Sphere.

"We spent months," the other assistant countered.

"I didn't say we didn't spend enough time, I said we didn't try hard enough. We didn't understand two things back then," Savina explained, pushing her glasses on top of her head. "First, we only half believed that the other Eysen might still exist."

"That shouldn't matter," one of the assistants interrupted.

"Oh, but it does," she said, a subtle hint of awe in her voice. The assistants didn't completely believe Savina's long held theory that the Eysen was "in tune" and able to understand and react to one's thoughts. "That's why we didn't get the second part," she continued as projections of light beamed from the Eysen, showing cross-sections of the Earth, spinning, divided by levels of color in a manner they still did not comprehend. "We didn't understand that we were not looking for something separate."

"What does that mean?" one of them asked while checking on the video recording equipment. They tracked and recorded the Eysen from multiple angles whenever it was "on." The system was automated, but a few years earlier they had lost hours of crucial data to a glitch. Ever since, they constantly inspected the gear to make sure it was working. In spite of being meticulous, about once every few weeks they would discover it had inexplicably stopped.

"The Eysens belong to the same source," she said, as if it should be obvious. "We were looking for another one because it isn't here, and therefore we see it as separate, but just as two particles can react when separated by great distance —"

"Action at a distance, quantum entanglement?"

"Yes . . . sort of."

"But that's a murky area of disagreement."

"And the Eysen isn't?" she asked rhetorically. "I'm saying they are *one*. If the Eysen-Sphere has taught us anything, it's that it is connected to some kind of undying, recharging, enormous energy that we don't understand. It may even be incomprehensible given the limitations of current human intelligence."

"And yet here we are."

"Right, but what did I tell you each on your first day in this lab?"

"And you've told us again at least a thousand times since," one of them said. "In fact, we should make a sign so you could just point to it."

"'You cannot think of the Eysen in terms of anything you understand because it is too far beyond our

knowledge to apply the limitations of our understanding,'"
they recited in unison.

"Right," she said. "It must show us. We're all simply
wanderers in the universe trying to find our way home."

"A home we don't remember."

"Yes," she said. "Whenever you hit a wall and aren't
sure what to do, stop thinking and unleash your
imagination. Instead of trying to answer the question
you're working on, try to answer the question you're *about*
to ask. This relates to the other Eysen *because* it's a piece of
this Eysen."

"Then how many pieces are there?"

"I don't know," she said, rubbing her eyes and staring
off into nothingness, as if contemplating that question for a
moment before shaking it off. "But I do know that there's
at least one other piece, and Ripley Gaines has it."

The assistants had become like family to Savina, and
yet they did not know of the Judge's mission. They
believed the secrecy was to protect the Eysen from
exploitation by nefarious people or governments until it
could be fully dissected. They each took their charge of
secrecy very seriously because they had seen things in the
Eysen that made them understand the world was radically
different than they, and all other scientists, had previously
believed.

fifteen

At NSA Headquarters in Fort Meade, Maryland, a high level videoconference, which included the Directors of the CIA and the NSA, concluded with a renewal of the Scorch and Burn, or "SAB," order given seven years earlier. SABs were so rare that none had been issued since the first hunt for Gaines and Asher. In fact, only two others had ever been initiated. One concerned Edward Snowden's leaks, and the other, no one left alive outside the secret committee which dictated NSA tasks could remember.

The two lead agents, Claude Rathmore of the NSA, a gung-ho super-patriot who always appeared ready for a fight, and Quinn Murik of the CIA, a man who thought every event in life, no matter how tragic, could be turned into a joke, left the meeting together. Murik thought Rathmore looked like he had perpetual indigestion, but imagined Rathmore thought himself determined looking. The CIA officer believed one could tell a lot by personal appearances. He noted Rathmore's slits for eyes, straight, narrow lips, and a small, but noticeable scar on his cheek. Add to that a close-cropped head of gray and brown hair he might have cut himself, and it all totaled lack of warmth and an uptight personality.

Murik, however, still used mousse in his hair, ensuring that it was always perfect. He was handsome, with twinkling, aware brown eyes and a comical smirk, constantly looking for the next punch line. Rathmore didn't appreciate Murik's junk food habit, or his proclivity for using his INU to the point of distraction.

The two polar opposite agents would answer to Tolis King, the head of the NSA's Veiled Ops. The invisible division, a blind budget entry, enforced what other agencies could not. Although King technically ranked lower than the NSA Director in the government's hierarchy, his authority actually exceeded that of his public boss.

King could call on the power and authority of every civilian and military asset of the US government. Most agencies had a MONSTER, "Mission of National Security Transfer Every Resource," point person, a secret post, even within top-secret clearances. The MONSTER could access all the resources of an agency, department, or any military branch instantly, and often invisibly, for the Veiled Ops unit, known to the MONSTERs simply as "the Unit."

The MONSTER structure was put into place as part of the Patriot Act following the September 11, 2001 terrorist attacks. MONSTER, like so many other provisions, was hidden from public knowledge and withheld from Congress. Even within the government, the few who knew about it believed it to be a resource-sharing plan which could be used to cut through red tape in times of national emergencies and threats to national security. MONSTER was unique because the program had been created by the NSA without input or oversight. Not even the President was aware of its full extent. MONSTER really existed only for a single reason: to make the Unit the most powerful force in the world. With that, it would ensure the NSA agenda was implicitly followed.

Rathmore, a take-no-prisoners patriot who had an odd habit of punctuating orders with rabble-rouser's clichés, didn't much like Murik, first because he didn't think he was serious enough, and second because he was CIA. Rathmore had initially discovered the personality conflict when the pair had worked together once before on a case when a foreign leader needed to be "corrected."

Rathmore's perpetually angry look and his never-without-a-cup-of-coffee habit were well known in the NSA, and translated to a simple rule of *stay out of his way.*

Murik saw it more as a challenge to find humor in the dark. He teased Rathmore for having two cups of coffee in his hands as they walked. "Both for you?"

To his surprise Rathmore nodded and grunted, "Yes." Then, upon seeing Murik's grin added, "What? I believe in always having a backup plan," one of his mottos that apparently applied to consumption of his favorite beverage. They continued down one of the underground corridors toward a situation room.

Murik shook his head, laughing, then changed the subject back to the assignment. "A real life Scotch and Brandy." As usual, Murik was staring into his INU. Rathmore assumed the guy had a porn addiction or something.

"Hey, real life here!" he snapped startling the CIA agent, who stopped walking and looked at Rathmore.

"Relax, Claude. INUs are part of life too," Murik said smugly. "I might even be able to find a date in here for you. I think you could use a little warmth and charm."

"No thanks," Rathmore replied. He couldn't imagine that other people didn't admire his reputation as a hardliner the way he himself did.

"Relax," Murik repeated, giving his shoulder a friendly shove.

Rathmore shook off as if ready for a fistfight. "Relax?" he asked. "Tension *is* how I relax."

Murik laughed and shook his head. "Yikes."

"Gaines loose with that Sphere is pure tension."

"It's difficult to believe, after all this time, that Gaines is really alive," Murik said, moving again, his eyes back on his INU.

Rathmore, who had been assigned the Gaines and Asher case years earlier as part of an ongoing investigation into Booker Lipton, had, like everyone else, assumed that with the passing of each successive year with no traces or clues surfacing, Gaines and Asher were most likely dead. It was now the biggest case in the world. He wondered how a frat boy like Murik had drawn such a critical assignment for the CIA.

"I didn't even think Scotch and Brandy cases were real," Murik said. "Well, it made sense for Snowden, but a dead archeologist and some chick from National Geographic—"

"Murik, how did you land this case?"

"I'm dating the Director's daughter."

Rathmore stopped walking. "Are you kidding?"

Murik laughed. "Of course, I'm kidding. The Director doesn't even have a daughter, and anyway, I'm married."

"Even that doesn't make sense," Rathmore said. "SABs are not safe assignments. Plenty of single agents could take the risk. We may have to go into the field."

"Maybe they figure I'm dispensable," Murik replied, grinning. "But I doubt we'll ever get out of the situation room."

"Yeah," Rathmore halfheartedly agreed as they reached the entrance to one of the highly secured mission-critical situation rooms at NSA headquarters. Rathmore slid his ID card into the reader, then both took turns placing their hands against a screen which authenticated their palm prints. The steel door slid open to reveal a tiny room, which they entered. Once the door behind them closed, they were subjected to door retina scans. The final barrier glided noiselessly out of the way and revealed a wide, dark room full of large monitors, blinking with maps, images, and data. Three technicians were busily attending to the machines, downloading all the information.

One of the technicians stood and briefed the two senior agents. "Here's where we are," the technicians began. "It appears as if Gaines might not have been in Fiji at the time of the accident."

"Where was he?" Murik asked, surprised.

"Possibly, Hawaii. We're running that down now."

"Wait," Rathmore said. "He travels? To the United States?"

"Apparently, although we still don't know how often, or even for sure," the tech cautioned. "We don't even know for sure if he's actually alive."

"Well, he sure as hell survived the helicopter crash in Arizona seven years ago. It's his DNA in that six-year-old girl in the Fiji hospital. Think people, think!" Rathmore snapped. "Let's have someone pick up that FBI agent who was on the scene. What was his name?"

"Barbeau. Dixon Barbeau. He's no longer with the Bureau, but he's around," Murik said, punching the commands into his Eysen-INU.

"Word just in that Gaines' daughter was discharged," the tech said.

"What? I thought we gave orders—" Rathmore began.

"It seems the Fijians don't know we run the world," Murik offered with a slight laugh.

"Damn it, Murik, this is serious," Rathmore barked. "The girl is how we found them. She's the only lead. Where did she go? We gotta do this!"

"We're just getting that data in now," the tech said. "Look." He pointed to another monitor, which showed images of Gale, Kruse, and Cira leaving the hospital.

"Thankfully they took a chopper," Murik said. "Cars are much harder to track from space."

The tech nodded their agreement. "You can see this is from about two hours ago, but now that we're onto them, we're catching up and moving closer to real time."

"They went to that?" Rathmore asked, indicating an area on the giant monitor which appeared to be a field. "Is that a developed airstrip?"

"Yes," the tech answered. "We had the airport closed by then."

As the system continued tracing Gale's race via chopper, then plane, the agents sped through time until they caught up with the synch.

"There they are in-flight," the tech said.

"Can you pro*ject* their tra*ject*ory?" Murik asked, emphasizing the words dramatically. When a few of the techs laughed, he was temporarily content.

"Obviously they didn't file a flight plan," Rathmore said. "Or at least not a legitimate one. What's the range of that plane?"

"The simulations are kicking in," the tech said. "There seem to be three possibilities. The Philippines, Indonesia, or possibly Malaysia."

"Cross-check those destinations with Booker Lipton holdings," Rathmore said. "Come on, people, crank it up!"

"As if that will help," Murik said. "Booker has more things hidden than—"

"What the hell!" Rathmore yelled as they all watched the plane crash into the sea.

"Are you kidding me?" Murik said.

"I don't believe it's real," Rathmore snapped. "I've seen this movie before."

"What?" Murik protested. "Do you think they *staged* that?"

"It's Booker Lipton. Of course they staged it."

"It looks mighty convincing," the tech added.

"Very," Murik agreed.

"I'm not buying it," Rathmore said. "This is the Canyon de Chelly copter explosion all over again. How quickly can we get someone to that crash site?"

"Let me see," the tech replied, checking various monitors. "If you can get a MONSTER to move the Navy, I'd say ETA seventy-five or eighty minutes."

"Seventy-five minutes?" Rathmore barked, slamming his fist on the table. "Unacceptable!"

"If we had anyone closer, we would've been able to stop them at the hospital," Murik said as Rathmore started a conversation with the Navy MONSTER.

"Okay, we think we can be there in sixty-four minutes," Rathmore said, shooting a look to the tech as if his estimate had been way off. "Meantime, keep everything we've got all over that site. Any boats or planes come within a mile of it, I want to know. Let's do this!"

"What about Gaines?" Murik asked. "He wasn't even on that plane."

"Right," Rathmore agreed. "What do we have on Gaines?"

"An address," the tech said, looking at a screen.

"Seriously?" Murik asked.

"Not where he is now, but where he was yesterday," the tech replied.

"That's a hell of a lot more than we had five minutes ago," Rathmore said. "Rock and roll!"

"A hell of a lot more than we've had for the past seven years," Murik added.

"I want someone there fifteen minutes ago," Rathmore ordered one of the other technicians. "Talk to everyone who might have even had coffee with him, arrest them if you have to. Anyone who recognizes his face should be in custody. Clear?

"Yes, sir."

"Asher and their daughter don't even matter if we can find Gaines first." Rathmore downed another gulp of hot caffeine.

"I'm already tracing everything that moved out from that address," the first tech said. "But, as you know, it can be a slow process."

"Not if you have additional inputs," Rathmore said. "Cross everything with Booker Lipton, his companies, known associates, properties, any assets, everything. Burn down the town!"

"Are you sure Booker is still helping them?" Murik asked.

"How else have they stayed under the radar for seven years?" Rathmore shot back.

"The artifact," Murik offered. "If it's everything they say it is, Gaines and Asher might not need Booker Lipton, and we may need a lot more than a MONSTER to bring them in."

sixteen

Stellard snapped up his down vest as he listened to the report from Wattington in audio text mode. The NSA had renewed the Scorch and Burn against Gaines and Asher. That was not unexpected, but upon learning of the MONSTERs, Stellard realized the Foundation was in a much weaker position than he'd previously thought.

"The SAB and MONSTERs change everything," Stellard said, his INU instantly converting his voice into scrambled text. "Can you get a list of MONSTERs?"

Wattington read the text and sighed. "Mission of National Security Transfer Every Resource" personnel weren't called MONSTERs just because DC loved acronyms. MONSTERs were scary. They could override generals and command enormous resources. With that power came the need for extra-classified appointments. "You ask too much," he texted back.

Stellard's early career had been spent in the CIA, so he knew about the unchecked power that both the CIA and the NSA possessed, in spite of the media-friendly illusion of congressional oversight. But back in his days with the agency, MONSTERs didn't exist, at least not formally. Occasionally, a well-connected, well-liked official in one agency, department, or branch could trade favors with another. However, that was unusual. The typical behavior was one of competition, for credit, turf, or personnel, but primarily for budget dollars.

"The Foundation simply has to reach the Sphere first," Stellard replied. "Get the list. Do anything necessary. Do you understand? This is the time."

"We should not overstep now, or the future is in danger," Wattington said.

"You don't understand. The future will not matter if HITE gets the Eysen. You're authorized and ordered to take every risk." Implicit in Stellard's directive were bribery, espionage, and assassination, up to the highest levels, whatever it took.

Wattington read the text and then clicked off. HITE, another acronym, belonged to one of the US government's most guarded secrets. Even the name, Hidden Information and Technology Exchange, belied the science fiction world, which lay behind the gates of the top-secret HITE facility in the Nevada mountains.

Impossible, he thought as he began a different text conversation with a Foundation operative who'd been working on cracking HITE.

Stellard mumbled something even he didn't understand after the contact with Wattington ended, hitting the thermostat remote to pump more heat, and then connected back to Taz.

His INU projected images from the operation in Fiji, and he suddenly felt optimistic. Earlier his hopes had been dashed when initial police reports stated that Cira Bradley, aka Gaines and Asher's six-year-old daughter, had been discharged. Now, however, they were talking about a fresh lead in the hospital.

"While we're waiting on the patient testimony," Taz said, still aboard the plane racing to Fiji, "they've discovered hidden cameras at the Bradley residence. The cameras aren't saving their recordings onto any devices on the premises, so we can't access the footage, but the video is being transmitted across the Internet, so it's possible we may be able to trace the link and find out who's been monitoring them."

"I can already tell you that it's Booker Lipton. He's been monitoring them, and wherever you go, the trace will lead either to a dead-end or an Asian sweat shop," Stellard said, raising his voice. "Is that *all* we've got?"

"The residence is clean. They've been careful. Indications are they left in a hurry, but there isn't so much as a scrap of paper with any adult writing on it, just some kid's crayon drawings. The 'I love mommy' and 'I love daddy' type of stuff."

Stellard took a deep breath. He had to remind himself that when the day began, the odds said Gaines and Asher were long dead and the Eysen-Sphere destroyed. Now they knew that to be false. They'd come a million miles. Unfortunately, the miles were not in the direction of the Aylantic Foundation's goals.

Stellard thought about how they had arrived at this point. During the years leading up to the discovery of the Eysen-Sphere, and particularly those after, the world had become increasingly dangerous. Income inequality had grown horribly out of control with the five hundred richest people owning about eighty-seven percent of the world's wealth. Terrorism was exploding around the globe, with the buzz of revolution in nearly every country, including the United States. The Foundation had been formed out of this environment and had only two objectives: one, solve the problem, meaning stop the uprising by any means necessary, and two, preserve the wealth and power of the members.

A brilliant and controversial plan had been developed in secret. A core group within the Foundation decided it was the only way, the final option. They dubbed the plan the Phoenix Initiative, and embraced it completely. Although not all members were aware of the entire scope of the Phoenix Initiative, they signed off, believing in the leadership and concerned for their futures.

The Initiative actually began with a simple idea — consolidate all the nations on Earth under a single government and force peace with a single, powerful, police-army-force. Turning the Initiative into reality was incredibly complex, but most of the membership didn't worry about exactly how it would happen. The leadership had convinced them that there was a plan that could only succeed in secret.

Stellard, a member of powerful furtive organizations such as the Trilateral Commission and the Bilderberg Group, was one of the few privy to the Aylantik Foundation's entire scheme. He'd come from wealth, not the hard-working, create-a-great-idea kind of riches, but rather money that was so old and ran so deep it was contained in the fibers of the currency. Stellard knew two things to be absolute: that the Foundation's plan could work, and that only one person and one thing could stop it.

Booker Lipton and the Eysen-Sphere.

$-O-$

The sound of the local police coming online with an update for Taz brought Stellard back to the present.

"There is a patient, a woman. She identified a photo of Gale Asher and claims to have witnessed Asher and the girl leaving the hospital," the officer-in-charge reported from Fiji. "The patient told us Asher and the girl boarded a helicopter."

"Was Gaines with her?" Taz asked.

"She said there was a man with them. We showed her a photo of Gaines, but the patient insisted it was not him. Her recollection was that the man appeared younger than Gaines, and might have been Asher's brother, or even a bodyguard or something."

Stellard muted all links except the one with Taz. "What do you think?" he asked.

"Gaines could have been disguised."

"Yes, but wouldn't they have had at least one of Booker's agents with them?" Stellard asked, studying the images feeding through his INU.

"Perhaps they were meeting on the helicopter," Taz said. "Wait, here comes security camera footage showing images of Asher and her daughter leaving the hospital. See the man? No way that's Gaines."

"Agreed. We'll run him down, but that's definitely one of Booker's people," Stellard said, suddenly distracted by an urgent text from Wattington. He read it twice, then said to Taz, "We need to change your flight plan. I know where Gaines is."

seventeen

In all the years since the Eysen-Sphere first came to life, Crying Man had never spoken to them. Instead, he'd always conveyed meaning through his expression, hand gestures, and his eyes, yet Gale and Rip had hoped, even expected, that one day he might speak.

There were times when it seemed as if he were about to, or at least was thinking about it, but something between hesitation or loss seemed to stop him. Gale and Rip didn't even know if the Cosegans were capable of speaking. After the first few years of studying the Sphere, Rip theorized that perhaps the vocal chords of the Cosegans had not yet evolved eleven million years ago because they didn't need to speak verbally.

Crying Man looked at Rip with a sorrowful expression.

"Thank you," were the first words that made it to Rip's lips.

Crying Man's stare was filled with concern.

"Please," Rip said. "Can you *please* speak to me?"

Crying Man walked around the skyroom, staring out the windows, seemingly admiring the view, until a single tree caught his attention. It was the largest tree on the island, twisting up among the palms and other spindly, tropical trees. Its thick, smooth bark and broad trunk appeared to have emerged from a Tolkien realm, the only tree that reached above the skyroom, but it mostly curved around the southern corner of the tower as if purposely trying to avoid obstructing the view. Crying Man appeared to be concentrating intently on the tree.

Rip didn't wish to interrupt him. It almost seemed as if the Cosegan was having a psychic conversation with the tree. If that were possible, and the Cosegans had already proven that almost anything was, what would that mean to be able to traverse into the secrets of the natural world? Gale believed that every living thing was connected in some way. Was this proof?

Crying Man's expression changed repeatedly as he stared at the tree, then he abruptly turned to Rip and nodded.

Although Crying Man didn't say anything, Rip had the sense that he was answering yes. He wanted to look at the Eysen to see if it was filled with yellow flowers, which early on in their research had seemed to indicate a positive response to questions posed to the Sphere. In this case, however, Crying Man held his gaze, and that was how the silent conversation began.

"How are you here?" Rip asked in his thoughts.

"The same as you. I am a resident of this moment," Crying Man answered mentally.

"But you're from eleven million years ago."

Crying Man nodded. "In any form of measurement, so many rotations around the sun star are long in duration, impossible to imagine. But it is not as simple as that. Time becomes heavy when measured, and heavier still when experienced. Yet that is only because of human perceptions. In truth, time is in the eyes." He pointed to his eyes. "That is where we see everything."

"Yes vision, but—"

"No, not *vision*." Crying Man shook his head. "Not looking out from the eyes, looking *into* them."

"Into what?"

"The universe."

"In the eyes?"

Crying Man nodded. "Without this," he pointed to his eyes again, "time does not exist. Time is only something we made up. Understand?"

Rip wasn't sure.

"I am alive eleven million circles ago, and yet I am here now with you, just like that." Crying Man snapped his fingers.

"But how do you do it?"

"To understand the answer, you would need to come to my world. You may try to think of all those years compressed, forced into the Sphere so that we both may stand around that duration, gaze upon it, sample from it, consider its meaning, and be joined through it."

"It's hard for me to fathom."

"You will understand this completely when you die."

Rip wanted to ask about Cira and Gale, but another question suddenly overtook his thoughts. He tried to push it from his mind, forgetting that by even thinking it, he'd already asked it in their silent conversation.

"What happens when a person dies . . . " Crying Man repeated Rip's unspoken query. "When you die, the light of stars fills you again, the energy of all who have ever lived flows into your being, and you remember everything."

"How do you know this?"

"We, whom you call the Cosegans, have mastered the restraints of human limitations."

"But then, what happened to your society?"

He turned and looked back out to the ocean for a moment before returning his stare to Rip's. "It is stable at this moment."

"This moment? When is that exactly? I see the Cosegan world from afar, across the divide of more than ten thousand millennia. Where is this moment in all of that?"

"You must understand that when you see me, I am not coming to you in a linear way. The last time you saw me may not have happened 'yet.' When you next see me, it may be 'before' this occasion." Crying Man grimaced, as if remembering something painful.

Rip tried to process the Cosegan concept of time. Assuming Crying Man was a sophisticated artificial Intelligence "guide" or interface into the Sphere's "operating system," then accessing "him" at various random out-of-sequence points made sense. Still, Rip wondered what had happened to them.

"So your civilization, or what we see as cities and call the Cosegan world, are as powerful and beautiful now as they were when we first saw them seven years ago?" Rip asked, then pushed, "What happened to your people?"

"I'm sorry. I must go now."

"Wait," Rip said, worried he may have offended Crying Man somehow and needing him to help.

"Cira and Gale," Crying Man said, detecting Rip's concern in his thoughts.

"Yes. I need help protecting Cira and Gale," Rip said breathlessly as Crying Man projected their names. "Can you do something? Will you?"

"Do you see the Sphere that you call the Eysen?"

"Yes," Rip said, turning toward it.

"And yet you question if I can protect your loved ones today?" Crying Man was suddenly just a face inside the Sphere. "After all the days you have spent looking within the Sphere, you still have no idea what we are capable of."

eighteen

Booker's submarine, propelled by a Cosegan water-powered turbine, surged toward an unlikely destination. The propulsion system plans had been gleaned years earlier from the Sphere, and made the sub by far the fastest in the world. Equipped with the latest stealth technology, it was also almost completely undetectable. Even without the special attributes of the sub, Booker hardly thought the Americans would be looking for an underwater vessel. It was a guarded secret that Booker even possessed a fleet of such crafts, more advanced than the US Navy's best, but Booker was preparing for more than just evacuations.

Along with the glimpses of the future they'd seen in the Eysen-Sphere, Booker had also spent more than a decade studying a long-hidden secret manuscript relating to the Sphere, known as the Clastier Papers. Clastier, a nineteenth century priest, had also found an Eysen, and had written extensively on what he learned.

His papers were divided into three sections: the Attestations, the Divinations, and the Inspirations. It was the second section which haunted Booker. The Divinations were Clastier's prophecies, and the final four tormented all who had read them.

1. Global pandemics and super-viruses wipe out vast numbers of the world's population.

2. A utopian period after a great plague.

3. Climate destabilization resulting in uncertain levels of mass destruction.

4. World War III, a conflict of such proportion that humanity might not survive.

Clastier had accurately foretold the rise of the United States, Hitler's atrocities during World War II, the development and dropping of the atomic bomb, the moon landing, the fall of religions, and many other significant world events, long before they'd happened. Booker, Gale, and Rip had extensively debated on the order of the Divinations, specifically when the predicted events were expected to occur, and the actual impact of each. The three of them were somehow determined to stop them from happening.

Booker enlisted the help of the leaders of the Inner Movement. The Movement, or "IM," as they were usually known, had begun years earlier, and had gained traction when a group of young people, who were reported to have supernatural gifts, exposed government corruption and demanded an end to war. Although the claims of extraordinary abilities had never been proven, many believed that the human mind had unlimited potential and could achieve remarkable things. Indeed, the discovery of the Eysen-Sphere and its seemingly endless stream of data emboldened those beliefs. Consequently, the Movement had grown.

The prophesized fall of the world's religions had left a void which IM filled for many. The ranks of IM were full of people who could be categorized in one of three ways: those still seeking something bigger than themselves, those searching for answers to the great questions of life, and those who thought the world should find a way to avoid war and violence because humans were meant to live in a perpetual state of peace. Most fit into all three categories, but the IM had slowly and quietly become something of a force in the world. Not surprisingly, Booker secretly funded most of its operations, and he also knew that the Aylantik Foundation wanted to destroy the Movement.

The Foundation had three natural enemies who were preventing it from putting its Phoenix Initiative into action. Booker was one. The US government was another. The Aylantik Foundation could not put its plan into place while the United States remained the world's sole superpower, but Booker knew from Gale and Rip's Eysen research that the Foundation would soon find a way to circumvent the US government. That was the reason the Foundation's third enemy, the Inner Movement, must be strengthened.

In one of his secret offices, Booker sat in front of a large bank of Eysen-INUs. He was about to contact Linh, the leader of the Inner Movement, to update her on the situation, when he noticed Gale and Kruse in a heated conversation. Booker had micro-cameras everywhere. It was another technology he'd discovered in the Eysen-Sphere, and it allowed him to instantly monitor people and events all over the globe.

He listened in on Gale and Kruse.

"How are we going to get to *El Prison* without the NSA, or who knows else, finding us?" Gale demanded.

"We're going to put you on a commercial flight from Nadi Airport," Kruse said.

"We're going *back* to Fiji? And I'm going to just walk through security and board a regular plane?" Gale looked flabbergasted. "Am I at least flying first class so I'll be comfortable when they shoot me?"

"We have a way to bypass security. We'll get on while they're prepping the plane," Kruse said. "We'll fly in the crew rest area, behind the cockpit. No one will see us. But US intelligence, if they're still even checking flights out of Fiji, will assume security would pick you up trying to board. It's actually the private planes they'll be triple-checking."

"Wait, if we're going back to Fiji, I can see Cira," Gale said, her face suddenly lighting up.

"No."

"There must be a way."

"You're out of your mind."

"Then you're going to have to drug me again to stop me."

"Fine."

"Don't even think about it."

"Gale, if you went near that hospital, Cira would be doomed."

"You're right," Gale said after a moment, staring into the distance, lost in thought, unknowingly looking right into one of Booker's cameras. "Okay then."

Booker spoke quietly into Kruse's earpiece. "Drug her. She's going to make a break for it at the airport."

Kruse closed his eyes. He'd had the same hunch, but he knew if he drugged her again it would likely mean he'd have to be reassigned, because there's no way in hell Gale would ever trust him again, and it's impossible to protect someone who doesn't trust you.

−O−

While trapped under trillions of gallons of water, Gale pondered the thing that had caused all of this, the thing that could fix it all.

The Sphere. It could show them any point in time across billions of years. Booker's study of Universe Quantum Physics had begun prior to their discovery of the Sphere, almost in anticipation of it, and although they had never heard an actual voice from the Crying Man, they could feel his communication.

Somehow the Cosegans built a machine that could contain all the knowledge of the universe, she thought, as she had hundreds of times since they had first realized the power of the Eysen-Sphere. *How did they accumulate that knowledge? How did they get it into a small, basketball-sized sphere that could withstand the passage of millions of years?*

These questions had burned in her mind for seven years, and with each stunning view into the Sphere, they were more amazed, but seemingly no closer to the answers. Perhaps the most remarkable thing about the

Sphere was that it had exact, and one-hundred-percent complete, detailed visual accounts of the eleven million years since its creation, continuing on indefinitely into the future.

Gale recalled the pivotal conversation she'd had with Rip after discovering she was pregnant with Cira.

"What do you want to do?" Rip asked somberly after first embracing Gale and telling her how much he loved her.

Gale took a deep breath. She understood his question and its implications, not because they didn't want a child, but because they both knew too much about the future.

"This child could be important," Gale said.

"A lot of parents believe that about their children."

"But in our case it could be true. We have the Eysen-Sphere. We have the Clastier Papers. This child will be a descendent of the Builders."

"The child will grow up here on El Perdido in hiding, and could lose her parents at anytime."

"Her?" Gale asked, catching his reference to the yet unknown sex of the child.

"Just a guess."

"Have you seen anything?" Gale asked, wondering if the Sphere had revealed something about the child's future.

"No, I would have told you." Rip looked at her. The blue of her eyes had changed him as much as the Sphere had. He called them "magic eyes," and often, when he struggled for an answer to some dilemma, he would find the solution in her eyes. "Gale, if we have this child, she may not live through the plague. She'll be eight or nine when it starts, ten or twelve when it completely ravages the world. Could you take losing a child? Because I know I couldn't."

"What if she survives?" Gale asked. "She'll grow up learning from the Sphere. She'll inherit it one day."

Rip nodded.

"Somehow we escaped," Gale continued. "Clastier and the Sphere will protect her . . . as they've been protecting us."

Not long after they made the decision to have Cira, the Sphere showed them a scene of the future so awful that they reconsidered, but by then it was too late to safely terminate the pregnancy. They wanted the baby, but could not imagine bringing her into the world that was coming. Plague and war, a pause, and then more war and another plague. It was one thing to read Clastier's Divinations, they had committed their lives to preventing the Final Four, but to see them projected from the Sphere, as if they were watching footage of something that had already occurred, was horrifying. Viewing the world that their child would face made Gale and Rip more determined, desperate actually, to find a way to stop it.

−O−

Gale found herself wishing the Crying Man was real instead of just the face of an ancient computer. Maybe he could save Cira.

Why hadn't they seen this coming? Even after seven years of seeing everything inside the Sphere, Rip didn't completely buy Gale's theory that the Eysen-Sphere was what many people called the Akashic Records. Akasha, an ancient word meaning sky, had been used to describe all the accumulated knowledge and experience that has ever occurred, or ever will exist. They were somehow stored, and could theoretically be accessed in the ethereal.

Although the Sphere seemed to match the description, even exceed it, Rip needed a more scientific explanation. Gale had argued that it didn't matter what you called it− the Sphere fit the story. The Akashic Records had long been considered part legend, part myth, and a matter of faith for many, but perhaps the story had originated from someone who had seen a Sphere hundreds or thousands of years earlier. They knew there had been at least two others, but what if there had been *hundreds*? What if a carpenter in Nazareth found one, two thousand years earlier? What if Leonardo da Vinci, Nostradamus, or Einstein got a glimpse into one? What about Hitler?

They had asked every question, but even while holding this object Rip called "an instrument to view eternity," they were not able to find the answers they needed most, those they labeled the Five Cosega Mysteries.

1. What is the Sphere
2. Who were the Cosegans?
3. Where did they come from?
4. Why did they leave the Sphere?
5. What happened to them?

They were constantly frustrated because, while possessing the most powerful object in the universe, they were mostly navigating blind, like an infant with an INU. Yet inside the Sphere, Gale knew there were the answers, not just to the Five Cosega Mysteries, but also how to save Cira, and the future.

nineteen

Savina flipped her dark, luxurious mane behind her lean, muscled shoulders, flexing them as she took the call from the Judge in her private office. Although he was considerably older, he'd made his feelings clear. He was in love with her, would leave his wife, do anything for her, but she viewed him as a father figure.

"Infatuation," she'd told him, many times. "You love my mind because you love power, and what is more powerful than a brilliant mind?"

He agreed to not pursue a romantic relationship, but only reluctantly. In either case, an affair with her would have complicated the mission, and the Phoenix Initiative was already complicated enough.

"So you think you can find him?" the Judge asked as he sketched a lingering detail into his latest mechanical drawing. A frustrated engineer whose pursuit of perfect artificial limbs had somehow landed him in the pharmaceutical industry. He now controlled one-third of the world's prescription drug market. His father had become a quadriplegic after an accident when the Judge was still a teen. Seeing his father suffer, the Judge was determined to create artificial limbs and sleeves for amputees and paralyzed patients. Many advancements had been made, but he still worked constantly, always seeking the elusive miracle solution.

"I'm almost certain of it," Savina responded.

The Judge was delighted with her answer because he wanted the other Eysen-Sphere. He had no doubt that Savina was smarter than Gaines, and therefore had progressed farther into the Sphere than the archaeologist, but only a Sphere could stop the Phoenix Initiative. With a second Sphere, the Foundation would discover more of the Cosegan secrets, secrets they could use to ensure the successful launch of Phoenix. Perhaps even more important would be taking away the greatest power from the Foundation's greatest threat—Booker Lipton would be much easier to defeat.

Savina wanted to know what Gaines had found, wanted to see if his Sphere was different, if the two Spheres together would be more powerful. She knew there was more than just eleven million years of information to traverse. The Sphere actually held what was equivalent to the size and age of the entire universe. How could the exploration ever be completed?

"We may find Gaines before you do," the Judge said as mini robots walked across his desk. "But when it comes to slipping away, his track record is perfect."

"The Sphere can lead us to Gaines," she said, her voice filled with excitement. The Eysen-Sphere had become her life. Beyond all the extraordinary discoveries already made lay the real addiction, the infinite possibilities.

The Judge had shown her how the flaws of the future could be corrected, how the world could be saved from itself. She believed in the power of that, and even more. Savina was certain that her reason for existing, the purpose of her life, and the most important job on Earth, was to use the secrets of the Cosega Sequence to ensure the future of humanity. In that, she and Gaines were very similar, but their methods, motives, and vision made them diametrically opposed to one another.

"Let me know when we get there. *If* we get there," the Judge said.

"*When* we get there," she corrected.

"Savina!" one of her assistants yelled. "Come quick!"

She ended the call and ran back into the main lab in time to see the Eysen-Sphere spinning so fast it'd became a blur.

"How long has it been doing this?" she whispered.

"It started just before we called you."

"What was happening before it began?"

"It showed another Sphere!" one of them said. "Another Eysen-Sphere appeared inside this one."

Savina walked around the spinning Eysen, worried that at any second it might fly across the room, that it would somehow destroy itself by rising up to the ceiling and crashing back down to the floor.

In order for Spheres to levitate and project elaborately, they required a second ancient artifact known as an Odeon Chip. The Foundation's Sphere, formerly belonging to the Vatican, no longer had its original Chip. The Vatican hadn't even known they needed one until Savina figured it out. The Judge discovered an obscure mention of it while reviewing NSA files on Gaines' time in Mexico before his "death." As it turned out, the Vatican also had a Chip in their secret archives, but had not known what it did, or if it was even connected to the Eysen-Sphere. The Judge acquired the Chip and the Sphere after the Church fell, but it was not the original Chip for that Sphere. According to Archive records, the Church had come into possession of the Chip in the year 321, and they didn't capture the Sphere until the mid-1800s. Savina had long been concerned that the mismatch might cause problems or limit her access.

"Do you think it's the Chip's compatibility issue, or because the two Spheres are connecting?" an assistant asked.

"Maybe there can't be two Spheres on the same spectrum," she said, thinking out loud.

"I think the Eysen is way beyond the spectrum," one of the assistants replied.

"Not the spectrum of frequencies or the energy spectrum. Not as we know it in physics. I'm talking about a dimensional spectrum," she explained, moving closer to the Sphere. "Look, the spinning is causing friction with the surrounding particles. It's going so fast that it's distorting the space around it. Do you see?"

The assistants crouched next to her and stared at the Sphere. "Yes," they both agreed. The air around the Sphere appeared wavy, like heat coming off a hot road in the summer.

"So it's getting ready to move," one of them asked, hesitantly, "into another dimension?"

"I don't know what it's doing," she answered. "Look. It's *incredible*." She involuntarily moved her hand in front of her mouth, as if to silence anything that might disturb the moment.

The distortion moved out in ripples, micro-thin circles, similar to a pebble dropped into a pond. The ripples were difficult to see, but they were there. The assistants backed up a couple of feet, apparently not wanting to get hit by the waves.

Savina dipped her hand in between the ripples, gasping as her hand disappeared.

"Pull it out!" one of the assistants shouted.

Savina held it steady for a moment and contemplated how she could get her entire body into the distortion waves. "Do you realize what this is?" she asked in a mesmerized tone.

"Where is your hand?" one asked, still alarmed.

"Another dimension," the other answered. "Savina, how does it feel?"

"My hand . . . it . . . it's as if I could fly. All the sensations from my hand are gone, but there's no pain . . . Instead of what it was, now I . . . anything I think I feel, heat, cold, pain, pleasure, it's instantaneous. It fills my body, but it comes from the place or dimension where my hand is."

"Are we getting this?" one of them asked, looking for the indicator light on the recording master control.

The sound of wind came from the Sphere and Savina's hand began to emerge; however, it remained translucent.

"It's winding down," one of them said.

As the Sphere slowed, its color turned a deep shade of purple. Images of galaxies radiated outward, transforming the room into a giant planetarium.

Savina looked down at her hand, already knowing it was back because the infinite sensations, as she would later describe, were gone.

The Eysen-Sphere stopped, and then suddenly went black. Savina and her assistants looked at each other. Before any of them could speak, the entire lab went dark. Battery backups began beeping and emergency lights popped on.

"The generator will kick in any second," one of the assistants assured them. He'd barely finished his sentence when the room dropped back into silent darkness.

"We're totally down," someone said.

"What's going on?" the first voice asked.

"It's the Sphere," Savina said.

They turned to where they thought it should be, but the darkness allowed nothing. One of them reached for the penlight he kept in his pocket. He tried it several times, but it also failed.

"I'm telling you, it's the Eysen," Savina repeated. "Just wait."

"For what?"

"I think we found the other one," Savina whispered reverently. "We found Gaines' Eysen."

"How?" he asked, suddenly aware of the sensation of floating.

"Just before I took that call, I had inputted all we know of Gaines' Eysen."

"You can't *input* anything into the Eysen-Sphere. It's read-only."

"Oh yeah? Look."

The Eysen they'd all been staring at, without being able to see it, had, at its center, a pinpoint of light. Within the absolute blackness of the room, the tiny glow appeared as a spotlight.

"What's it doing now?" an assistant asked.

The room instantly filled with colors, swirling in a vortex of exaggerated hues.

"We're not getting this recorded," an assistant reminded them.

"It doesn't matter," Savina shouted above a gathering roar of white noise, sounding as if an enormous waterfall was pouring in on them. "I'm not sure the equipment is in the room anymore anyway!"

The assistants looked around, finding that there was nothing left of the lab. No tables, no equipment, not even any walls.

"I don't think *we're* in the lab anymore!" one of them yelled.

"I-It's as if," Savina stuttered, but they couldn't hear her above the roar. "It's as if we're inside the Eysen."

"Savina, the Eysen has engulfed the lab ... It's consumed us!" one of them yelled.

"And it feels glorious!" she shouted back.

"Where is it taking us?"

"To Ripley Gaines!"

twenty

Rip wasn't really sure if he had dreamed the episode with Crying Man or not. He did remember being asleep, but he also recalled being awake through much of the night. It seemed so astonishing that it didn't feel real. The Sphere only showed the present day Earth. Before Rip had a chance to delve back into the Cosegan world, his INU lit up. It was Huang.

"I have a connection to Booker."

"A thousand thank yous, Huang. Once again, you've proved yourself amazing."

"Anytime, Rip. Here you go," Huang said, switching the connection.

"Rip," Booker began, "now before you go all ballistic on me—"

"Booker, you get me off this goddamned island and take me to Gale and Cira, or so help me I'll *destroy* the Sphere."

"Damn it, Rip. Calm down. They're both safe."

"But you *lied*. You knew the breach was caused by Cira going to the hospital. Her eye... her *eyes*!" Rip shouted. "How dare you? This is my family."

"How dare I?" Booker shot back "How dare *you*. Do you think this is only about *you*? What about the millions of other families? *Billions* are in jeopardy."

"My family is the only one *I* can save."

"That's not true. You may care only about yours, but you know the world will not be fit for even *your* precious family if we lose the Eysen-Sphere . . . It's the Sphere, Rip. The Sphere is more important than your family, you, or me, because without the Sphere we can't save anything. NOTHING! And you know it."

"Screw that, Booker, and screw you!"

Rip stormed over to the window and, for the first time, viewed El Perdido like Gale did. As a prison. He knew Booker was right, he just couldn't allow that thought in. The possibility of losing his family.

Rip began to shake. A terrible wail overtook him, building, consuming his insides, bursting to explode, desperate to be released, frantically needing to relieve the pressure of all that his life had become. He turned to the Sphere, still floating where he left it. The miraculous object could be more accurately described as a curse.

"Let. Me. GOOOOOO!" he screamed with all the surging, pent-up emotion.

Booker, of course, assumed Rip was yelling at him, but Rip was actually raging at the Sphere. The thing that had stolen his life. The object of his obsession had trapped him. Beyond that, his anger flew in a thousand directions.

He was furious because Booker was right. How could his family survive in the world that was coming? How could Cira grow up and live a life in a world that was no longer real? It would be impossible to grow in a society where the scars from karmic crimes could never be healed, but he saved his greatest disdain for himself.

How had he not been able to get deep enough into the infinite pool that was the Eysen-Sphere to save them all, to solve all the problems, to stop the evil pursuing them? That evil, dressed and masquerading as real people? Billionaires, politicians, terrorists, extremists, everyday average folks in comfort and complacency, not bothering to notice the danger? He'd learned that from Gale. "We're not here to eat fast food, watch television, and accumulate stuff." She'd said it a hundred times since they'd met.

The Sphere had shown him she was right. Something more was out there.

Booker, as if reading his mind, launched a tirade.

"Haven't you seen enough? The Eysen has taken you across the universe, shown you the meaning of time, taught you we're not a random accident, adrift and alone. We have *purpose*. We have done this, and yet you still act as if this is just an artifact. Stop being a damned archaeologist! The Eysen-Sphere is our hope, Rip. It's the dream of us. The Sphere is *everything!*"

"But we still don't understand it."

"Can we? Are we *capable* of understanding something like this? Something that is more than all of everything we've ever imagined? You named it correctly all those years ago. 'Eysen, to hold all the stars in your hand.' The entire universe is in there. How can we grasp all of that? You have to trust that Cira and Gale will survive . . . but if they don't, that is how it was meant to be. I can assure you they will still exist somewhere, and you, Rip, you're the fortunate one who possesses the keys to find them."

"That is not fair. You can't write people off like that."

He thought of Crying Man. Was he already protecting them? Would he? Could he? Did it really happen?

"I'm not writing them off, but this is about more than attachment."

"Attachment? Booker, you're talking about the same thing. You're attached to the world, this world, the way it is, the way you think it should be. You want to be a hero and save the world—"

"*Change* it," Booker corrected.

"Change the world, save it, orbit it, blow it up, I don't give a damn. Why don't you try letting go of that?"

"And what will that do? Will that save Gale and Cira?"

"Maybe."

"For how long?" Booker asked.

"Long enough for me to find a way. "

"Contrary to what you see in the movies, the end of the world doesn't come all at once. It slips away from us, bit by bit. One bad decision, one compromise, one fear filled second at a time."

"And?" Rip asked.

"There isn't much time left . . . There is a history of the future, and some things are irreversible."

twenty-one

The police officers hurrying down the corridor toward Cira's hidden hospital room were high-ranking deputy commissioners. The nurse and orderly watched the image in the INU, then turned to Harmer with panicked looks.

"We're done now," the orderly whispered too loudly.

"No," Harmer said, waving her arm in a silencing motion. "Their weapons are still holstered."

The orderly checked the live view again, seeing that the men were twenty feet away from the door to the bogus supply room.

Booker watched the same video feed, ready to give airborne AX agents the go-ahead as soon as Harmer signaled. Booker's assistant filled his glass for the third time, a concoction of Amazonian herbs. As he drank, Booker never took his eyes away from the images coming from Fiji.

Harmer remained calm. Only when the police were about five feet from the door did she move to a forward position next to the false panel. She held her weapon steady, an unlit cigarette pursed tightly between her dry lips. Her free hand pointed at the orderly, as if willing him to remain calm. Harmer could hear the click of the officer's boots as they approached. She mentally measured the remaining distance—three feet, two, one ... Harmer kept her eyes fixed on the back of the panel even as the footsteps passed. Then, as she heard them enter the next room, she went back to the INU.

For six more tense minutes they waited. Finally, all four officers came noisily back into the corridor. Harmer returned to the panel and listened as they walked by. She clearly heard them saying that the patient had seen Gale, her daughter, and a bodyguard leave the hospital hours earlier. The police seemed to believe it.

She exhaled a long sigh as their voices faded in the distance and she returned to check the feed.

"Dodged a bullet," Booker said in her ear. He'd already given the stand-down order to the AX agents in the air.

"Looks like it." Harmer replied, scanning all the feeds from around the hospital. Police officers were slowly returning to the lobby. Both the relief and the antiseptic smell, left her feeling nauseous, desperate for a cigarette.

−O−

"Who the hell is this patient?" Taz asked once he had the Police Commissioner back on the line. In spite of all the evidence, based on what he knew about Asher, and he'd studied her for seven years, she was not the type of mother who would abandon her daughter under such conditions.

"As I said, she's an eyewitness. She identified the subjects. Her story corroborates that of the doctor and other staff members and, most importantly, the footage of them leaving. Her room has a clear view of the helipad where Gale Asher arrived and departed. I'm sorry to say your fugitives are no longer here. Probably long gone from Fiji would be my guess."

"Check again!" Taz demanded, wanting to punch his gold-ring-clad hand through his INU. "They wouldn't move that girl right after surgery." The Foundation had managed to get into the medical records, and already had two doctors review the case. Both were in complete agreement that moving the girl immediately following surgery would almost certainly result in permanent vision loss. They insisted a minimum of ten days would be required to avert any post-op risks.

"Okay," the Commissioner said in an annoyed tone. "We'll give it one more run-through, but then, unless you have any specific leads, we're done. Contrary to what you big shots in America might think, we actually do have important cases to attend to and other matters to pursue."

As usual, Taz quick-punched the air in frustration. He wanted to say something more, but thought better of it. He might well need their help. The chase could still lead him to Fiji, although that seemed unlikely now that they believed Gaines was in Hawaii.

Instead, he muted the lines and calmly resumed his conversation with Stellard. "They wouldn't move the girl," he repeated.

"You've seen the footage," Stellard said, positioning his custom-made hot water bottle.

"As if that footage couldn't be faked," Taz cried. "And did you notice Gale Asher? She looked like she was being held upright as they went to the helicopter. They practically lifted her into the thing."

"Maybe they had to sedate her to get her to agree to move the girl, who knows. I don't really care right now. Gaines and the Sphere are what we want, and they're in Hawaii."

"All right," Taz said, still unconvinced, but resigned, knowing his new assignment was much more important. He was less than twenty minutes from landing at Honolulu International Airport, but this time there would be no advantage. The NSA, CIA, FBI, and multiple levels of Hawaiian law enforcement would be all over the university, or anywhere else Gaines might have been.

The United States, Taz thought, *is the last place I ever would have expected Gaines to turn up. All that federal manpower on the ground... I'll be lucky to pick up a few scraps.* But the Foundation also had plenty of contacts and clout in the fiftieth state. *I might catch a break.*

"Who else do we have in Hawaii? How much help will I have?" Taz asked, wondering how he even communicated with this cold, dull man. Taz played his fingers as if touching imaginary piano keys, catching the light of the bobbing line of his gold rings. He calculated, pushing back his impatience as a hundred strategies ran across the mountains in his mind. One day he'd be in charge, then things would go right.

"Wait," Stellard said. "I just got word from one of our guys inside. They traced Gale Asher and her daughter to a plane heading toward Indonesia."

"As good as any place to hide, I guess," Taz replied.

"The plane just crashed into the ocean."

"Booker Lipton's plane?" Taz asked flatly.

"A good assumption," Stellard said, his voice trailing off in an incoherent mumble.

"Survivors?"

"None."

"Of course not," Taz sighed. "I need to go to Fiji. Get someone else to handle things in Hawaii."

"Are you kidding? The Eysen-Sphere is in Hawaii."

"Maybe, and so are a few hundred agents of the US government," Taz said. "But no one is going to Fiji now except maybe Gale Asher because her daughter is still there in that damned hospital!"

twenty-two

The search for wreckage at the site of Gale's crash yielded only minor debris. Although the NSA had satellite verification that the plane did in fact enter the ocean and break up, Rathmore did not believe "crash" was the accurate word for what had occurred. He'd ordered technicians to review everything and see if they could have gotten off the plane somewhere.

"Booker's people could have CWS," Rathmore said. "CWS", or Cloaked Wing Suits, allowed personnel to be dropped out of aircrafts and soar to the ground, yet remain almost completely invisible while in the air. The wing suits were made from a fabric which digitally replicated the environment around it. "We have suspicions that Booker may even secretly own the company that is developing it for the military."

Murik flinched. Booker's possession of the technology would be dangerous for the US government. If he were actually the owner of the contractor manufacturing CWS, it could be a major setback for the CIA, which was counting on CWS to give it an edge in the war on terror.

"Hell," Rathmore began, "maybe they never got on that plane. Maybe they didn't even board the helicopter at the hospital. Get our people in Fiji to make damned sure they actually left there."

Fiji was Murik's department. He made a call.

"Sir," an analyst broke in, "Vax is indicating that we have a leech."

Rathmore froze, knowing that a leech, the NSA term for an outside hacker sucking data from the agency's highly secured and encrypted system, meant they'd lose the race for the Sphere. Vax, a radically sophisticated internal monitoring system that hunted for any anomalies in data movement and usage, had been put into place after the Snowden affair.

"What do you have?" Rathmore demanded, attempting to mask his panic.

"It's still early, we don't have any clear source, but Vax is showing abnormal usage centering around the Gaines situation."

"What about abnormal movement?" Rathmore asked hesitantly.

"Yes, sir," the analyst replied. "Data has left our system."

"Dammit! How soon until you close it? How soon until you locate it?" Rathmore knew the answers he wanted were impossible to give. He began running through names of people with access to the current crisis.

"It could be days," the analyst responded.

"We don't *have* days," Rathmore barked. "Send me the personnel files on every person in this. I will find that leech and destroy him myself."

"How do you know it's a him?" Murik asked, done with his call and catching up to the conversation.

Rathmore scowled. "Odds," he answered as he stood. "Let's see what King has to say about this. It may take the analysts days to find the leech, but Veiled Ops should be able to find it in under an hour."

"Veiled Ops for internal investigation?"

"You may do things differently at the CIA, but here at the National Security Agency, we do whatever it takes."

"What if King is the leech?" Murik asked, ignoring the dig.

"King? Are you out of your mind? What if *you're* the leech, Murik?"

"I'm just saying that with these stakes and with Booker Lipton involved, don't be surprised how high the corruption goes."

Rathmore sat back down. He'd wait until he reviewed all the files, *including* King's, and even the NSA Director's. Murik was right. Booker could get to anyone.

−O−

A short time later, Murik and Rathmore entered the interrogation room in another part of the NSA building. The man sitting across from them was an expert at interrogation techniques, and one of the world's most knowledgeable people about Gaines, Asher, and the artifacts.

But he wasn't there to help Murik and Rathmore. He was there to defend himself against charges of treason, espionage, aiding and abetting federal fugitives, falsifying reports, murder, and dozens of other crimes that were being outlined and readied in a sealed, one-hundred-and-thirty-count indictment that a secret grand jury would quickly issue.

Dixon Barbeau had known for seven years that this day might come. He felt relieved, and his lighthearted demeanor and amused expression infuriated the two agents there to get to the truth. Rathmore, in particular, was on the cusp of rage.

"I guess you're the bad cop," Barbeau said to the bristling NSA agent.

"I'm not a cop," Rathmore snapped.

"The FBI wouldn't take you? Is that why you landed at the NSA?"

"Hey, Barbeau," Rathmore said, opening a file on his INU, "we ask the questions."

"Do you? And I don't get a lawyer?" Barbeau asked, smiling. "Your boys who arrested me pulled me out of a fine restaurant, by the way. I expect to be reimbursed for the meal I didn't get to finish. Anyway, I told them repeatedly that I had nothing to say without a lawyer."

"Really?"

"I know you said you aren't a cop, but you look like a guy who's watched some television. Even the TV cops get it right most of the time. Read me my rights, let me call an attorney, you know the drill."

"Oh, no, you have it all wrong," Murik said. "You aren't under arrest. We just want to talk. See, there's been a big misunderstanding. Some people think you may have done some questionable things during the Gaines case seven years ago."

"A long time ago," Barbeau added, still smiling.

"Yes," Rathmore replied. "And as my colleague stated, you're not under arrest. We're here to help you clear up all this confusion. If you didn't do anything wrong, then there's nothing to hide, right?"

"Wrong. Are you, an agent for the NSA, going to define what right and wrong is for me? I didn't think you bothered with such difficult concepts."

Murik couldn't help but laugh.

Rathmore shot him a dirty look before turning back to Barbeau. "Listen to me, Barbeau, we can save you a lot of trouble. You don't need an attorney right now, but if you don't cooperate with us, tomorrow morning you will. Right now a grand jury is preparing a one-hundred-and-thirty-count indictment against you. And you know what that means?"

Barbeau nodded.

"Do you want to go to prison?" Rathmore asked. "Because you know, if those other inmates find out you're an ex-FBI agent, well . . . "

He stood, walked around behind Barbeau, and began massaging his shoulders. Barbeau tried to shrug him off, but one of his hands was cuffed to a steel rail under the table. Rathmore squeezed harder and leaned down until his mouth was almost touching Barbeau's ear.

"They'll be real nice to you for a few days, passing you around, taking turns making you their wife, but once they get bored with you, they'll kick your head in."

Rathmore shoved Barbeau's head forward, hard enough that it just missed hitting the table. Even as he straightened up, Barbeau still smiled.

"There's no need for any of that," Murik said. "I'm sure Barbeau understands the consequences of all this. He's not a street punk. He's done this a lot more than the two of us combined."

"I think you're mixed up," Barbeau said. "I'm happy to help."

"Good," Rathmore replied, unable to hide his pleasure. "Why don't you start by telling us how it is that you testified you saw Gaines and Asher get on the chopper before it exploded?"

A screen across from the table lit up with photos of the burning helicopter in Canyon de Chelly. Next to them, satellite images overlaid with maps of the area and markings of the incidents glowed. Maps comforted Barbeau. They were like friends to him in some strange way. He stared at them a long time, as if recalling that day.

"They shot me and boarded the chopper. It took off and exploded. I was injured and pinned on the ground. I almost burned to death," Barbeau said bitterly. "That's what happened."

"So you're saying they died?" Murik asked.

"Who?"

"Gaines and Asher!" Rathmore snapped.

"No one could survive that inferno," Barbeau said. "Of course they died."

"But they didn't," Rathmore said. "They're very much alive. Even have a nice little family now, but you probably know that. You're probably on their damned Christmas card list!"

"Alive?" Barbeau asked.

"You're going to prison forever," Rathmore said, "unless you tell me what really happened right now."

Barbeau smiled. "I guess they don't train you how to do this in the NSA."

"Do what?"

"Find the truth," Barbeau said. "The intelligence community is so concerned with collecting facts that they constantly miss the truth."

"Facts are truth," Rathmore barked.

"Not always," Barbeau continued. "More often, particularly with the government, I've learned that Don Quixote had it right. 'Facts are the enemy of truth.'"

"Well, here's a *fact* for you," Rathmore whispered in a slithery tone, leaning toward Barbeau. "You're *never* going to talk to an attorney. The fact is we have places to hold you indefinitely. The fact is we can make you disappear. The fact is you're going to pay for your treason in the worst possible way. So start telling the truth or the *facts* are going to bury you so deep you'll forget your own name . . . and I know for a fact that that's the truth."

Barbeau shook his head, then reluctantly spoke. "I'm telling you what I know. I was there. They got on that chopper. It exploded. If you're certain they're still alive, then maybe something else happened, but that doesn't change what I saw."

"You're lying."

"Give me a polygraph," Barbeau offered.

"I'm sure a star like you would have no trouble beating it," Rathmore jeered, staring into Barbeau's eyes. "How about a drink? Vodka and something?"

"No thanks."

"Right, you don't do that anymore, but you used to. Used to have a real bad drinking problem, didn't you? Kind of cost you your family and almost your career . . . What have you been doing since you left the Bureau?"

"I work in the private sector."

"For Booker Lipton."

"No."

"You know what?" Rathmore said. "They want us back in the situation room. But I'm going to send a couple people in to see you. You'll like them better. They specialize in getting folks like you to cooperate."

"I'm sure they do," Barbeau replied.

"Oh, don't worry. They aren't going to beat you up or anything," Rathmore said, as Murik and he stood at the door. "It'll be more like a party. They'll bring the booze. And Barbeau? I know you want the drink, so save us all some trouble and just take it. You'll enjoy it a lot more than if they have to force it into you."

Once they were in the hall heading back to the situation room, Murik asked, "Is that really necessary? His file said he's been sober for nine years. Seems a shame to push him back onto that road."

"Oh, relax. After today, he won't be able to get another drink where he's going. We have to know what he knows. What *really* happened back in Arizona when Gaines and Asher 'died.' I want to know everything they did from that moment until we find them because that's *how* we'll find them."

Murik nodded. "What's going on in the situation room?"

"Agents are at the University of Hawaii. We've got confirmation Gaines was in Honolulu yesterday."

"Is he still?" Murik glanced into his INU.

"Not sure, but we have a ton of leads and information piling up. Gaines and scores of scientists have been secretly doing research on the Sphere there. We've already seized INUs containing thousands of encrypted files which allegedly detail the research— *years* of it. The data is streaming in right now. We've got a team working it."

"Can we decrypt it?" Murik asked, as they jogged down the corridor.

Rathmore looked back, genuinely smiling for the first time that day. "We're the NSA. Encryption? Now they've moved the game to our playground."

twenty-three

Stellard looked over the reports detailing the worsening situation. Shivering, he stepped over to the window and stood in the sun. "When is summer coming?" he mumbled.

An assistant looked up, but made no attempt to answer. Summer in DC would still be cold inside of all the ridiculously air-conditioned buildings, but outside, the heat and high humidity that gave the nation's capital a swamp-like environment always felt like a comfortable blanket to him.

"If nature meant for us to be cooled like refrigerated sandwich meats, we'd all be wrapped in butcher paper, wouldn't we?" he said, not for the first time.

"Taz has just landed in Hawaii," his assistant announced.

Stellard reluctantly left the window's sunshine and walked over to his giant interactive globe. Another involuntary shiver shuddered through him as he found Hawaii. Every military base, police station, federal building, hospital, and school lit up and became zoomable.

His assistant elaborated on the report he'd just read, giving personnel counts by agency for the US agents all over Honolulu. This meant Taz would have difficulty discovering anything new. However, the Foundation had enough people placed in power positions around the world that they would benefit from the work of others, something they did often.

"It would be nice to get it first," Stellard mumbled to himself. "But as long as we get it . . . "

$-O-$

Taz was still angry he couldn't go to Fiji, but even if Stellard would authorize it, the plane didn't have enough fuel. He'd have to go to Hawaii, as planned, and trust the police the Foundation crew who had just arrived in Fiji from the Philippines.

The Foundation team consisted of eighteen highly trained military-type men in their twenties who were not worried about breaking laws, life, or property. They were paid well, and the Foundation was very powerful. The agents did not know of the Foundation's mission, but what did that matter? The team had the best weapons, lived on the edge, enjoyed adventure, and even had great benefits.

$-O-$

Harmer, having survived the second police sweep of the hospital, thought they were in the clear. The push and focus of the search for the Eysen-Sphere had moved to Hawaii after the flawless "crash" of the plane carrying Gale and Cira.

Then Harmer saw the team of mercenaries entering the building.

"Foundation?" she asked Booker through her INU.

"It's not CIA, NSA, US military, or Mossad, so Foundation is the most likely," Booker replied soberly as he ordered his AX team back into the air.

"Damn it, how much luck do we have left?" Harmer asked, reaching for a cigarette that she couldn't light. "We may need some help from above on this one."

"Help is scrambling now. The AX team will be above you in about twelve minutes," Booker said, watching the Foundation men take positions at all the hospital entrances and exits.

Harmer watched too. She could tell the Foundation men were treating it as a hostile operation. They believed someone was hiding in the hospital. "They know," she whispered to herself.

The orderly heard her. "What do they know?"

"Nothing," Harmer said, not taking her eyes off the INU where she could now also see that the Foundation unit leader was talking to the head of the Fiji Police. They met in the main lobby, where a police command center had been set up when they first arrived. The Foundation unit leader looked directly into a hospital camera several times.

"They know we're in here, don't they?" the orderly asked. "Who are those guys? They aren't police. They look dangerous."

"Don't worry. They aren't going to find us."

But the orderly could see the same thing Harmer could: the Foundation men were moving swiftly though the building, searching far more thoroughly than the police had.

Booker spoke into Harmer's ear. "Seven minutes and we'll be in striking distance."

That hardly relaxed Harmer. She knew the team would be ordered in only to save Cira. Harmer would already be dead.

She looked back at the nurse and the orderly, who were both craning to see the images flashing from the INU. Even the nurse looked terrified now, and the orderly might be on the verge of tears.

"Can you reach Mr. Bradley?" she asked Booker, using the alias for Rip.

"Yes."

"Then you better do it," Harmer said. "This may go down bad. I think you want him involved with the decisions."

Booker understood. Rip's daughter could be made permanently blind or killed as a result of the Foundation raid. If either happened, Booker would be blamed. Getting

Rip involved might not change that, but it could minimize the damage to their relationship.

Harmer always thought of the mission. She'd been around the Eysen-Sphere and Gaines long enough to know what was at stake. Her earliest AX training had taught her that emotions had no place in this line of work. Rip had not had that training, and the future of the world depended on Rip's not disintegrating from whatever was about to happen in Fiji.

Booker connected to Rip through his INU and patched him in on the feed. El Perdido was a safe contact point. Booker quickly caught him up on the developments at the hospital.

"Oh no," Rip groaned. "The Foundation will kill her. They don't care about anything." He looked around frantically, as if trying to find a way to get to his daughter, to get himself off the damned island.

"I've got an AX unit ready to drop in," Booker said. "We can take them."

"Can you guarantee me that Cira won't get hurt?"

Booker hesitated. He looked at the clock . . . three minutes. "No."

"No? No! No . . . no, you can't." Rip's voice faded. He moved over to the floating Eysen-Sphere. "Crying Man," he whispered, "what am I supposed to do?"

The only response was a strange silence, seemingly full of something he couldn't quite detect, but nonetheless felt.

And then, all at once, from the confusion of fear, the tragic despair of a helpless father, and the malaise of misery, came clarity.

Rip knew just how to save his daughter.

twenty-four

Kruse looked over at Gale. *She'll be waking up soon, angry as firecrackers*, he thought.

Drugging her had been necessary. The risks were too great that she would have run, or at least caused a scene, once back in Fiji. And how could she argue with success? Rip was out of harm's way on El Perdido. Cira was protected by Harmer in the hidden hospital room. The police had bought the story that Cira had left and had not discovered them. Gale was safely on her way, via Hawaii, to be reunited with Rip. Booker, Kruse, and Harmer had navigated Gale's entire family through a crisis that rightfully should have resulted in their imprisonment or death.

Still, Kruse was nervous. Being on a commercial airliner meant he had no weapons. Even though they were tucked into the crew's quarters behind the cockpit, hidden from scrutiny, Kruse felt unable to suppress a welling tension.

He couldn't recall the last time he'd been without at least one gun. He preferred his Glock-19, but owned a varied arsenal of weaponry, most of it scattered around the world. The latest repository had been the helicopter, which had flown them to the plane used in the crash. He knew several disciplines of martial arts, but it wasn't his strong suit. Booker would make sure his collection caught up with Kruse.

Stop worrying, he told himself. *Booker's plane, picking us up in Hawaii, will have a fresh supply of weaponry. The rough part was making it through Nadi Airport. Hawaii will be a piece of cake.*

The chemicals in Gale's system would wear off in time for him to calm her down and prep her at least a couple of hours before landing in Honolulu. Kruse sat on the edge of the narrow, elevated bed, trying to reach Booker through his INU. All kinds of apocalyptic images were going through his head—two fighter jets escorting the commercial airliner to the airport so they could be arrested when they landed, a crazed Foundation member hijacking the plane, maybe the Israelis shooting them out of the sky, a dozen different scenarios, and all with Kruse powerless to defend against any of them.

No one knows where we are, he reminded himself. He looked around for anything he could make into a weapon. "Come on, Booker," he whispered out loud, silently begging the INU to connect.

Finally, Booker's voice came into his earpiece. "Bad news."

Kruse's first thought was that they'd found Cira and Harmer in the hospital. He stole a quick look at Gale. In the same instant, he suddenly realized it could be that Rip had somehow been captured or killed. Then, before even finishing his breath, he knew it was actually Gale and he who were in trouble. "Hawaii?"

"Yeah. The CIA, NSA, FBI, the Foundation . . . it's a damn party."

"And we're the guests of honor?" Kruse asked, already thinking of how he could hijack the plane. Otherwise, they were trapped, and flying right into a hornets' nest.

"But there is good news," Booker said as he finished sucking down the last of a black raspberry and almond smoothie. "They don't know you're on this plane, or that Gale is even heading to Hawaii."

"Not yet," Kruse said, only partially relieved. "Then they're there for the university?"

"Right. They raided the school and are ripping through all the data right now."

"But you have something in place that will screw the NSA. What did Rip call it? Eroders or something?"

"You don't miss much, Kruse."

"Anything that might make it easier to protect them."

"I know, and yes, we have eroders built into all the INUs used in Eysen-Sphere research, but some of the data is so valuable that it will not be destroyed. It gets swallowed into a digital-cocoon that should be impossible for anyone to access without the encryption key."

"The NSA is fairly good at that type of thing."

"So were the Cosegans," Booker said.

"Oh, you're using their technology?"

"Yes. So the NSA can have at it, but unless they've got eleven million years to work on it, I'm not too worried. Still, I'd like to retrieve the digital-cocoons just to be sure."

"Why weren't they transmitted?"

"The data is simply too enormous. Even if we could move it in smaller packets, the NSA would have noticed."

"Okay, correct me if I'm wrong, but that's a problem for another day, or a BLAX crew to handle. I need to know what to expect when we land in Honolulu."

"It might be nothing. They have agents at the airport, but they assume Rip is long gone. They aren't looking for Gale. Private planes are still going out without hassle."

"Uh-huh," Kruse said. "But it might be something."

"You know as well as I do that a lot can change in two hours and twenty-eight minutes."

"A lot of people can die in that amount of time."

"We do have a decent AX force in Hawaii. They're getting in position at the airport now. If it does turn bad, you'll have help."

"Any way to use your influence and divert this plane somewhere else?"

"Even if I could, there's nowhere to go."

"Then I guess we'll ride this thing through."

"Tarks will meet you. He'll have a suitcase full of guns."

"A Glock?" Kruse asked hopefully.

"Of course."

"Thanks. Hope I don't need it today, but I'll feel much better when my hands are wrapped around the handle," Kruse said. "Is our escape plane ready?"

"Ready and waiting, but even if there is no welcoming committee, it's going to be tricky. We obviously don't want Gale in the terminal building. I've sent the airport maps, runway layouts, and building plans to your INU."

"I see them," Kruse confirmed, looking at the schematics and making them larger as they projected from his Eysen-INU.

"Good. You'll be coming into the EWA Concourse, gate thirty-four. Our jet is at the next terminal over, but we're lucky. Thirty-four is the last gate. As soon as you get inside, go into the men's room, it will be immediately on the left. There is a locked door in there, the code will be sent to your INU as soon as we get it. That leads to a maintenance corridor, and from there you can get out to the next terminal. Our blue and white Gulfstream—tail number N72908—will be there waiting to taxi."

"Okay. As long as Gale doesn't kill me first, we might just make it."

"Tell her Cira is doing well. They're still safely tucked away."

"Maybe we can get her a quick video connection inside the room," Kruse suggested. "It would go a long way to calm her down."

"I'll see what I can do. Just make sure she knows our plan is working and she'll be with Rip soon." Booker made an exasperated sound while, unbeknownst to Kruse, he watched the hospital situation worsen. "I've got to jump off. I'll talk to you when you're on our plane. Good luck."

Kruse studied the airport maps again. *It should be easy,* he thought, but he was consumed with worry. *It's just because I don't have a gun. I'm on a commercial airliner and flying into the home field advantage of my enemy . . . otherwise, everything is fine.*

twenty-five

Savina breathlessly attempted to regain her bearings in the star-filled lab. She spun until her two assistants surfaced and then shouted at them, "I saw him!"

"Gaines?" one of the assistants called back in a voice that echoed across millions of miles.

Savina didn't hear the response as she fought to get back to Gaines. "He's in the ocean! Alive! His Sphere is so beautiful. Oh, I can't imagine what he's seen."

Actually she could. Savina was one of the few people on the planet who had any idea of the things Gaines had witnessed in the depths of the Eysen-Sphere. But her all-consuming addiction to the object caused her physical pain, especially when she dreamed of the things he'd experienced with his Sphere that she had not.

What I could do with two, she thought. *And linking them together . . . incredible. The power wouldn't just be doubled, it would expand exponentially like two cubed to the hundredth power.*

A rushing noise, sounding like what Savina expected stars forming would, pushed all her senses to the brink of uselessness. Only the sound remained, and then just the swirl of light. It created a sensation of dimension that she felt, but couldn't understand, and it lasted f o r e v e r.

Then, she seemed to see time twisting. The slow melting of particles as if they were components of time, a blending of consciousness and immortal protons. Next, she could actually *see* gravitons, the building blocks of gravity.

Everything went purple, blue, and then black, and in that spatial blur, Savina's thoughts spilled from her mind and became completely visible across the view of endlessness before them.

She looked around, wondering if her assistants could see it all—everything she had ever thought— but they were lost in the dark edges somewhere. Like a million movies playing at once, a collage of images, each mental creation appeared as if it were independent of her, as if in its own lifetime.

Each is a single dimension of its own, she thought.

The assistants called again. Nothing. Then again, louder, their voices cascading a reverb across a tumbling sense of time and an expanding space. The lab, no longer physical, had become the ultimate virtual lab for all of life as something more like a concept. Everything had transformed. Their very existence was now just a sudden experiment.

"What?" Savina finally called back to them, annoyed at being brought out of the dream. She was so close to solving it . . . whatever *it* was. She wasn't sure just then, but knew it was much more than finding Gaines. She felt an urgent need to know who built the Eysen-Spheres. Where were they from? Where had they gone? How had they done it? How? How? How? And, what did it mean?

To Savina, the Spheres contained all that could be known, and she craved to feel every bit of it. Her emptiness was a mystery to her. She'd always felt different. Maybe it was from knowing too much, seeing things that others couldn't. The answer to the cause of that emptiness, in spite of her astronomical IQ scores, had always eluded her.

Gaines, his Sphere, and the ocean that surrounded them faded. In the place of their glowing presence, her assistants surfaced. Savina clawed at the air, trying to bring Gaines and his Sphere back. She tried to dive into the surrounding ocean. All at once, the lab slipped back into view, back into order, back, yet different. *Everything is different now*, Savina thought as she grappled with the frustration of loss and the fascination of discovery.

"What in the world was that?" one of the assistants asked.

"Proof," Savina said as the colors and air in the room cooled.

They all stared at the floating Sphere, seeming so normal and quiet now, but terrifying just the same.

"Proof of what?"

"The Sphere is not subject to the laws of physics . . . It's proof that there's something beyond what we know, something beyond everything." Savina's voice carried the trembling awe of someone who had defied death while those around her had perished. "Did you see what it did, where it took us?"

"If I'd been alone, I would have thought it a dream," one of them said.

"I saw the other Sphere," the other added.

"You saw it, too?" Savina asked, delighted. "Did you see Gaines?"

"In an ocean."

Savina squealed. "We're going to get him. Wait until I tell the Judge." She ran to her office. "Was any of it recorded?" she asked over her shoulder.

One of the assistants was already at the controls. "Nothing," he said dejectedly.

"How could it have been?" she asked, stopping at the office door. "No matter. Log everything you can recall into the system. Don't worry. We'll just have to repeat the journey." She closed the door.

"Repeat?" one of the assistants said to the other. "Does she really think we can control that?"

"I think Savina thinks *she* can."

He looked over at the Sphere. "What the hell *is* this thing?"

—O—

The Judge sat in his penthouse office overlooking Manhattan and listened to Savina's incredible story. "It's hard to believe," he said, tinkering with a new neuro-controlled robotic set of legs.

The Judge, in his mid-sixties, still had the look of the old college quarterback he had been, his slightly crooked, twice-broken nose a testament to his days in the gridiron trenches. He wore his gray hair a little long, bordering a chiseled cheek line and salt and pepper stubble, a handsome man, and there was that earring which always seemed out of place on his gruff, tough-guy appearance.

"No," she said. "It's so easy to believe. Humans have been living in a self-imposed closet for the past five thousand years."

Seeing her face light up on the video call had made him think of a child on Christmas morning. "I don't disagree with that statement, just the extent to which you now say we're deficient in what's actually occurring in the universe."

"We'll find out once I talk to Gaines and can use his Eysen-Sphere."

"Confident."

"Don't you realize? I *saw* him. The Spheres are directly connected."

"Savina, I need to know where he is."

"I know that. And you shall."

The Judge did believe in the power of the Spheres, which is why they had committed virtually unlimited resources to finding the other one. "This is a unique time in human history," he began, the speech one that Savina had heard often. "We can shape the future like never before. Booker, with his collection of UQP oddballs and Inner Movement weirdoes, have one vision. The US government, specifically the Pentagon and intelligence agencies, has another . . . but it's the Foundation that—"

"I know that, too," Savina said. "I'm leading the charge, remember. Every one of the groups you just mentioned sees the risk, and everyone wants to save the world . . . three very different approaches."

"Yes," he said, putting down a precision screwdriver. "I've brought it up again because I'm concerned that the Sphere might lead you down a different path. You're seeing things no one has ever seen, experiencing mind-altering events — "

"You've cautioned me many times. I know you think that the more I delve into the Sphere, the closer I'll get to the metaphysical philosophies of the Inner Movement, but those people are following some New Age dream. They aren't dealing with science."

The Judge thought of Booker Lipton's own team of physicists, working on research into a new field called Universe Quantum Physics, or UQP. Booker's originally secret pet project had grown so large that it was now well known in the scientific community. UQP was the ambitious attempt to create a new area of science involving quantum mechanics, aspects of physics at the nanoscopic level, metaphysics, subatomic particles, the theory of everything, infinite layers, energetic manipulations, extreme neurological control, forces of space, and concepts of time, all within the reality of a multiverse.

UQP was generally regarded as a rich man's folly, but it scared the Judge because he had seen into an Eysen-Sphere, and the Foundation had been born out of the remnants of a group that had been defeated by the Inner Movement. Booker Lipton had tried to recruit Savina, and he had far more people on his team exploring UQP than the Foundation did, trying to develop the potential of their Sphere. Now the Judge realized that it wasn't just Booker chasing what he'd lost when the Gaines' Eysen-Sphere supposedly disintegrated seven years earlier.

"Booker has obviously been concealing Eysen-Sphere research in his UQP program," the Judge said. "He could be way ahead of us on what the Spheres can do."

"UQP is not a legitimate area of any science," Savina replied. "The only way Booker has attracted so many prominent scientists to his fantasy factory is because he pays them like professional athletes. Million dollar contracts, signing bonuses, it's insane. He's turned the academic world of science into an ostentatious and garish carnival, like watching Wall Street bid for top MBAs. Believe me, I know. You saw what he offered me."

"But what does he get for that investment?"

"Not what you think," she said. "Many of his recruits take the salaries and Booker's extra funding for their side projects, but they aren't on board with his dream of a fairy tale world."

The Judge was surprised that after what Savina had just experienced with the Sphere, she was still maintaining that Booker's search for other dimensions, wormholes, portals, and his belief in psychic phenomena, time travel, and related phenomena, was a joke. The Spheres had the potential to answer the great questions; where did we come from, why is it all here, what holds everything together, when did it start, when does it end? The exact questions Booker had asked her while trying to hire her.

There were two reasons Savina had committed herself to the Judge. The obvious one was her addiction to the Sphere. When she began with the Foundation, she didn't believe the other Sphere still existed, and Booker had not said differently. Nothing in the world offered more excitement, or a chance for greater discovery. More importantly, however, the Judge had showed her the future inside the Sphere.

The vision had terrified her. A real and complete Armageddon, worse than anything science fiction had conjured, was coming ... and soon. She believed the Judge's Phoenix Initiative had the best chance of succeeding in saving the human race from those horrors, as well as possible extinction.

"And you *still* feel Booker's UQP is just a fanciful hobby? Even after today?" the Judge asked while he fitted a miniscule titanium bearing into a socket with a pair of precision tweezers.

"Absolutely," she said, but as she felt pulled back toward the Sphere, guilt clouded in.

Her answer was partially a lie. Savina didn't know anything for sure now except that she needed more time with the Sphere, and with that thought, the words of Booker Lipton replayed in her mind.

Time is a funny thing.

twenty-six

Rathmore and Murik surveyed the vast amounts of data pouring in from Hawaii, grateful that the hunt for Gaines and the Sphere had taken an easy turn onto US soil. The NSA and CIA could, of course, operate anywhere on the planet, but things always went more simply when no one needed to be shoved out of their way.

Hundreds of agents and law enforcement were involved in interviewing, detaining, arresting, and collecting data. "Lady Checkmate," as the top brass in the Pentagon called the woman in charge, coordinated eight jurisdictions and agencies, as well as the US Navy's involvement. Her official title was "the Conductor," a kind of super MONSTER. Famous in Washington intelligence circles, the plump African-American had a mind filled with contacts and ideas, even before she earned her current moniker, because of her use of bold strategies to achieve her objectives.

"We're getting a much clearer picture now of what's been going on," Rathmore said as Murik adjusted the volume on several interrogations going on simultaneously. "An anonymous donor, most likely Booker Lipton, poured tens of millions of dollars into research. The Eysen-Sphere has been to the university on at least three occasions in recent years, possibly many more times."

"Amazing," Murik said. "Right under our noses."

"Yeah, well, that will prove to be their biggest mistake. Booker's arrogance is incredible," Rathmore growled. "Let's eat this guy alive!"

"What do we have on Gaines' movements from the last sighting?" Murik asked, ignoring Rathmore's usual anger and popping a couple caramel candies into his mouth. "How did the NSA monitoring miss this?"

Rathmore glared at Murik.

Murik laughed. "Relax, Claude. I'm just trying to lighten the mood. You're going to give yourself a heart attack. Candy?" He held out an open pack of caramel-creams.

"No thanks," Rathmore said irritably, shaking his head. "The Conductor is piecing together Gaines' time in Hawaii, but these damned academics aren't cooperating too much," Rathmore said, shaking his head. "Here she is now."

The Conductor's face came through on the large screen. Her age, difficult to guess, could have been anywhere between forty-five and sixty-five.

"What's the story on these scientists not talking?" Rathmore asked, resisting the urge to call her Lady Checkmate and wondering if she could be the leech. "It's not like these eggheads are hardened criminals. They should be easy pickings."

Murik recalled meeting the Conductor at a conference a couple of years earlier. She was a force. Intense. Way smarter than he was. He was glad they were on the same side.

"It's strange, really," she said distractedly. "It's as if they're afraid."

"Of whom? Us?" Rathmore asked. "Or Booker Lipton?"

"Neither. I think possibly the Sphere."

"*What?*" Rathmore exclaimed. "These are scientists, and you're telling me that an eleven-million-year-old artifact is *scaring* them?"

"If you don't realize that the Sphere is much more than an ordinary artifact, then I'm not sure how you got this assignment," she said as if chiding a student who had not done his homework.

"Fair enough," Rathmore said, his normally bristly personality no match for the Conductor, whose ramrod reputation and edgy nature exuded both powerful calm and fury waiting just below the surface. Her personnel file was filled with classified sections that even he hadn't been able to access. The only one with more redacted parts was King. Investigating a mole within the hierarchy of the US intelligence community was like trying to find stolen goods in prison. *Too many balls in the air*, Rathmore thought. *If I can just get to Gaines and the Sphere, the leech will either be revealed, or won't matter as much.*

Of course, Rathmore knew that the Sphere had led to the stunning collapse of virtually all of the world's religions. He'd read every top-secret intelligence briefing on the Eysen-Sphere, even the impact papers which assessed the effect of the Eysen-INUs on the world. Rathmore was an expert on the INU's role in disrupting industries, geopolitical stability, and economic conditions across the globe, yet he was actually surprised, even shaken, by the latest developments, specifically those at the University of Hawaii.

Up until then, the Sphere had been more mythical than real. Almost everyone who had seen it had either disappeared, or died. Even the dozen or so grad students who had been on the original dig, when Gaines had first pulled the Sphere from the Virginia cliff, had all died within months of the find. Like many in the government, he simply didn't believe all the lore which had grown around the object. He also liked his jeans ironed and no spots on his bananas, so there wasn't much room for anything which didn't fit the mold.

Yet after he'd seen the files compiled on the happenings in Hawaii, his mind began to open. Hundreds of archeologists, scientists, astrophysicists, cryptologists, astronomers, and a shocking number of physicists were now on the staff at the university. Among the best in the world, the Nobel laureates, Einstein World Award winners, and geniuses of extraordinary merit, had been assembled there, working secretly for years on one thing: the Eysen-Sphere.

Damn it to hell, Rathmore thought. *We haven't been overestimating the power of this object, we've clearly been underestimating it.*

"We need to squeeze these brainiacs," Rathmore said, glaring at the Conductor. "They can lead us to Gaines."

"Do they all know they were working with a fugitive? Do they know Gaines is alive?" Murik asked.

"Most are denying this, of course. But how could they not know?" the Conductor responded. "Remember, Gaines had quite a reputation before the Cosegan find."

"Gaines was there yesterday! These people know!" Rathmore cried.

"The search for Gaines is ongoing," the Conductor said. "Our best assessment, at this point, is that he left Hawaii at least twelve hours ago. We're running through the data, crossing satellite footage. We'll find him."

"Yeah," Murik agreed. "We're tracking everything that's moved off Oahu for the past twenty-four hours, but now it appears EAMI might be a real phenomena."

EAMI, or Eysen Anomaly Matter Interference, a theory put forth by one of the top government scientists who'd been assigned to the original Eysen case, hypothesized that the Sphere may have the ability to create anomalies and interfere in scientific measurement and technologically based equipment, in effect, changing reality, or at least making it appear to have been changed.

The controversial idea had some basis in the laws of quantum mechanics, but when a physicist had tried to explain it to Rathmore, he'd been unable to follow the logic—something about the Sphere's unknown origin, purported age, and properties in relation to the details known and specific episodes surrounding it. The EAMI theory had been used to explain the disappearance of the Eysen-Sphere at the time of Gaines and Asher's purported deaths. The NSA's satellite images of the minutes leading up to the helicopter explosion were analyzed, and everything matched the testimony of FBI Special Agent Dixon Barbeau, which they now knew to be false.

Every aspect, every second, every piece of evidence or data, no matter how seemingly insignificant, had been analyzed dozens of ways in the wake of losing the Sphere. EAMI also explained how Gaines and Asher had escaped so many close calls even before the explosion in Canyon de Chelly. "As if the Sphere were protecting them," one scientist argued.

The official story stated that the remains of Gaines, Asher, and the Sphere had been destroyed in the fireball, which had burned thousands of degrees hotter than a normal crash of that type. Although the NSA, CIA, and FBI had continued searching, Gaines and Asher were never spotted again — another point for EAMI.

Instead of the EAMI theory falling apart after Booker's companies released commercial INUs, and then churned out steady advancements in the devices, as well as all manner of other technology, it actually strengthened the case for it.

"It defies all that we know about reality," the NSA's top-secret report concluded. That report, the definitive work on the Sphere, prepared with input from HITE, as well as former Vatican officials, the National Science Foundation, NASA, Sandia National Laboratories, the Smithsonian, and CERN, did not endorse the EAMI theory, but definitely leaned toward it. The scientists and engineers at HITE had especially favored EAMI.

The Conductor nodded. The Eysen Anomaly Matter Interference had been read by only a few dozen people. The Conductor had received it just hours earlier. "I'm still getting through the EAMI report," she began, "and now we're up to our necks in new material on the strange and unusual abilities of the Sphere."

"I've hardly had time to investigate some of the new research we've been able to access from Hawaii myself,"

Murik added. "It's crazy stuff. Reality bending, detailed views into the past. Startling predictions of the future. Eysen Anomaly might be a problem, but if these other reports are true—"

"The 'crazy stuff,' as you call it, is a matter for HITE and others above our pay grade, but we need to find the thing first," the Conductor interrupted. "Eysen Anomaly could prevent us from doing that. I think we've all seen enough to agree that clearly EAMI is real, and we need to accept that it's going to be perhaps *our* greatest challenge going forward."

"And not just for this case," Rathmore added. "EAMI is going to change how we do everything." Then he quoted from the report: "'EAMI has the potential to change perception and balance of power so significantly that it threatens to erode the dominance of the United States in the world.'"

twenty-seven

Rip was certain that a firefight between AX and Foundation forces, within the tight confines of the narrow hospital corridors and the tiny paneled off room where his precious daughter lay unconscious, would result in her death. However, there was no way to move her. Nothing could be done except to trust the one person who had done more to upend his life than any other, the Crying Man.

"Tell AX to stand down," Rip said to Booker.

"Rip, they'll find her," the trillionaire shot back.

"Damn it, Booker, there's nothing in that hospital that belongs to you. Nothing that warrants your authority. Cira is *my* daughter. This is *my* call."

"Are you sure?" Booker asked. "When they find her, they'll move her, and the risks to her eyes—"

"Doing it this way is the best hope I've got to keep her alive."

Booker gave the command to the waiting AX team. "Stand down."

"Bradley," Harmer began after listening to the exchange in her ear, calling Rip by his alias, "do you want me to defend this room?"

"No. If they discover the room, I want you to surrender." Rip knew it was a tough request. For Harmer, who had been trained to protect, to fight, surrendering to the Foundation meant that even if she survived the encounter, she'd be imprisoned and tortured until Gaines was found. Harmer could wind up locked away for years. Rip met her eyes through the INU.

Harmer nodded. She understood that giving up might be the only chance that Cira had. The room couldn't be defended indefinitely against so many.

"Okay," she said quietly. "Maybe they won't find us."

Rip, Booker, and Harmer all turned their attention to the feeds from the hospital security cameras. Four men were working the floor where Cira's secret room was located. They came from opposite ends of the building. It looked like they had less than five minutes before one of them got to the "supply closet."

Rip looked back at the Eysen-Sphere, hoping Crying Man would appear. He wondered where Gale was, and wanted to ask Booker, but decided to wait until . . . until whatever was about to happen, happened.

"Are you going to surrender?" the orderly asked Harmer, watching the armed men scour the hospital.

"If they find us."

"Wouldn't it be safer to just give up now?" the orderly asked.

"Not while there's still a chance they won't find us," Harmer said without turning around. "Look, I get that this is scary for you. Why don't you just lie on the floor and it'll all be over soon."

The orderly stayed where he was and kept watching as the men drew closer. Harmer reached again for a cigarette, looked up at the ceiling, eyes darting to the walls, the tiled floor, and back to the ceiling. The men from the north end of the building looked like they would reach them first. The air in their room felt smothering; a stale mix of antiseptic, newly cut sheetrock, sweat, and fear.

Rip and Booker also counted the men's steps. How long until they reached Cira's room? All Rip wanted to do was scoop his daughter out of that bed and run to safety. Had he known, back in Virginia, that one day he'd be a father to that sweet little girl, he never would have run with the artifacts. But how different the world would be based on everything that had happened. Everyone else on the dig was dead. He and Gale were the only survivors, but for how much longer?

Two armed men entered the supply closet. There was no camera in there, but Harmer could hear them easily as they moved and shuffled through the supplies. It gave her the same feeling as hearing a rat scratching inside a wall. She tensed, waiting for them to find the secret door, to burst through, guns blaring. Then, they left. Harmer had been holding her breath and exhaled quietly. Even the orderly smiled.

Rip cheered loud enough that he startled a bird on the roof of the skyroom. It flew to another part of El Perdido Island as Rip continued his brief celebration.

Then he saw the team coming from the other direction. They waited outside the room next to Cira's.

The first team came out and went to the next room that the second team had already checked. The second team went into Cira's neighbor's room. They were double-checking! Harmer saw the same thing. So did Booker.

"Everyone sit tight," Booker said. "We've got one more pass."

"We have another coming," Harmer whispered.

The orderly, who'd been about to hug the nurse, let out a whimper as though he'd been kicked. Harmer held up her hand.

The new team left the room next door and entered the supply closest. They made less noise than the first team, but spent more time. Harmer imagined them looking for trap doors, hidden panels, moving boxes and five-gallon buckets.

How could they be in there this long and not find our entrance?

Then, suddenly, they went back into the hall.

Everyone relaxed. Rip closed his eyes and whispered, "Thank you."

Harmer turned briefly to the nurse and orderly, allowing a slight smile. They had done it!

Booker didn't move, never took his eyes off the feed. He had a bad feeling. He knew how professional soldiers and mercenaries thought. He had thousands working for him. Something about the eyes of one of the men bothered him. Too serious, too intent, too thorough.

Then that man swung his automatic rifle around and turned back to look at the supply closet's door. He looked at the room number on the wall next to the door, then went back to the neighbor's room and looked at hers.

"What?" his comrade asked.

"Something . . ." the man said, jogging slowly down the hall in the direction they had come. At the far end he stopped and looked at another door. He went into that room. It was a supply closet. A real one. A half-second later he came out, speaking into his wrist, and ran back to the door near Cira's.

"Damn," Harmer said so faintly that not even the orderly could hear. She quietly laid down her gun and tiptoed to the opposite side of the small room from where Cira was. She watched in the INU while eight armed men congregated outside the closet. One of them entered with a high-powered light.

The Foundation soldier had been in the closet for only a few seconds when suddenly from behind Harmer the orderly yelled, "Help!"

The nurse gasped.

Harmer shook her head and looked at her gun on the floor across the room. She wouldn't have really shot the orderly. The guy had just been scared. It didn't matter anyway. They'd already been discovered.

Harmer could see from the hall camera in the INU that one of the Foundation forces had entered the closet with a black canister. They were going to gas them. A second later a soldier located the hidden panel and kicked it in.

"We're unarmed! We surrender!" Harmer yelled. "We have an injured child in here."

"You're welcome to come out," a gruff voice shouted from the other side of the wall.

"No tricks," Harmer yelled. "We're coming out . . . unarmed. Civilian hospital staff first." Harmer motioned to the orderly. "You first."

"No way," he said.

"I've got a hospital orderly in here. He's scared you're going to hurt him," Harmer yelled out.

"We don't want to hurt anyone," the voice replied. "Come out. You'll be safe."

Harmer nodded again to the orderly. He didn't budge. The nurse stepped slowly toward the opening.

"Nurse coming out first," Harmer yelled. "Unarmed."

Once the nurse was safely out, the orderly followed.

Harmer took a deep breath and looked at Cira. Just the two of them left. One final moment to decide to fight, or give up. Rip could almost feel Harmer struggling against her training and instincts.

"You next," came the voice.

"I can't leave the girl," Harmer said. "My weapon is on the floor."

"You have to come out or we'll come in and take you out."

"I've got an INU in here. Give me an address and I'll link its camera to you. I'll show you the whole room."

After a few moments of silence there came an, "Okay." A minute later they told her the address. She programmed it into the INU and at the same time signed off to Booker and Rip.

"I'll take care of her," Harmer promised as the connection went dark.

—O—

Rip and Booker remained connected to each other. Booker had already "back-filled" Harmer's INU so that nothing useful and no traces of AX data could be found in it.

From a place of hellish agony, and in a barely recognizable raspy voice, Rip asked Booker, "Where's Gale?"

"She's landing in Hawaii soon, and then on to El Perdido," he reported. "With any luck she'll be in your arms in about six hours."

"And when will she find out that Cira is a prisoner of the Foundation?" Rip asked in a painful moan.

"When you tell her."

twenty-eight

It took longer for Gale to regain consciousness and recover from the effects of the narcotics than Kruse had anticipated. With less than sixty minutes until Hawaii, he worried she might not wake up in time. Twenty-one minutes from landing though, she finally came to. Gale looked at him for a long time before speaking. He could almost see the brain cells clicking back into place, and along with them, her seething anger.

"You bastard," she said coolly. "Where are we?"

"We're about to land in Hawaii."

"When we get to El Per-rison, I want you off that island before I sleep. In fact, I prefer you don't even get off the plane. Understood?"

"Yes."

She shook her head as if expecting an argument, as if wanting one. "I don't believe you. I am not . . . " Gale didn't finish. "Is there any news on Cira?"

"I just spoke with Booker. They're still safely tucked in the hidden room. Cira is doing fine."

"As if I can believe anything either of you say . . . but I want so badly to believe that." Her voice trembled.

Kruse just nodded, maintaining eye contact. "There are some things we have to do before you can get rid of me."

"Hawaii?"

"Yes. The transfer should be easy. We're on a commercial flight and need to get onto Booker's plane.

We'll be gating close to where his is waiting, but... the CIA, NSA, FBI, and probably the Foundation are *all* in Hawaii."

"They found out about our work at the university?" she asked calmly, used to being hunted.

"Yes."

"That should keep them busy."

"We hope so. There's no reason to believe they know we're anywhere near Hawaii, so it should be just a quick off and on, then straight to El Perdido. Rip is waiting."

Gale looked around the cramped crew quarters. She didn't know how Booker had managed to get them hidden on the plane. Perhaps he owned the airline, or maybe he'd paid off the entire crew, but that seemed unlikely. Something about the arrangement made her extra nervous. It felt as if she was about to be arrested, or the plane was going to crash. An eerie intuition.

What if it was Cira? What if something bad had happened to her?

"Are you sure Cira is okay?" she asked.

"Yes."

"Can't I talk to Harmer, or see inside the room?"

"Not safe now. Maybe on the flight to El Perdido."

"How did Booker manage to get us on this plane?"

"I don't know exactly, but—"

"It seems risky," Gale interrupted. "Too many people know we're here."

"Just the crew, and they don't know who you are. I believe the story is that you're in the witness protection program."

Gale nodded, but she didn't feel any better, and because she no longer trusted Kruse, the reasons for her unrest were not clear.

When she wasn't thinking about Cira, the Sphere filled her mind. It was always difficult whenever Rip took it away. She'd become as much of a researcher as he had over the years, often referring to it as "the other world," because although it was a portal into the world in which they lived, its limitless coverage of the history of the universe meant that the period of time they recognized within the Sphere was as significant as a split second.

After a few weeks of jumping across billions of years recorded by the Sphere, Gale had understood what Booker meant when he said "time's a funny thing." *Time is something we made up to allow us to cope with the enormity of existence,* she thought. *We know nothing about what time really is. Time away from Cira is different though.*

Gale realized she was shaking, thinking of her daughter all alone in a strange hospital room, hunted by the most dangerous people in the world.

She forced herself to focus. The Sphere, the thing they'd been counting on to save the world, she'd be back to it and Rip very soon. Together, the two of them could figure out how to use it to help Cira. One of the many anomalies of the Sphere was how it functioned from some type of intelligence. It seemed incredibly intuitive, and it could actually answer questions. The Eysen-Sphere, just like the Eysen-INUs modeled after it, grew smarter and evolved as its users did.

The scientists described the Sphere as the most advanced Artificial Intelligence program they'd ever seen, way beyond what many of them had warned could one day circumvent humans. A coalition of top minds had been warning the world since the beginning of the century that AI could, in the future, cause the end of humanity. But now Gale, Rip, and Booker's UQP scientists knew it would be something else. Either one, or all of the Death Divinations, or the Phoenix Initiative.

AI might cause a problem in the middle of all that though. It was a scary thing to imagine machines outthinking humans and being in control of our fate, yet the Eysen-Sphere's AI operated almost as a benevolent entity, and Gale often had to remind herself that it was mechanical and not some kind of god.

Still, here she was, praying to the Eysen as if it were divine.

−O−

The plane touched down at Honolulu International Airport without incident. It taxied to gate thirty-four and readied to disembark the one hundred seventy-seven passengers. Then there was a delay.

"What's going on?" Gale asked after a few minutes of unusual stillness.

Kruse listened carefully at the door, but just raised his eyebrows and slowly shook his head.

The minutes crawled by as if they were insects burrowing down Gale's throat, invading her gut with determined fury.

"Ladies and gentleman," the captain finally said over the intercom. "We apologize for this brief delay. After a quick inspection, we'll be ready to go."

"Inspection? What the hell is that?" Gale whispered sharply.

Kruse opened the narrow door less than an inch and peered out. He closed it quietly after less than a second. His eyes closed for a moment.

"What?" Gale asked.

"There are two federal agents checking the plane!" he snapped in a hushed tone.

"They know we're on board," Gale said, trying to push through a wash of despair. Would she ever see Cira again?

"No, no way. If they knew we were here, it would be a dozen agents. We'd still be in the middle of the runway," Kruse said. "No, they're probably just checking any flights coming from Australia, New Zealand, Fiji, anywhere we might have gone."

"That hardly helps us. They're bound to check in here."

Kruse pulled one of the curtains that separated the sleeping areas and handed it to Gale. "If the agents get this far, try to pull this over their heads."

"What will you be doing?" Gale asked.

Kruse took the fire extinguisher off the wall and stood behind the door. They waited in the narrow space, suddenly stuffy and warm, bracing for a final, desperate fight.

I can't believe seven years of running and hiding has come down to this, Gale thought. *Cira blind in a hospital, Rip alone on El Perdido, and me, shanghaied onto a passenger jet and arrested at the gate.*

The rumbling of voices permeated through the thin door. It wouldn't be long before the first agent reached them. Kruse held the fire extinguisher above his head and concentrated. If he got the angle right, he could kill the first one with the initial blow and then swing the blunt object into the next one's face. Either way, he'd have to get the first agent's gun. When he'd seen the agent, his gun was still holstered, but hopefully he'd have it drawn by the time he opened the door.

"What's in there?" they heard the muffled voice of the agent on the other side of the door ask.

"Crew quarters," a female flight attendant responded.

"Anyone in there?" the gruff voice asked.

"No," she replied, a little too stilted. Unbeknownst to Kruse, while the flight attendant answered "no," she was nodding her head "yes." In the moments that followed, Kruse could detect an awkward silence and some shuffling. He guessed the other agent was joining his partner.

Kruse knew the door was locked, and could almost picture the flight attendant holding up her hands indicating the numbers of the four-digit code. A second later, he heard each button being pushed as if in slow motion.

One. He looked at Gale. She was ready.

Two. He took a deep breath and steadied the extinguisher above his head.

Three. He felt the adrenaline surge.

Four. Click. The door opened.

Kruse brought the extinguisher down, hitting only the agent's arm, but it was enough. His gun crashed to the floor. All in an instant, against the sound of screams from passengers, the agent tried to push his way in as the second agent called for backup. Wedged between the wall and the door, Kruse had leverage on his side and pushed back. Gale dropped the curtain and went for the gun.

She couldn't quite get it, as it had slid into a small space under the lower bunk. Kruse suddenly won the battle and the door slammed shut. His face met hers and they were both shocked to be closed in again, alone and alive.

"The gun," she said, pointing.

He reached down and could just touch it with his fingertips. "Stay down," he said. "They're probably evacuating the plane and may start shooting through the door as soon as the area's clear." He maneuvered and stretched. "Got it!" he exclaimed triumphantly.

"Kruse!" a man's voice shouted from the other side of the door. Kruse, startled, looked at Gale.

"No one out there could know my name."

"AX-0317."

Kruse looked at Gale for a split second and then pulled the door open.

twenty-nine

Savina thought of her assistants as brothers. They had shared countless, exciting hours exploring the Sphere and witnessing many extraordinary scenes, but nothing like the adventure of being swallowed by it. Savina had full confidence in her "brothers," believing they would do anything for her, and for the Sphere.

"We need to talk about what just happened," one of them said as she came out of her office after her call with the Judge.

"Let's go for a walk," she said. "We'll get some lunch."

Outside, the northern California air held a chill. The grey April day gave no sign that spring was trying to fight its way into the meteorological schedule. Savina shivered, but didn't want to go back through all the security to get her jacket.

"Let's drive to that sushi place," she suggested, looking at the other two a moment longer, knowing a bond had formed among them, forged in the surreal aspects of their mission to help save the world.

The three of them piled into her Acura and Savina negotiated the mid-day traffic to her favorite eatery, about fifteen minutes away.

"Savina," one of the assistants began, "where did we go? Where did the Sphere take us? *How* did it take us?" His voice sounded different now, holding an understanding of the unbelievable things they'd seen.

"When I started this project, the Judge told me that the Sphere shows the entire universe to us," Savina said. "But I think we now know it's much more than that." Her voice hushed, as if speaking in a sacred place, the three of them alone in the world of the Sphere. "The Sphere is like the *key* to the universe and all that the universe might be part of. The multiverse, other dimensions, the truth of time . . . everything."

"To hold all the stars in your hands," one of them said.

"Yes," she whispered, distracted by the memory of it.

"But it sounds a lot like you're talking about UQP," the other one added.

"I know," she said quietly. "Universe Quantum Physics. It's more than Booker's pet project. He must be on to something."

Savina recalled the many wonders of the Sphere, how it often seemed to respond to their needs, even when unvoiced. The wondrous hours spent watching hundreds of animals that no longer existed, that were not even in the fossil record. Plants, trees, water creatures — such things as Dr. Seuss could never have dreamt. She thought of the violet trees that stretched taller than redwoods, and pink rainstorms falling across hundreds of miles of tangled, yellow-leaved, blue vines as thick as passenger trains.

One of her favorite views into the Sphere had been the cities constructed entirely of light. Some ancient or future civilization — she didn't know which — had mastered photons and electromagnetic waves. It had been a glorious thing to behold, cities the size of any modern metropolis with no solid structures, only light in every imaginable color and intensity creating the buildings. *How had they harnessed the energy for such a place*, she still wondered.

Now it seemed the answers were surfacing, and many of them might already be known by Booker's UQP project.

— O —

The Judge sat, three thousand miles away, listening to the

private conversation between Savina and her assistants. He tinkered with a robotic sleeve that could be worn by quadriplegics, giving them back the use of their arms. It wasn't quite ready, but the technology had come from the Sphere. It would work soon.

The conversation concerned the Judge. Savina might have assumed the lab was bugged, but she obviously hadn't guessed that the Foundation's invasion went as far as her car, and that was only the start. The Judge could listen to her while she showered, hear her talking to the carrots growing in her vegetable garden, and knew more about Savina's routines and habits than she herself did. The Foundation could take no chances with their Sphere and those who handled it, and her words confirmed what he already suspected. The Sphere had seduced her.

With so much at stake, he would have to think through his next move very carefully. There were others who could take her place, although Booker had most of the best. Even if she were irreplaceable, with Gaines back in the world, each moment held the potential to crash the Phoenix Initiative, taking with it humanity's best chance for survival. No, somehow he needed to keep her on board.

The Judge continued to listen in on his three employees in Savina's Acura.

"Gaines has been working on the Sphere for seven years!" one of them said. "Seven long years. And do you think he's had access to Booker's UQP resources?"

"It's hard to imagine Booker allowing scientists to see the Sphere, or to even know it still exists," the other assistant said.

"But the Foundation allows us to see ours," Savina countered. "And they've kept it secret. We haven't said anything to anyone. Booker could do the same. Through bribery, legal intimidation, even threats of death."

"Would it take that much?" one of them asked. "Once a scientist spends a little time with the Sphere, he would do anything to continue. It's the most important scientific discovery ever! Look at us. What could compare to the work we're doing? Would you want to do anything else? I mean, if the Foundation cut your pay in half, wouldn't you still stay? Wouldn't you do this work for free?"

They all agreed.

"So Booker has how many scientists in his UQP program?" one of them asked.

"No one knows for sure," Savina replied, "but it could be hundreds. And it's not just quantity. He has the best."

"What do you think they've discovered?"

"Maybe the same as us. It's not like we have a manual for the thing."

Savina and her team had never seen Crying Man. During their four years on the project, they'd seen remarkable scientific data, including information relating to the origin of the universe and the recent history of humanity, but they'd concentrated much of their efforts on the future. It's what the Foundation wanted. Technology was the other push. The Judge had ordered them to pursue every sign of engineering. Savina assumed that was an effort to keep up with Booker and to develop machines which could help the Foundation win the future.

In all that time, they had not seen anything to explain who built the Eysen and why. Each of them had wondered, but even if it had been their assignment, the Eysen was not cooperating. Sometimes days had been spent unable to get the Sphere to get off the growth and molecular structure of a single flower, or the formation of one of Jupiter's moons.

It had not all been minutia though. They had gleaned incredible plans for solar power plants, levitating vehicles, aerospace design, and many other technological advancements. A host of those discoveries had already been put into production, or were in some form of development. Still more, some of the most important and fantastical technologies, were being secretly held by the Foundation to be used or introduced years, even decades, into the future. The Sphere was like a trillion-dollar research and development department.

"What are we going to do when we get back to the lab?" one of them asked.

"We have no choice," Savina responded, deep in thought. "We have to go farther. We have to let the Sphere show us its secrets. I don't know what risks we may face . . . " She paused, thinking back on how the lab had been consumed, how they were all floating in some unknown realm, untethered from anything they knew. "But we must press on. Before we find Gaines again, we have to find someone else inside the Sphere."

"Who?"

"The Cosegans."

thirty

Taz handled the Fiji hospital operation from his INU as he was driven toward the university. He wished he could have been there, but it was satisfying to know he'd been right. Gale Asher and Booker's people had not moved the little girl. He tried to imagine how difficult it had been for Gale to leave her daughter, knowing she would almost certainly be captured.

The leader of the Foundation's mercenary unit had been relaying a play-by-play until they were able to get a video to connect via a satellite link. Technology made it almost unnecessary for Taz to be in Fiji anyway, but still he believed in "smelling the air," and "tasting the blood," as he put it.

"Taz, we're linking to an INU inside the hospital room," the mercenary leader said. "We're about to get live images."

And then, suddenly, there was the prize; the bandaged little daughter of Asher and Gaines. A few feet away stood a tough-looking woman whom Taz recalled from the files. *Hammer or Harson or something*, he thought. She worked for Booker Lipton, proof of what they already knew. Booker had been hiding them all these years, and if Asher and Gaines had survived, then so had the Eysen-Sphere. *Only a matter of time.*

"Take the room," Taz ordered. "But be extremely careful. I want both of them alive. And don't touch the girl. No need to risk her vision until we have to."

Taz knew that soon enough the competition would arrive in Fiji to claim the girl for themselves. The NSA and CIA were going to find out. They always did. He might have to move Cira, but in the meantime he would get Harmer — he finally remembered her name — on a plane to Hawaii. He wanted to talk to her in person. Gaines and Asher had trusted the woman with their daughter's life. She had to know where they were.

Taz had already sent another team to Fiji, but they were still a few hours away. *Would the parents really have left their precious daughter behind? Alone?* He contemplated doubts and logic, which had often opposed one another in this case.

"There are three-hundred-thirty-some odd islands they could be hiding on without even leaving the country," Taz told Stellard. "You know as much as I do about Asher and Gaines. Would they abandon their wounded little girl?"

Stellard didn't think so either, and now that they knew their daughter hadn't really been on the plane that crashed, it was very possible that Gale Asher had also not been on board. "I think there's a fifty-fifty chance that Asher is still somewhere in Fiji."

"Yeah, and I'm stuck in Hawaii following the cold trail of Gaines, who's probably a thousand miles from here now."

"But we have a contact," Stellard said. "This guy, Dabnowski, has worked on Booker's UQP team for years. He's probably seen the Sphere, and may well have been with Gaines over the past few days."

"I know," Taz said, not as excited as his boss about the prospect of grilling a nerdy scientist when his real targets, Gaines and Asher, were so close. "I'll work him over. Why won't he talk to me on the phone?"

"He doesn't trust the NSA," Stellard replied.

"Who does?" Taz asked as he saw the shabby concrete sign for Kamanele Park. Old metal jungle gyms and rusty swing sets gave the small area between busy neighborhood streets a dated feel. It was only the giant shade trees and palms swaying in the warm breeze that came close to making it a worthwhile "park." His contact had chosen it for the meeting, no doubt due to its proximity to the university, and the fact that no one important would ever bother with the place.

Taz promised Stellard a full update as he signed off and wandered over to one of the worn benches. He was a few minutes early, but twenty minutes later, when no one had shown up, he was ready to leave. Taz had almost reached his car when his driver pointed to the trees bordering the opposite end of the park.

A man in his early thirties, wearing glasses and carrying a beat-up, old-fashioned leather briefcase, stumbled over the exposed roots of a nearby tree, then quickly looked back as if someone might have shoved him. Taz headed toward the man.

"Are you Dabnowski?" Taz asked once he was close enough.

He nodded and checked behind him again. "Taz?"

"That's me," Taz said. "Thanks for coming." He wanted to scold him for being late, for wasting his time, but the guy already looked as if he'd been chewed out a few times that day. Taz, believing he was a thousand miles from the action, needed to catch a break.

Actually, Taz thought, *he looks wildly nervous. Scared even.*

Taz pointed back to his bench. "Should we sit?"

Dabnowski looked around again, scanning the whole area. "This one's better," he said, pointing to another bench nestled in a cluster of trees. Once they were sitting down, Dabnowski, dressed in a rumpled cotton suit with no tie, asked, "So you're with the Foundation?"

"Yes."

"There are agents all over the university, you know?" he asked, fumbling with one of the plastic buttons on his shirt. Taz noticed a light stain, maybe coffee.

"I know," Taz said. "Have they talked to you?"

"No. I've been staying out of the way. They, the NSA, interviewed me a long time ago. I was friends with Snowden." His voice was strained, as if he was constantly suffering from indigestion.

"Really?" Taz said with a combination of respect and nervousness as he too scanned the area.

"We were neighbors. Met when he first moved to Hawaii." Dabnowski looked out through the trees again. "I told them I didn't know him well, but we were close."

"Wasn't he only here a year?"

"Fifteen months. Fifteen very serious months."

Taz nodded. Although curious about the Snowden connection, he didn't have the luxury of digging around in history. He needed information about current events, namely Gaines. "Did you work with Gaines?"

"Yeah, I knew him. I mean, we met a couple of times, but I mostly worked on the project when he was gone."

"Gone where?"

"I don't know where he went when he wasn't here. He wasn't here much, but we kept working."

"What did you work on?"

Dabnowski stood up and paced. "I'm not sure I should tell you."

"Then why are you here? Why are you meeting with us?"

"Because the Foundation is the best chance we have to change things. Well, the Inner Movement might be able to . . ." Dabnowski looked off into the near distance, but it was as if he was seeing something a million miles away. "Anyway, the Foundation is working against the NSA on this."

"And how do you know that exactly?"

"I've done work for Sky Race."

"Right." Taz recalled Stellard telling him about that, but he'd been distracted with the Fiji hospital raid. Sky Race, Inc., a huge corporation involved in space technologies, controlled by a Foundation member, was an extremely influential company. "It must have been more than work, if you know all that."

"Look, Taz, I can see you'd rather be somewhere else, and you may think I'm some loser-nerd, but you're the weak player at this meeting. I know enough to be scared because I don't want to die, but there are things in life that we're obligated to do. I'm an astrophysicist, but that doesn't mean I'm not interested in earthly affairs." He glared at Taz, as if annoyed at needing to explain his qualifications and motivations. "It's exactly because of my interest in space that I'm so concerned about this planet."

"Okay, okay. Relax," Taz said.

"It's impossible to relax when the Sphere is in danger of falling into the hands of the US government."

"Who should have it?"

"Gaines."

Taz gave him a quizzical look.

"I know the Foundation is seeking it for its own purposes, and that's a distant second to Gaines keeping it, but a heck of a lot better than the NSA giving it to HITE."

Taz didn't know who or what HITE was, but they'd wasted enough time. "What did you do with the Eysen?"

"I was on the Mauna Kea team."

From a bar bet he'd lost in college, Taz knew that a dormant volcano on the island of Hawaii called Mauna Kea, measured from base to summit, stood nearly a mile taller than Mt. Everest. He was also vaguely aware that it housed some "telescopes," but that was the extent of his knowledge. "What's the Mauna Kea team?"

"We work at the observatories," Dabnowski said. "There are thirteen telescopes, the most advanced in the world, funded by eleven countries. It's the largest astronomical observation facility on Earth — electromagnetic spectrum, infrared, visible light, submillimeter, radio . . ."

"Must be like Disneyland for you," Taz said. "But what are you doing with the Eysen-Sphere up there?"

Dabnowski looked at him as if he'd just asked what color the sky was. "Do you know *anything* about the object you're looking for?"

Taz suddenly felt self-conscious. "I know what I need to know."

"I don't think so," Dabnowski said. "You have no idea what the Sphere is." Then he paused and looked directly into Taz's sunglasses until Taz took them off. "You don't have a clue about what's going on."

thirty-one

Rip stumbled away from his INU. Cira, their innocent child, was now in the hands of one of his mortal enemies. There had been no choice.

There's always a choice, he thought. *At least she's alive. Gale will be destroyed.*

Booker had said he'd contact people in the Foundation to plead for Cira. "Just keep her stable. Save her eyesight," he'd tell them. "Gale and Rip might make a deal, but not until the girl is healed. They couldn't possibly do one now while it was unsafe to move Cira."

It might work. The Eysen-Sphere was a huge bargaining chip. However, Rip had absolutely no doubt that the secretive trillionaire would never trade the Sphere, even to save his own child.

There was a strange glow emanating from the Sphere, the kind the full moon had on foggy winter nights. He'd never seen it look quite like that. Then the room filled with blue mist. Not just projected light, but actual cool, moist air. Rip lost the Sphere in the fog. For a moment, he wasn't sure it was safe to breathe in the mist, but then he had to, and it entered his lungs through an involuntary inhale.

Everything went strange. He couldn't tell where the floor was, or even where up was, lost in an avalanche of thick, colored, now purple, fog, having passed through deep shades of teal, indigo, and finally, violet. Then the rush of sound began, like a volcano, or as if ocean waves were crashing all around the skyroom. Rip had no idea where he was, no logical explanation for what was happening.

Minutes passed, maybe even hours. Explaining the event later, he would say that if he'd come out of that fog days later, it would not have surprised him. When absolute quiet overtook the roar of volcanic waves, he realized the mist had become black. It terrified him for an instant as he considered the vacuum in which he found himself. All that had happened must have been his death. *Seeing Cira captured was too much for me. In my overwhelming grief and stress, I had a heart attack and died. Damn it… I let my family down.*

Then he saw a face. She was lovely, but the image before him did not belong to Gale or Cira. He did not recognize her; young, thin, with intelligent eyes. As she came more fully into his view, all that he could see was the woman and where she stood in a dark room, filled with stars and a large glowing planet.

But, that's no planet, he thought. *It's the Eysen-Sphere! Who is she? How did she get the Sphere? Is this a dream?*

Rip was agitated. Nothing like this had ever happened. He knew the Sphere was able to show the future. He'd even been projected into the future, and the past, as a holographic figure. Those episodes had allowed him to interact with people of the time where he'd "gone." The era's inhabitants had mostly been startled, even afraid of him, but a few, on specific occasions, in both the past and future, had almost expected him.

But this didn't feel like those situations. *It feels like now, immediate in the breath I just took,* he thought, alarmed, unable to see the Sphere through the fog. On those other "trips" he'd been completely immersed, able to see every detail as if he were a current resident of where and when he had found himself.

Pushing through the black mist, Rip tried to walk to the Sphere, but there was nothing firm under his feet. He dropped onto his hands and knees to what he believed was the floor, but he really wasn't sure. It felt more like standing on a waterbed covered with silk and sand. Trying to crawl, then attempting to swim, to the Sphere proved futile. All the while the young woman stared into the Sphere in front of her as if seeing the most amazing images.

"It is now?" Rip shouted. He didn't know how he knew it, but he did. *And she isn't here on El Perdido. She has another Eysen-Sphere. Is it Clastier's? Or Malachy's?* He didn't know, but he knew where it had come from.

The Vatican. Booker had tried, ever since the Church collapsed, to locate and acquire artifacts related to Cosega and other items from their secret archives with little success. The Church had long seen the end coming and had prepared well: secrets hidden, treasures buried, waiting until the "second coming," when the force of the Vatican's concealed collections could empower those who would resurrect Catholicism. Rip knew too much about the next hundred years to know that was not going to happen, but beyond that . . . it was hard to say.

But the Catholic Church didn't care about decades or even a few centuries. They dealt in millennia, and the world was a constantly changing creation. Anything could happen given enough time and the right circumstances.

Rip stood, at least that's what he thought he was doing, shrouded in the blackness. Somehow he believed the woman could see him. The Spheres' connecting with each other had been an early lesson, but he had searched and found nothing.

How did she locate me? And then he panicked. *Who is she working for? Does she know where I am physically?* He thought about stopping Gale from coming. *Agents could be heading to El Perdido at this very moment!*

thirty-two

As Kruse lunged out of the crew's quarters, he saw the bodies of the two now unconscious federal agents, bound with zip-cuffs . Gale followed closely, and saw, even before Kruse did, that two other men were keeping the crew and passengers down and quiet.

"Kruse, this way," one of them yelled.

"AX agents," he mouthed to Gale, as they started briskly down the aisles. Dread quickly replaced Gale's brief sense of relief, imagining the gauntlet that lay ahead.

Two more AX agents waited at the front of the plane, where the door was already opened and joined to the gate's gangway.

"How did you get here?" Kruse asked.

"We were on the plane the whole time," one of them answered. "The boss doesn't like to take chances. But we were unarmed, and had to wait until they rushed the door to act."

"Just in time," Kruse said as they ran down the gangway. "Thanks!"

One of the agents stayed on the plane to stop an immediate rush of panicked passengers toward the exits. The other three hurried Gale and Kruse to the restroom, one remaining in the hall for cover as the others all dashed inside. Kruse remembered this room and its tunnel from Booker's instructions.

"The pilot and one of the feds had both called in from the plane," one of the agents said as they used the code to unlock the maintenance door. "We may be only ninety seconds ahead of an army of pursuers."

Once in that tunnel, they were only fifty yards from freedom. Rounding the last turn before the exit which led to Booker's plane, they ran into a security guard. Kruse barreled into the man, instantly knocking him down.

The security guard seemed oblivious to the fact that he had just stumbled upon one of the world's most wanted people, but was upset to be knocked over. "Hey!" he yelled as he tried to get up. Just as his radio announced the highest-level emergency code, one of the AX agents put him back down on the ground, where he would stay until medical attention arrived.

Kruse and Gale burst through the door and raced for the plane. Its engines were on, and the plane was already slowly rolling. They expected to be dodging bullets, but all seemed clear. They timed their steps and Kruse helped Gale jump onto the folded, extended staircase as the plane picked up speed. She heard Kruse land behind her, then he was pushing her up toward the entrance.

As she reached the top step, about to duck inside, she turned around and realized that it wasn't Kruse behind her. It was one of the other AX agents. She glanced around and saw Kruse sprinting back into the airport. *One last fight*, she thought, as the agent shoved Gale into the plane and pulled the hatch shut.

"Happy you could make it," the pilot said. "We've been cleared for take-off."

"It still might get rough," the AX agent said to Gale. "Better buckle up."

"Where are we going?" Gale asked, still afraid to trust anyone.

"El Perdido," the man replied. "I believe Rip is waiting there for you."

Gale smiled as she buckled up, but she worried about Kruse. Although furious at what he had done, she knew she owed him her life many times over, and there was a very good chance that he would not live through the day.

–O–

Murik and Rathmore watched in disbelief as images streamed into the NSA situation room in Fort Meade, Maryland.

"That's Gale Asher," Rathmore said. "No question about it. What the hell is she doing in Hawaii?"

"Leaving in a hurry," Murik said, pointing to satellite footage of the plane that security video had just showed her climbing into, now rolling toward takeoff.

"Bang-bang, you're dead, fifty bullets in your head," Rathmore said. "She's not going anywhere. I'll have that runway blocked in less than a minute." He began shouting orders into another line, but the Conductor interrupted.

"Let her go," she said.

"Are you crazy? I'm not letting her go!" Rathmore argued. Then he had to clarify his order to federal agents at the airport.

"Where do you think she's going?" the Conductor asked calmly from the backseat of a black SUV racing toward Honolulu International Airport. It was her operation, but Rathmore had the final say.

"How the hell should I know? She's running for her life. I can't believe she flew to US soil in the first place, and on a commercial airline!" He laughed. "Maybe she *wants* to get caught."

"She's trying to get to Gaines," the Conductor said.

"Right," Murik agreed. "Why Hawaii? She could have flown in *any* direction. She'd lost us. She was *free*. Why fly into Hawaii, even if she didn't know about the massive presence of agents and military personnel? It's the United States, and she isn't crazy."

"She's going to Gaines," the Conductor repeated. "Gaines was here yesterday. He may not be far from here."

"Maybe she thinks he's still in Hawaii. Maybe he still is," Rathmore said as Gale's plane moved closer to the runway. Trucks were on standby to block it, military jets ready to scramble.

"That Gulfstream was waiting for her," the Conductor continued. "She wasn't planning to stay here, she was just switching planes. Let her go."

"Oh," Rathmore breathed, finally catching up to her thinking. "Let her go and she'll lead us to Gaines."

"That's the idea," the Conductor said. "She's our best chance to find him and the Sphere."

"I completely agree," Murik added. "We can have half a dozen Navy jets in the air tailing her from a safe distance. Let's see where she goes."

Rathmore didn't like to gamble. He knew getting Gale Asher to talk would not be easy. He already had authorization to torture her if necessary, but the moment she was captured, Gaines would most likely flee his current location, knowing she might crack.

Then again, Rathmore couldn't resist the chance to finally be ahead of the leech. They could lock this down and have the situation wrapped up in a matter of hours.

"If this goes bad," Rathmore said, looking from Murik to the Conductor on the monitor, "you are both sharing the blame when the Director wants blood."

The Conductor nodded. "What about King?"

"I have my own director to deal with," Murik said, referring to the CIA Director, but the NSA had the lead on this one because of HITE. Back in the late forties, and through most of the fifties, HITE had belonged to the CIA. Under the Kennedy administration, it was moved to the NSA. The Eysen-Sphere was the most advanced piece of technology ever known, and the NSA believed that the future stability of the world depended on who possessed it. Booker and the Foundation knew for a fact that it did. The Sphere owned the future, and both were determined to keep it out of the other's hands.

"No one outside this room needs to know yet," Rathmore said, answering all their questions. He motioned to the Vax analyst. "Track everything. If any data about

Gale Asher, airplanes, or even the State of Hawaii moves, I want the report. Clear?"

"Yes sir," the analyst said.

"If we're lucky," Rathmore began, "we'll get Asher. If we're not, at least we'll flush out the damned leech. Now let's do this!"

thirty-three

Harmer had done everything possible to avoid leaving Cira without actually endangering the child. Now she sat, dejected and bruised, on a private plane speeding toward Hawaii and Foundation interrogation. Harmer knew where the rendezvous point was. She had lived with them on El Perdido in those early years. The Foundation would eventually employ torture experts to extract the information from her. Booker would know that, and he would have BLAX, the dark ops section of AX, come for her.

If they can't rescue me, they'll make sure I'm dead before I can talk, she thought. *It's for the best.* Thinking of Booker brought her some inner peace.

Taz had excused himself to check the update. Cira was an issue. Booker Lipton had already been in touch with top Foundation members to make a case for leaving her put, but Stellard and Taz knew the NSA would be there soon, and if the little girl were still there, they would take her. The Foundation needed Cira because her parents, like most parents, would do anything to save their child. But if the Foundation caused her permanent blindness, that would make things more difficult.

Still, she wouldn't be dead, Taz thought, *and that's better than nothing.*

Stellard and Taz agreed to utilize the same strategy that AX had used: hide the girl behind the phony supply closet. In the meantime, they would rely on their contacts within the NSA and the CIA to warn them if the agencies were close to moving on the hospital. Wattington would also work to promote a diversion that would transfer attention away from Fiji. A fabricated but reliable Gale Asher sighting should do it.

But who would report it, and where? they wondered. Developing a plausible story became a top priority.

Taz apologized to Dabnowski, who was growing impatient with him. Dabnowski believed Taz was "in way over his head." If it weren't for Dabnowski's need to have the cooperation and protection of the Foundation, he would have already left.

"You were saying?" Taz prompted. "About the Sphere?"

"This is not a latent artifact created by some afore-unknown advanced prehistoric civilization," Dabnowski said, pushing his eyeglasses up on the bridge of his sweaty nose. "I mean it is that, of course, but it is infinitely *more*. It proves everything that we do not know. It didn't just show us the *Cosega* part 'before the beginning,' that what people believed about the Bible, about religion in general, was false. It showed that our *whole history* was false. Everything we thought we knew about where we came from, who we are, what we are, it's all wrong."

"I get that much."

"Good," Dabnowski said, allowing the brief beginnings of a smile. "I doubt you'll 'get' much more than that." He tried not to sound or appear condescending, but the truth was that Dabnowski, an astrophysicist, and his peers, some of the greatest minds in the scientific community, also had a hard time with the rest of it. "Because as mind-boggling as all that is," Dabnowski continued, his face lighting up, "it's the *Eysen* aspect of the Sphere, the 'to hold all the stars in your hand' part that really bends reality, distorts time, and connects *everything*."

Taz looked at him, wondering if this nut would ever get to the point. "I know the Sphere is amazing. Why do you think we're moving heaven and Earth to get the damned thing?" Taz wanted to move along and either get something that would help him locate Gaines and the Sphere, or, barring that, go pursue another lead. "So tell me about the telescopes. You never finished that."

"Is there someone else I can talk to?" Dabnowski asked, exasperated. "No disrespect, but if you don't understand what it is you're after, how can you ever hope to find it?" Dabnowski asked this knowing that there was no chance in the world a person like Taz could ever "understand" the Sphere, but someone at the Foundation obviously had a sense of the awesome significance of the Eysen-Sphere, and that was the person Dabnowski needed to speak with.

Taz's phone went off. He glanced at it and saw Stellard was interrupting again. "Sorry, but I have to take this."

Dabnowski shook his head, sighed, and contemplated another way to save the Eysen-Sphere.

"We've received a gift from the gods. No diversion necessary," Stellard began. "Word just came in. You'll never believe where Gale Asher is at this very minute."

"Could you just tell me?" Taz asked, looking back at a very impatient Dabnowski.

"Gale Asher just landed at Honolulu International!" Stellard said happily, actually clapping his hands as he said it.

"I can be there in fifteen minutes," Taz said, already heading to the car. "What the hell is she doing in Hawaii?" He was sprinting now. "Do you think that means Gaines is still here?"

"I have no details yet," Stellard responded. "Just get to the airport and hope we get to her first!"

As soon as Taz opened the car door, his driver pointed back at Dabnowski, who was standing, staring back at them with his hands on his hips.

"Damn, I forgot about him," Taz muttered. "I'll just be a second, and then we're returning to the airport."

He ran back to the astrophysicist.

"Sorry, we just got a major lead," Taz said, panting. "We'll need to finish this another time."

"No," Dabnowski said. "Here, take this." He pushed his briefcase into Taz's gut a little too hard. "If you find the information in there useful, if you can even *comprehend* what it is and you have questions, then get your boss or, better yet, whoever is in charge of the Foundation, to contact me."

"Hey man, I said I'm sorry, but this is a big deal, and I'm being pulled in a few directions," Taz said, nearly fumbling the briefcase.

Dabnowski looked around nervously, and then directly back into Taz's sunglass-shielded eyes. "I can assure you that nothing you're doing, no one you're chasing, is as important as what the documents in that case will tell you."

Taz looked down at the worn leather straps of the satchel, wondering why the astrophysicist hadn't put the information on a flash drive. "Okay," Taz said in his most conciliatory voice. "Thanks for your help. We'll be back in touch."

Dabnowski took one last look around, then, without a word, walked back the way he had come. Taz, baffled by Dabnowski's attitude, turned and darted back to his waiting car.

"Nothing is more important than getting to the airport and finding Gale Asher," he said to himself as he tossed the battered leather briefcase on the backseat and called Stellard for an update.

thirty-four

The Judge listened to every word of the conversation between Savina and her assistants. Whatever the brilliant physicist did next would determine everything. Not only did her actions relate to the Sphere the Foundation already had, it also affected the one they hoped to get from Gaines. The fate of the Phoenix Initiative, and indeed civilization itself, depended on the Foundation's controlling both Spheres. Even with the one they had though, it might mean their plans could still have a chance to succeed, as long as the one that Gaines had wasn't used against them.

"Don't betray me, Savina," he whispered to the air as the group arrived back at the lab.

In the time it took them to get through security, the Judge took a call from Stellard and learned of Gale Asher's arrival in Honolulu. The Foundation had a team in Hawaii on their way to assist Taz at the airport, but Stellard agreed with the Judge. The chances of getting around the NSA, CIA, and FBI were not likely.

"Assuming they take Asher alive," Stellard said, warming his hands on a hot mug, "having her daughter will be even more important. Taz wants to preserve her eyesight and keep her in place, but it's risky not moving her."

"I agree with Taz," the Judge said. "We have no indication that the US government is sending anyone to the hospital. Now with Asher found, they may just leave it alone. They know Gaines isn't there since he was in Hawaii yesterday."

"Okay," Stellard said. "We'll continue with the conceal and wait strategy."

"Good," the Judge replied. "Now, I want you to prepare for a 'Fort Knox.'"

"It will require enormous resources," Stellard warned, not surprised to hear the Judge reference their code word for an assault on a US government installation. As soon as Stellard had learned Gale was at the airport in Honolulu and that one of the American agencies was going to arrest her, he knew the Judge would order a Fort Knox.

"You have a blank check," the Judge said. "You know that. A thousand men, more, I don't care what it costs. If the government has her, they'll get the Sphere. That cannot happen. That is doomsday, you understand? I don't care if we have to blow up an entire military base."

"Roger." Stellard knew that whatever was necessary meant just that. "It would help if you can find out where they'll be taking her."

"Wattington should be able to get that, but I'll send out feelers. I assume they'll put her on a plane the minute they get her. Maybe we can get that plane."

"Not sure we'll have time unless you just want her destroyed."

The Judge thought about that for a moment. Once they transferred Asher, it would be extremely risky to get to her. It would be better to have her dead than to have the American government have her.

"Shoot her down."

—O—

Back in the lab after lunch, Savina pulled her owl-like glasses down from the top of her head and began a desperate search for the Cosegans. She'd looked before, but now everything was different. She knew Gaines was alive, she knew there was another Sphere, and she knew her

Sphere was much more than an object from an out-of-place, advanced civilization.

"I don't know what it is," she said as the familiar Sequence cycled through, "but it makes me think that Booker Lipton's new UQP science isn't so crazy after all. He didn't attract all those scientists to study it just by throwing a pile of money around. He knows something, and he most likely got it from Gaines' Sphere."

"A buddy of mine's worked in UQP for a few years now," one of the assistants offered. "I know they're big into observations and experiments with gravitational waves."

"That makes sense," Savina said. "Gravitational waves changed everything."

"Booker's got people spending fortunes on experiments with the waves. It's like he's trying to prove it's possible to move great distances through the universe, even across time. Once they proved Einstein's 'invisible' waves existed, they took it to an extreme. As you know, the waves occur whenever an object moves in space, like ripples through a pond."

"Yeah, but the ripples are made of particles a million times smaller than the width of a hydrogen atom," the other assistant countered. "They're impossible to detect without LIGO."

They all knew about LIGO, the advanced Laser Interferometer Gravitational-Wave Observatory, which had first detected and continued to track gravitational waves. While exciting and astounding proof of distortions in spacetime, which in itself had enormous implications on what the universe is, the waves were so minute it seemed more like an astronomical Rosetta Stone than anything that would have a practical application.

"The size isn't the point," the first assistant continued. "At least not to the people working on UQP. Apparently they want to ride those ripples at their peaks. My friend explained it as instead of swimming across an ocean, imagine surfing across it on a big wave. You'd get to the other side much faster and with far less effort and energy."

"Wow!" Savina said, laughing in a moment of revelation. "Booker really thinks he can find a way to travel across time . . . and why not? Light does it."

"And all the information in the Eysen sure has."

thirty-five

Booker—through his own extensive surveillance network—learned of the meeting between Dabnowski and the Foundation too late. Prior to Cira's hospitalization, there had been an orderly system to monitoring the movements of all the scientists involved in Sphere research, but in the past twenty-four hours, all those procedures had gone by the wayside. AX agents had been reassigned and technicians monitoring the scientists suddenly had their caseloads tripled. Booker had been shocked by the meeting and contacted Dabnowski himself.

"Do you have any idea what the Foundation is trying to *do*?" Booker asked after the preliminaries, which included Dabnowski admitting to the meeting.

"They're trying to keep the Sphere away from the government."

"So am I."

"But Mr. Lipton, with all due respect, you're a profiteer, and—"

"I have funded the research and paid your salary!" Booker cried, incensed. "The only reason you know what you know about the Sphere, have even *seen* the Sphere, is because of me."

"But you're after the technology. You want to find ways to make the next great gadget, the next billion-dollar market, a way to crush another competitor. The Foundation does actual good in the world."

Booker knew people believed that. The Foundation had teams of public relations people making them look like angels on Earth when, in fact, he considered them as close to evil as any group he'd ever known. He'd said many times that even though he generally despised the CIA and NSA, those agencies were far more trustworthy and upstanding than the Foundation. Booker, on the other hand, was seen much as Dabnowski had described, even worse, depending on whom you talked to.

"While it's true, I have few advocates, Dr. Dabnowski, I can assure you that dealing with the Foundation will accomplish the exact opposite of what you're attempting to achieve."

"I'm glad I don't trust you, because that would be most unfortunate, if it were true. And if you're thinking of having some of your thugs or friends at the NSA pick me up, it's too late. I've already turned over my research to the Foundation."

"For such a brilliant man, Dabnowski, you're a fool," Booker said, trying to contain his anger. At the same time, he worked an INU and ordered an AX agent to pick up Dabnowski immediately. He knew the Foundation would have already ordered Dabnowski's assassination or abduction, and wanted to save the man, and his knowledge, if possible. "Whom did you meet with at the Foundation?"

"Why should I tell you?"

"Because you have made a colossal mistake, and this is your last chance to minimize the damage you've done. I should also remind you that you signed a non-disclosure agreement which is binding, and will ruin you, should I decide to enforce it."

"You know this is about more than one man's career. I've already decided it's worth my job, my future, even my life, if it comes to that. History may never know my sacrifice, but I've done what I *know* is right. The future of all of us is more important than the life of one of us."

Booker knew AX would get it out of him, and he also had other ways of finding the information. There weren't that many Foundation agents in Hawaii, and Booker had access to NSA tracking systems. It might take a few hours, but he'd find out. The problem was that with so much at stake, a few hours could mean everything.

The monitors in Booker's office were filled with images of urgency; Gale Asher on the Gulfstream, taxiing toward the runway, Rip Gaines on El Perdido, the hospital in Fiji, his link to the security cameras still live. Others showed BLAX and AX operatives in various parts of the world, yet with all that activity, Dabnowski troubled him most at the moment.

He muted the call and gave the order to pick up the astrophysicist. Once the Foundation realized what Dabnowski really knew, they would grab him. If not them, then the NSA would find him once they caught up in the game, which shouldn't take long after their raid on the university. The world had largely ignored Booker's Universe Quantum Physics project, but if the government got enough of the scientists to talk, UQP was about to become the hottest topic in the intelligence community.

The global balance of power had been fairly lopsided for decades. The US had the edge in all areas of technology, health and medicine, space, weapons, and more. For the past seventy-five years, the US owed almost all of that "good fortune" to HITE, but everything HITE had ever accumulated paled next to the Eysen-Sphere. It was the reason they never stopped looking, and now, with what the UQP team had discovered, the stakes were even higher.

Booker watched Rip struggle in the skyroom, trying to understand the unfathomable object, and imagined what it would have been like for those in earlier times, like Clastier, Malachy, and the others who had encountered Spheres.

"It's all we've ever sought," Booker whispered. "*Understanding* . . . answers to all the great questions . . .

and yet we may destroy ourselves before we uncover that which can save us."

thirty-six

Rathmore watched the plane carrying Gale turn onto the runway at the Honolulu International Airport. He knew his options: block the runway and storm the plane, have the plane fired upon and destroyed, or let it takeoff.

"Ninety seconds," the team at the runway announced.

"Let her go and we'll get Gaines," the Conductor urged again.

"Where is she going to go?" Murik asked Rathmore rhetorically. "Is that Gulfstream going to outrun an F/A-18 Hornet?"

"Sixty seconds."

"We have her on satellite. We'll know every turn the pilot makes and our Navy MONSTER just put eight Hornets in the air."

Rathmore looked at the live feed from the runway. On another screen, several men, who had been on the plane from Fiji with Gale, were involved in a shoot-out with federal agents that had spilled onto the main concourse. It wasn't a matter that particularly concerned him. That was definitely within the Conductor's domain, but he did want at least one of the men alive. He was certain they worked for Booker Lipton, and he hadn't had many opportunities to question AX agents.

"Thirty seconds."

Murik looked at Rathmore. The team had to start moving if they were going to safely block the runway. The

Gulfstream had been cleared by the tower and was accelerating.

"Okay," Rathmore finally said. "Let them fly." He stood up and addressed the entire room in a loud, bursting shout. "Do. Not. Lose. This. Plane!" He then made eye contact with some of the younger techs and continued his rant. "Loose lips sink ships! That means no one outside this room is to know we have Gale Asher. No one!" Rathmore had become concerned, over the course of the past twelve hours, that the NSA had a leak. "Let me remind you that this is a Scorch and Burn, meaning a violation of clearance carries a mandatory death sentence."

While the room buzzed with tense and determined activity, Rathmore's thoughts turned to his prisoner down the hall, former FBI Special Agent Dixon Barbeau. Rathmore had read every file relating to the Eysen case. At the very beginning of the investigation into Gaines' theft of the artifacts, Barbeau had made a critical decision to let a key witness go in the hopes that he would lead them to Gaines. It had not worked. The witness was later killed, and Gaines had never been caught.

Rathmore closed his eyes and said a quick prayer. He needed to have another conversation with Barbeau, but something nagged at him. Something in how Barbeau was so sure of himself, so damned self-righteous, but that would have to wait. He didn't plan to leave the situation room until Gale Asher's plane landed.

"Sir, King is on the line, looking for an update," a technician said.

Rathmore looked at Murik.

"You have to tell him," Murik said slowly.

Rathmore took the call. A few minutes later, he turned back to Murik. "King's got the Unit moving toward the flight path."

"Let's hope he's not the leech."

"He's not," Rathmore said.

"We just got the report back on the tail number of the Gulfstream," another analyst announced, as they all watched the plane soar into the sky. "It belongs to Buchta Broadcasting, a media company that owns a slew of radio and television stations in the southwest, including, are you ready for this, the one where Gaines' father works."

"So Booker owns everything," Rathmore said, disgusted. "Arrest Gaines' father. Pick up Asher's parents too. In fact, get every relative either one of them might have spoken with during the past seven years. Boom. Boom. Boom." He clapped his hands in exclamation.

—O—

The Conductor reported that the scientists were slow in providing information about the Sphere research and UQP. "We've still got nothing useful from the drives. Our experts are now saying it could take weeks, even months, to crack the encryptions."

"That may be optimistic," Murik said. "I talked to one source who said it could be years, if *ever*. Booker's companies are all protected by insanely complex firewalls that have never been hacked, and ever since Gaines discovered the Eysen-Sphere, encryption has advanced rapidly."

"It's one of my areas of expertise," Rathmore said. "I think we can crack it."

"What about CryptFast, a firm suspected to be controlled by Booker?" Murik asked. CryptFast had begun selling software five years earlier. It came with a million-dollar guarantee if it was to ever be hacked. "I'll take that check. Might even buy you a new personality, Claude."

"Marketing gimmick," Rathmore said, ignoring Murik's weak attempt at humor while nervously watching the Gulfstream flying out over the Pacific Ocean.

"No one's beat it. They even host an annual contest where they up the guarantee to ten million."

"Publicity stunt," Rathmore snapped. "The NSA could get through it easily, but you know we're prohibited by law from taking part. None of our technicians could privately try such a stunt either or they'd face prosecution."

"I don't know," Murik said, staring into his INU, his fingers manipulating data like a concert pianist. "Booker isn't some software startup company."

"It doesn't matter anyway. Even if they crack the university drives in a week, that's too late to help us right now," Rathmore said. "What are the scientists saying? That's where our information is going to come from."

"The biggest news is that there are at least one thousand scientists on Booker's payroll."

"More than a *thousand*?" Rathmore repeated. "What the hell is Booker doing? It only took a few hundred to design and build the first atomic bomb."

"If I recall my history correctly," the Conductor began, "the Manhattan Project, which produced the bomb, took about five years and cost two billion dollars, even translating that into today's dollars, that's twenty-some billion. Booker has had seven years, and could spend twenty billion each year without even noticing."

"What the hell is he working on?" Rathmore asked again. "The Sphere has already made Booker rich beyond measure with his INU technology, but there's a lot more to it . . . Those damned scientists know. We'll arrest them all if we have to. I'm authorizing enhanced interrogation methods."

"On *scientists*?" Murik asked. "We're going to torture scientists? Maybe we should round up some of Gaines' daughter's preschool classmates and see how they do with water boarding."

"We need to know what they know *now*," Rathmore retorted. "You CIA boys invented this stuff. I would think you'd be leading the charge."

"They aren't all here," the Conductor said. "They're at universities, labs, and companies around the world. And something else . . . "

"What?" Murik asked, still ignoring Rathmore.

"They're afraid," the Conductor said. "Terrified, actually."

"Of what?" Rathmore asked.

"I don't know yet. They're too scared to tell us."

"Sir!" the Vax analyst shouted in alarm. "We've got data moving on Asher. Waves of it leaving our network!"

thirty-seven

Taz couldn't get anywhere near the gate purported to be Gale's location. He could hear the shootout though, and hoped the feds weren't dumb enough to kill their most valuable lead. Stellard fed him information from inside the NSA while he watched helplessly from behind a security barrier as a large section of the airport was evacuated.

"They found her and an unidentified man in a routine sweep of a plane from Fiji," Stellard told him through his earpiece.

"Fiji? Damn, they play wild," Taz said, hitting his left palm hard enough to feel the sting of his gold rings. One of them, an eagle in flight, had been his father's, a military man he barely remembered. KIA in Iraq.

"At least three other men were on board the plane as well. A passenger plane, by the way."

"They flew commercial?" Taz couldn't believe it. "Any chance the guy is Gaines?"

"The NSA doesn't believe so, but it hasn't been entirely ruled out. Still, if Gaines was traveling with her, why would they leave Fiji when there are plenty of places to hide down there and they would remain much closer to their daughter?"

"You're right. She's heading to Gaines. It's the only reason she would take this risk."

"We're working on getting you airport security credentials. We had an identity lined up as an airline employee—one of the members owns one of the airlines at that terminal — but in the time it took to get you here, they ordered all employees out and aren't letting any others inside."

Taz cursed the time he'd wasted with "that egghead" Dabnowski. "Ever since Gaines was 'resurrected,' I've been a little late for every party," Taz said. "We can't just rely on scraps of information from Wattington. By the time we learn anything, the NSA is already onto the next break."

"We've got the daughter."

"Exactly. If the NSA gets ahold of the kid, we'll be out of the game. Every minute that passes is a minute closer to the US government figuring that out. We have to cut a deal with Booker now."

"But we can't move the girl," Stellard said, standing in the Foundation's darkened conference room. The seldom-used space was a virtual "dome of silence," utilizing every known anti-monitoring technology, but Stellard came in for the heat. There was a giant gas fireplace set into one wall, surrounded by an ornately carved marble mantle. He loved the flames, generated instantly whenever he pressed the concealed switch. It was his favorite place in the building.

"There must be a way to safely immobilize a six-year-old kid and move her," Taz said. "I mean, they can replace a human heart. These are just eyes! If the NSA kills Gale Asher, there'll be far fewer demands on Gaines for a deal."

"What do you mean?"

"Asher is a 'mommy.' That maternal instinct means she'll betray Gaines, if need be, to save her kid, and she'll sure as hell put enough pressure on him to help make up his mind. The Sphere for the kid, or, at least, Gaines for the kid." Taz looked around at the mayhem continuing to build at the airport. "But we have to do it now while Asher is still alive!"

Stellard agreed and immediately made the call to Maxim Miner, also known as the Judge. As current head of the Foundation, the Judge was one of the most powerful people in the world, and he could reach Booker.

−O−

The Judge waited for a series of clicks and transfers. He'd spoken to Booker on numerous occasions and knew the routine — routers, faux stations, and satellite bounces that would make the heavily encrypted call totally untraceable. Booker was not just the world's wealthiest man, he was the world's most wanted.

Although he had never been prosecuted for any crime — his lawyers, lobbyists, and contacts were too good for that — the NSA and FBI had put him on a target list ever since the Gaines case. They couldn't prove any direct wrongdoing by Booker, but there had been enough confrontations with suspected AX agents that meant charges were always pending. There'd actually been open military conflict in Mexico with AX, but somehow Booker had bribed his way out of that mess. The Foundation, on the other hand, didn't care about proof or how much money the man had. They employed a team of four assassins who worked full time trying to find and kill the trillionaire.

"Maxim," Booker said, a false smile projected in his tone. "Hope you weren't kept waiting too long."

"We're ready to deal for the girl," the Judge said, not bothering with small talk.

"I thought we had an understanding that we would talk about that once the doctors had cleared her to move."

"Events have necessitated that we alter the timetable."

"Really?" Booker said, watching the same satellite link that Rathmore and Murik were seeing. The Hornets' stealth pursuit of his little Gulfstream had not been unexpected, and would be a problem, but he was still savoring Gale's escape from Honolulu.

"We'll give you the girl for the Sphere."

"Yes, I'm sure you would," Booker said, "but there's only one person who would make that deal with you. Gale

Asher, and she sure as hell doesn't want her daughter permanently blinded."

"We have reason to believe the US government has a team of agents about to land in Fiji, and the hospital will be their first stop," the Judge said. "I've also just spoken with the head of surgery at the Bascom Palmer Eye Institute and there is a protocol. There is a way to safely move her."

"Yes, I've spoken with people at the Wilmer Eye Institute at Johns Hopkins, and they have said it can be done, but not without some risk." Booker had been only a few minutes away from ordering a rescue mission on the hospital ever since Cira got out of surgery. He was aware of every possible option.

"Some risk? Don't you think the girl and her parents are way beyond 'some risk?' I mean the odds are quite good that none of them will make it out of this alive."

Booker glanced at the projections. Gale's plane, still a few hours away from El Perdido, had enough fuel to land anywhere in the US southwest, California, and most of Mexico or Central America. He had assets, including AX agents, in countless possible landing areas. Anything was possible.

"I won't give you the Sphere," Booker said.

The Judge knew he couldn't threaten to kill the girl or Booker would go to war. That was not something the Foundation could handle right now. They were ready to take Booker on once the Phoenix Initiative had launched, but not before.

"We'll take Gaines."

"And you think the father will sacrifice himself for his child?"

"Who said anything about sacrifice?" the Judge said. "We can always use a brilliant man of his caliber at the Foundation. You have so many geniuses, why not trade that one?"

"What's in it for me?"

"I don't know, but you're talking to me, so there must be something."

Booker watched the shootout at the airport. The link covered only a few cameras, so his view was not optimal, but he saw Kruse go down.

"Get her ready," Booker said. "Be sure to follow the Bascom Palmer Eye protocols to the letter. No mistakes."

"So we have a deal. Gaines for the girl?"

"I need to confirm a few things, but yes. Tentatively, we have a deal."

thirty-eight

Gale looked out the window at the ocean below. The world seemed calm and beautiful, belying the turmoil she knew was swirling around her. "Cira, I'm so sorry," she said softly as tears filled her eyes.

The AX agent who had gotten her onto the plane looked across at her, silently asking if she was all right. Gale nodded and wiped her eyes, turning back to the window. She could almost feel the jets following them. She imagined the satellites tracking her every breath. Gale understood that the NSA had let the plane take off, and knew the reason—Rip and the Sphere. Booker would be cooking up some complex plan, a great escape, but she knew he'd never fly her to El Perdido and the Sphere, not with the entire resources of US intelligence agencies massed against them.

She wondered if Cira was awake. *Maybe they're keeping her sedated. Is she dreaming of mommy, or maybe Winnie the Pooh? Is she holding her cat Earth?* The thoughts were so painful Gale felt as if she'd swallowed broken glass. Her request to speak with Booker had so far yielded no results. It apparently wasn't safe to speak with Rip either.

Kruse must be dead, she thought. Even though he'd drugged her twice and forced her away from Cira, she knew he'd just been doing his job. She would miss the man who, along with Harmer, had kept them all safe for seven years.

Harmer, she wondered. *Is she still with Cira? How could such a crazy plan ever work? Hiding in the hospital. Poor Cira.* Gale couldn't stop her tears from flowing for the next half hour, until the agent told her Booker was on the line. It was a short call, and what he told her made her more anxious than ever, but at least there was hope. Everything depended on perfect timing and utilizing one of the untested secrets of the Sphere.

The Sphere, an unpredictable swirling mass of energy that, somehow, the Cosegans had crafted into a usable entrance into all creation, offered them a chance. Relying on it was all they could do, but its awesome power thus far had proven difficult to harness.

She recalled the time they had spent more than two months watching dinosaurs. No matter what they tried, it was only dinosaurs every day, day after day. After the first month, Booker found the top paleontologist and Rip met him in Hawaii. All the dinosaur data was transferred to INUs at the university where it was still being studied.

Gale worried. What if the Sphere got stuck on dinosaurs again? Or tree frogs, or comets, or anything other than Cira?

—O—

"They let her *go!*?" Taz shouted into the phone. His fist of gold rings smashed into a plastic seat. He looked down at the one the Judge had given him a few years earlier, an inlay design of a mythical phoenix rising from flames. The next finger over held his father's eagle.

"Obviously they're following her," Stellard said, still standing by the fireplace.

"And obviously Booker knows they are," Taz countered.

"I'm sure, but it buys time."

"Until what?" Taz asked. "Where the hell are they going to hide?"

"I don't know, but he'll never lead them to the Sphere," Stellard said. "On that front though, I do have a piece of extremely good news. Booker has agreed to give us Gaines in exchange for the daughter."

"Wow! That is incredible news. Surprisingly good. Can we trust Booker?" Taz asked.

"Of course not, but Gaines and Asher are obviously willing to do anything to protect their daughter and get her back, and he's acting to protect the Sphere."

"Gaines must have a way to lock it," Taz said, then paused to follow a stray thought. "Hey, you don't think it's possible that Asher has the Sphere, do you?"

"Why would Gaines have come to Hawaii without it?"

"Who knows?" Taz said. "Maybe I'd better talk to Dabnowski again."

"Good idea," Stellard agreed. "I've already got the people in Fiji working on readying the girl for the move. I'll be back in touch as soon as we get a final go from Booker."

Taz headed toward the exit. His car and driver were waiting. Before he contacted Dabnowski, he thought he'd better spend at least ten minutes looking at the papers he'd left with him. There was certainly time, as Gale Asher was not coming back to Hawaii, and it would still be a couple of hours until Harmer arrived for questioning.

Taz sat in the backseat with the windows down, a warm, fragrant breeze filling the car. He opened the case and was immediately intrigued by the lengthy title "Past and Future Time Exchange: A Method Through Space. Study and Review of the Cosega Sphere." It was co-authored by Dabnowski and several other scientists, with input from the Inner Movement organization.

As soon as Taz completed reading the first page, he ordered the driver to immediately return to the airport. "Get me on the next flight to the Big Island."

I've got to get to the Mauna Kea Observatories now!

thirty-nine

Rip came out of the black fog wondering who the woman was, wondering what this latest surprising episode from the Sphere meant, and wondering how long he had to find the answers. As the otherworldly daze cleared, he immediately thought of Cira and Gale. Relief flowed through him as he realized his Sphere was there, safe, levitating where it had been left. It meant that the woman had her own. *There really is another one!*

First he tried to reach Booker, but when that didn't work, he went back to the Sphere. "Crying Man, where are you?" he asked out loud.

What if the woman with the Sphere is a Cosegan? She might be trying to show me something. Maybe she has the answers — who were the Cosegans, where did they come from, why did they leave the Sphere, and what happened to them? The same questions he'd asked thousands of times in the past seven years. Rip was convinced that they could not stop the final four Divinations without first fully understanding the Sphere, and that was impossible until they answered the five mysteries. He had hundreds of others questions, but those five were the core to the conundrum.

With Crying Man not responding, Rip wandered out onto the balcony and stared at the ocean. For so long, this view — what had become his deeply personal horizon — had always balanced him in both good and bad situations. Whether clouds or stars, blue, grey, or black . . . standing here in the constant breeze had always fed his soul.

But as he passed an aluminum patio chair, his foot got tangled and he stumbled. Getting up, the chair leg caught in the deck railing, which made him slip against the wall. Rip kicked at the chair, twisting, clawing, smashing it against the stucco wall. Picking it up, pulling the vinyl straps that formed the seat, beating and punching until it was a twisted, broken heap. In a huff, Rip threw the remnants off the balcony and watched it crash onto the rocks below. He slid back to the floor, hands shaking, cuts and scrapes on his knuckles, wrists, and ankles.

All he could see in the frustrated dismay that strangled him was Cira's face. He could hear her saying "Daddy," and remembered her first steps, hands raised in triumph. He saw her running to him whenever he came into a room, reading her books . . .

His clenched fist pounded his thigh. "Where are you, sweetie . . . where are you?" Rip wallowed for minutes or hours, there was no way to measure time against such misery. Everything had been torn apart, taken from him, all but the Eysen, and that he would gladly trade to see his daughter smile again.

A whooshing sound, coming from inside the skyroom, brought back his attention. Rip pulled himself off the deck as if collecting a broken thing from the scene of an accident. His steps were painful, slow, like he was trudging through crusty quicksand. Then he saw Crying Man.

Part of him wanted to attack the Cosegan, to banish even his memory back across the eleven million years. Yet gazing at such a person, the purity of his eyes, the depth of emotions, knowledge, and experience radiating from a face seemingly spun from starlight, made anything other than adoration impossible. Rip knew he'd been falling apart, and believed that Crying Man was there to save him.

"Thank you for coming," Rip said, so happy to see the vision of the wise man projecting out of the Eysen, full size, vibrant and steady as the morning. "I don't know what to do," he continued, hearing his own voice shaky and weak.

"For seven years, I've been trying to save the Eysen, trying to save the world . . . hoping to save the future."

Crying Man nodded.

"Now all I want is to save my daughter."

He stared into Crying Man's eyes. Layers of tears, oceans deep, gave his eyes the appearance of more than simple extensions of optical nerves. They spoke a language which conveyed the illusion of time.

As with their previous wordless conversation, Rip felt Crying Man's meaning. "Cira is safe."

"But the Foundation has her," Rip whispered painfully.

"She is safe."

Rip nodded. He believed him. Rip took a deep breath, relieved that someone or something more powerful than himself was watching over his daughter. After a few moments, Rip decided to push for everything. He didn't know when, or if he would see Crying Man again, and wasn't even sure he would have the Sphere much longer.

"Tell me how to stop the Death Divinations."

Although Rip was ready to elaborate on what the Death Divinations were, Crying Man, not surprisingly, knew exactly what Rip meant. He shook his head slowly.

Rip swallowed hard, his throat tight. The answer shocked him into silence. *They can't be stopped!* He wanted to mourn, thought of screaming a dozen rage-filled protests as if it were Crying Man's fault. Instead, he stared at the ancient figure, waiting for more, wishing for a change, a clarification.

Nothing.

"Then why?" Rip asked in a desperate voice. "Why did you leave the Spheres? Why let us see the future if we cannot change it?"

"For help," was the simple response.

"But how does it help? Billions will die! This beautiful, horrible object contains the wisdom of the universe, the history of time, the damned dream of the future, and you mean to tell me I can't find a way in all of that to stop a super plague, heal the eco-system, or prevent World War Three?"

"Help."

"How does it help?" *Make me understand.* "Who is the woman with the other Sphere? Can she speak?" Rip considered for a moment that the woman he'd seen could have been the person who created, or at least programmed the Sphere he was looking at. It might have been the same one.

Crying Man put his hands together and bowed slightly, then spread his arms full and wide, starting above his head and arcing out in a broad, wide reach. The motion opened a view. Rip, as if peering though an open window, looked through it. What he saw would forever change him.

forty

While Rathmore organized a team to uncover the leech siphoning NSA data, he simultaneously monitored reports from a separate team tracking Asher's plane. The satellites and Navy Hornets kept easy tabs on the Gulfstream for several hours as it flew toward the west coast of the continental United States.

"Are they crazy?" Rathmore asked after reviewing many projected flight paths for Gale's plane. "They may be heading for San Diego. What do they think is going to happen when they land? That no one will notice?"

"Maybe they're going to try to sneak in under the radar and land on a smuggler's strip somewhere in the California or Arizona desert," Murik offered.

The Conductor came back on their screen and interrupted the debate. "We've got a professor who's willing to talk about UQP and the Sphere," she said.

It had been a steady stream of denials and refusals with one scientist after another. The stone wall of secrecy made the top officials at the NSA even more determined to crack the encryption. Rathmore was desperate to get one of the geniuses to spill what they'd been working on with Gaines and the Sphere. UQP, Booker's Universe Quantum Physics, had previously been ridiculed by government scientists, but now it seemed it could prove to be the key, not just to finding the Sphere, but to actually understanding it.

"There's a break," Murik said, clapping his hands triumphantly. Even Rathmore smiled at the news.

"I warn you though," the Conductor cautioned. "You may not like what he has to say. You damn sure probably won't believe it."

The Conductor nodded to someone off camera and the view changed to a holding room in the Honolulu Federal building.

"Professor Yamane, this is Claude Rathmore of the NSA and Quinn Murik of the CIA. I'm sorry we're all talking to you on screens, but I'm at another location on the island," she said, having abandoned the airport and returned to her temporary command center at Pearl Harbor. "But at least technology allows us to all be in the same room."

"I understand," Professor Yamane said, scratching his bald head and shifting in the hard plastic seat.

"Well, professor," Rathmore began, "we appreciate your cooperating with us on this matter of national security."

"Oh, it's more than national security," Professor Yamane said, sniffling and wiping his nose.

"Meaning?" Rathmore asked.

"The Eysen-Sphere is about global security . . . survival of the species, really," Professor Yamane responded, urgency in his nasally voice.

"Species?"

"The human race," Professor Yamane clarified. "If the Sphere is not handled carefully, it will lead to an extinction event."

Rathmore looked at Murik as a classmate might when hearing a lecture in another language for the first time.

"How could the Sphere lead to the extinction of humans?" Murik asked the professor. "Last I checked, there were more than seven billion of us—"

"A little glass ball," Rathmore interjected. "Even with all the legends I've heard about it, destroying the world with a tiny object like the Sphere would be impossible."

"Oh, the world will be fine. It's the people who won't be," Professor Yamane corrected. "And it's not the 'glass ball' that will destroy us." The professor sniffed again and took a sip of hot liquid from a thick mug. "It's humans that will end it. We're going to do it to ourselves."

Rathmore turned his attention to another screen. Professor Yamane's credentials rolled down it, including a long list of degrees, awards, papers published, and other accolades. Yamane, a microbiologist, had even been on a Presidential Committee on pandemic response preparedness.

"What is a microbiologist doing involved with the Sphere anyway?" Rathmore asked.

"Because of the future scenes," Yamane replied.

Rathmore looked at Murik again. "Why can't this guy just answer a question in a way that doesn't lead to more questions?"

"Because he's a scientist," Murik replied, smiling. "Let me try. Professor, give us a little background about the Sphere and what your role with the project has been."

"Have you all seen the Sphere? Do you even know what it is?" Professor Yamane asked.

"Pretend we know nothing," Murik said. "Walk us through it."

"As you might imagine, I haven't had too much time with it myself, none of us have. Well, except the physicists. A few of them have logged more hours themselves than the rest of us combined. I'm not sure I agree with that method, given the severity of what we're facing, but—"

"Professor, please. The basics?"

"Right," he said, wiping his nose with a light blue handkerchief. "The Eysen-Sphere doesn't just show the past. There is also, of course, the amazing details it displays in the present, but the most powerful, or rather dangerous thing it does, is when it gives glimpses into the future."

Rathmore rolled his eyes and was about to interrupt Professor Yamane, but Murik held up a hand to stop him.

"Really more than glimpses," the professor continued. "Sometimes we see grand visions, and as strange as it seems, the physicists do a fairly good job at explaining how it's all possible. I could try to elucidate, convert amazement into simple language . . . " He looked at their shaking heads. "No? Okay. Anyway, in the beginning I was still skeptical, but I saw enough to convince me that what we were seeing was actually going to happen. We saw things that became the future."

Rathmore muted his end and leaned over to Murik. He muttered, "I thought this clown was a scientist. He's three ducks short of a quack. We have better things to do." Rathmore turned toward a shielded monitor, showing which bits of data had been accessed by the leech. Another composite graph overlaid the same information with everyone who had access. The two leading suspects were the Conductor and King. Both had far more clout and connections then he did. He had to be sure, and the team still hadn't discovered how the leech was getting the information out.

No doubt one of Booker's advanced technological tricks or gizmos, Rathmore thought as Murik called his attention back to the screen from Hawaii, as if this part of Yamane's testimony might be important.

"That's when I saw the plague," Professor Yamane continued, in mid-sentence. "And it's because of seeing it that I decided to cooperate with the government."

"Why wouldn't you cooperate?" Rathmore asked, annoyed.

"It's not that I'm not patriotic, you understand," he said sniffling. "It's just that we all agreed the science was more important than the competition."

"What competition?" Rathmore asked while checking the progress of Gale's plane.

"Between nations. The lines on the maps . . . it's kind of elementary when you stop and think about it. You can't see them from space because they aren't real. And anyway, the bacteria, the pandemics, they don't care about borders, not the imaginary ones that humans draw."

"So what you're saying," Rathmore began, "if I understand you, is that the Eysen-Sphere is like some kind of crystal ball, and it has shown you a future where all of humanity perishes in some massive worldwide pandemic?"

"Yes, but it should sound much scarier than it does when you say it."

"It might, if I believed it."

Professor Yamane just sniffled and wiped his nose.

"We know the Eysen-Sphere is some kind of ancient supercomputer," Rathmore said. "I'm even willing to believe that it might have been left here from some ancient aliens or something, although I doubt that."

"Supercomputer?" Yamane smiled, as if a child had just mispronounced a common word. "The Sphere is so much . . . you don't know." He shook his head.

Rathmore narrowed his eyes. "Look, professor, I'm sorry, but the future hasn't happened yet, so anything you've seen inside the Sphere is a prediction, not a *fact*."

"Really? What if I could prove it to you?" Professor Yamane asked. "Because I know how you feel, I felt the same way. I'm a microbiologist, sir. I assure you I revere facts and have no use for fantasy."

"How are you going to prove it to me?" Rathmore asked, intrigued.

"By telling you something that hasn't happened yet. Something important. Something you will not be able to deny."

Rathmore smiled at Murik, as if he was part of a gag, maybe a practical joke. But Rathmore couldn't decide if he was the victim or the perpetrator of the joke, worried he might even be the punch line. His smile turned sour. "Professor, we're busy, but thank you for your time. An agent will finish debriefing you."

"Mis-Mister R-Rathmore, aren't you even a little curious?" Professor Yamane stuttered.

"All I am is curious, professor, but I don't have years, or even months to wait. You'd have to show us something today. What could you possibly say right now that would prove to us that the Eysen-Sphere can predict the future?"

"What about a war? A *serious* war?"

"When?"

"It will erupt before the end of the day."

"Today?" Rathmore shot a look to Murik, as if the CIA might be involved or, at least know about this.

Murik shrugged.

"Between whom?" Rathmore asked.

"China and Russia."

forty-one

Savina knew she had to talk to Booker, and she knew the Judge would never allow it. Just how much her communications were monitored by the Foundation was unclear, but she couldn't chance it. She handwrote a letter and sealed it inside a small envelope, which she gave to one of her assistants. He had a friend, working on UQP at Cal Tech, who would know how to get this urgent message to Booker. Savina communicated wordlessly, with gestures and lip-reading, to the assistant, who soon signed out for the day.

There was plenty to do until she heard from Booker, which hopefully would be soon. She needed to talk with him before the Foundation or the NSA caught up with Gaines and got hold of the other Sphere. In the meantime, Savina had to work out a plan to slow down the future.

She knew what was coming, a dangerous period for humanity in which more than half the world's population would die. "We must make sure the 'right' half survives," the Judge had said many times. The Foundation was working to engineer just such a scenario. The Phoenix Initiative, years in the making, would launch in less than ninety days. The diabolical plan had been designed to circumvent the prophesized natural plague which was coming, whether the people were ready or not.

More than seven billion on the planet, and only about a thousand of them knew that it was all going to end soon.

The secret had been kept because only Booker and the Judge controlled who knew. The two powerful men had assembled people to solve the planetary death sentence, and those participants understood that if word got out, pandemonium would surely follow, spiraling civilization into an inescapable stew of anarchy and apocalyptic horrors.

Within the Sphere, Savina had seen views of the world after the plague. The Judge had convinced her that "designing the end" was the best way to ensure that it didn't *actually* become the end. But the risks were frightening: one miscalculation and it could quickly erode the population to numbers too low and too weakened to sustain themselves. "Earth would be left to the heartiest animals; ants and cockroaches," the Judge often repeated.

The same was possible with the natural plague. They'd seen it in the Sphere. Clastier saw it hundreds of years earlier in his Sphere, and Malachy discovered it nearly a thousand years before. Like everything else that had happened in the history of the planet, however, the Cosegans had known about it at least eleven million years ago.

"Time is a place," Savina reminded herself whenever she thought about how the Cosegans could have seen humanity's entire future. *They found a way to go there and look around,* she thought while searching the digital caverns of the Sphere. *It must have been an easy trip for those ancient people, since they were able to record everything and preserve it for me to access eleven million years later.*

She shook her head, still in awe and, at the same time, baffled by the technology that allowed them to provide a map into time. *How did they get it all contained in this indestructible crystal ball?*

She called it indestructible because it had lasted for eleven million years, but in truth, it had always been handled with the utmost care. Savina had a fantastical theory that she had not dared to share with the Judge, or even her assistants: that if one day she happened to drop the Sphere, it would shatter into a million splintered fragments, and with it, all existence would vanish, as if it had never been.

forty-two

It would be another hour until Taz's flight would leave for the Big Island. His driver had arranged for a four-wheel-drive rental car, which would be needed to get to the Mauna Kea Observatories. All the while, Taz had been reading more of Dabnowski's files and intermittently trying to reach the jumpy astrophysicist.

Finally, Dabnowski answered his phone. Taz begged him to meet at the Observatories.

"No, don't go to Mauna Kea!" Dabnowski hissed. "The NSA has a team there now." Instead, he reluctantly gave Taz an alternative location of a nearby oceanfront beach to meet.

On the way, Taz continued to read and struggled to comprehend it, but Stellard's words kept repeating in his head.

"You go and find Dabnowski. Find him before the NSA does and do whatever it takes to get him to start talking again. Make that crazy scientist trust you."

Taz knew that would not be easy. He had definitely made an awful first impression, but at least Dabnowski had agreed to see him again.

"Dr. Dabnowski, I'm sorry. I know I was acting like an idiot earlier. Please accept my apology," Taz said, extending his hand as the astrophysicist found him in a grove of palm trees, sitting on a beautifully carved bench overlooking the Pacific.

Dabnowski nodded, giving him an annoyed, skeptical look. He motioned his head toward the briefcase. "So you can read."

"Yes. I ... please, let me say again that I'm sorry. Science isn't my thing. I'm mostly just trying to track down Gaines and the Sphere."

"I know, but you read those papers, and now you realize how much is going on that you had no idea about. Science is king. Not money. Not weapons. *Science.*"

"Science without money is hard to do," Taz said, but immediately regretted initiating a debate with the person he was attempting to win over.

"Tell that to Booker Lipton. Booker may have been rich before, but once he got hold of the Sphere, he became more like a Pharaoh. And what was in that Sphere? Science." Dabnowski smiled. "Money and weapons may have been the power of the past, but it is science that will rule the future ... or, I should say, *save* the future."

"Okay," Taz said. "And you know that either the US government, Booker, or the Foundation will likely end up with the Sphere. Obviously you want the winner to be the Foundation or I wouldn't be holding this briefcase and you wouldn't be sitting here."

Dabnowski nodded. "I may be a scientist, but I know that the US government cannot be trusted with the Sphere. Either they will lose it, or, at the very least, vast quantities of its information will fall into the hands of Chinese spies, or some other country – the Russians, the Israelis – or they'll just filter it to the corporations."

Taz was not about to point out that the Foundation was run by the rich elites who controlled the most powerful corporations. Instead, he asked a nagging question. "But if Booker funded all this research and brought you and hundreds of others to study the Sphere, why not take this to him?"

"That was our original plan, but then the NSA discovered Gaines was alive. Booker is one man. What if he gets it wrong? What if he dies?" Dabnowski looked at his shoes, scuffed Nikes, years old. "Have you seen what's in there? The future . . . it's extremely dangerous."

Taz nodded knowingly.

"With the NSA back onto Gaines, Booker is in trouble. He may not survive," Dabnowski said. "Then I realized the Foundation, as a consortium of bright and influential people, would be a superior alternative. Spread the risk, spread the knowledge, spread the power. Do you see?"

Another nod from Taz

Dabnowski continued his manic rant. "Booker has helped advance the cumulative knowledge of what is now a whole new area of science, but UQP had grown bigger than he is, and he's too secretive. I've met him once. He's not very likable, and he runs his empire, the largest in the world, as a dictator."

"No argument from me," Taz said.

"In the scientific community, we like committees and shared, group efforts. There is too much at stake to trust this to the whims of one man," Dabnowski continued, thinking of the coming plague. He, like many of the UQP scientists, had seen the future in the Sphere. The unpredictable nature of the ancient object made it impossible to hide, so Booker, rather than trying to hide it, had used the apocalyptic visions to recruit and elicit written promises of secrecy. "Booker claims to want to understand the Sphere in order to save humanity from the horrors waiting in the near future, but he continues to use everything we and Gaines have gleaned from the Sphere to create new products. *Products*! And those products aren't going to help us change the future. All they're going to do is make Booker richer."

Taz could hardly believe his luck, and wondered if it was a trick. But Booker's reputation had never been one of a savior. Quite the opposite, in fact. "I assure you that the Foundation is quite different from Booker."

Dabnowski nodded nervously, allowing only a faint smile. "We have to act. Time is running out. Billions may die."

"It's the Foundation's greatest priority. We already have whole teams working to stop the plague." Taz thought he detected a hint of relief in Dabnowski's eyes. "And this, your great discovery, will make a huge difference." He patted the man's shoulder. "So you've actually done this? You've used coordinates that were found in the Eysen-Sphere and plugged them into certain telescopes at the observatory and they were there? You could see them?"

"Yes," Dabnowski said. "We detected anomalies at the precise points in space, right where they said we would."

"How did you find the coordinates?"

Dabnowski didn't know why this would matter, but he appreciated someone, especially an "idiot" like Taz, showing interest in his field, so he answered. "There is a Cosega Sequence that begins every session with the Eysen-Sphere. It's like a language. A universal language of science, if you will. Complex, yet simple. The key was the rotation of the Earth around the sun, representing a year in 'human time.' Far more than that though, it utilizes planetary movements and sizes, all types of astronomical data that's constant and knowable. Gaines decoded it. From there we can understand much of what we find in the Sphere." He looked out to the ocean as if trying to remain grounded while talking about such an enormous topic. "Of course," Dabnowski continued, "it is far too vast an object to really understand or attempt to control, but we have made great strides, particularly in the past year."

"But is this really true?"

"You mean time travel?" Dabnowski asked, knowing the layman would go for the sensational aspect of his report. "Not in the science-fiction sense of getting into a contraption, turning a dial, and then walking out into a medieval castle during a siege or some such thing." He looked around, certain the NSA would be there soon.

"I'm sure it's not like that."

"Are you? Good." Dabnowski couldn't help but smile. "If we hit those points in space, it is possible to project back in time, and because the world is made up of energy and matter, matter being composed of atoms, which in turn is made up of subatomic particles, protons and neutrons, electrons . . . Of course, when you talk about matter we should also bring up massless particles. There's photons, and then that leads us to quarks and leptons, but—"

"Please," Taz interrupted. "I'm not quite as bright as you."

"Of course you aren't." Dabnowski smiled in a curt, condescending way before continuing. "Because these particles make up all things in the universe, some theorize that we might be able to rearrange time by rearranging those particles. Kind of like genetic manipulation. We rearrange a few things and the corn grows bigger, a few more and the earworms and sap beetles won't eat the corn. Of course, if we do it wrong, it won't be fit for us to eat either, but no matter."

"Back to the time travel issue," Taz prompted.

"Yes, we rearrange a few particles at the right time in the right place in the universe, and voila. Everything after is different."

"But how would you control the outcome? It could be total chaos."

"The same way we do it with corn, or human embryos. We have a DNA map."

"But how do you map the universe?"

"We don't have to. The Eysen has already done it. That magical little Sphere has mapped all of time and space."

Forty-three

Inside the dimly lit NSA situation room, Rathmore stood up. "Come on, get this guy out of here." Professor Yamane's claim of knowing a war was about to break out between two of the world's largest countries was laughable. Rathmore turned to another wall of monitors and ignored the one with the sniffling professor.

"Wait a minute," Murik said. "Why would Russia and China go to war with each other, and why today?"

"As a distraction," Professor Yamane said, as if he were discussing the weather. "There is a group, a very influential one, that wants to stop the US government from getting the Sphere."

"So they arrange a last-minute war between two of the most powerful nations on Earth?" Rathmore scoffed. "Forget this delusional quack! He's wasting our time." He turned back to the monitor showing the satellite images of Gale's plane and followed the projected flight paths.

"Are you sure?" Murik asked.

"Aren't you?" Rathmore shot back. "Russia and China aren't going to war, period. And this guy wants us to believe it's *today*? Talk about a distraction. He's messing with us. He's on their team."

Murik cut off the connection.

A message appeared on Rathmore's primary monitor. King's Veiled Ops unit was twenty-two minutes from intercepting Asher's flight path. *Do not close in!* Rathmore typed back. If King was on Booker's payroll, this part of the mission, their best lead, was about to blow up.

Even without his doubts about the Conductor and King, Rathmore was strangely nervous about Gale's plane. Although it was being tracked from ground radar, numerous satellites, and the Hornets, he knew Booker was a sly and resourceful adversary.

"Where are they going to land?" he asked again.

The technicians were monitoring the computers that were continually updating projected flight paths and landing sites. Already teams were scrambling to be ready to hit the ground from Panama to San Diego.

"What the–!? " Rathmore shouted, checking another screen. "What's happened to my feed?" he yelled at the techs.

"That's strange," one of the techs murmured while switching through a series of monitors.

Rathmore stood and paced from screen to screen. "I don't like the word 'strange' coming up in any of my operations. Show me the plane! Where the hell is my plane?"

"I don't know."

"You don't know? You don't *know*! You get *paid* to know!" Rathmore said, more alarmed than Murik had ever seen him. "Come on, show me something people. Show. Me. Something!"

"It's got to be a glitch," Murik said.

"Asher's Gulfstream has disappeared from the satellite images and from radar." Rathmore chewed up each word and spit it out. "That's one hell of a glitch."

"See if the Hornets have a visual," Murik said, expecting it all to work out. "Planes don't just disappear."

"Negative," came the response from the flight leader of the Hornets. "The plane went into a cloud. It did not come out. We pursued and passed through to the clear. Target seems to have vanished."

"Is there weather? Was there another plane? This is *impossible*!" Rathmore whined.

"Clear and calm conditions, sir. No other crafts in the vicinity."

"Where are they?" Rathmore demanded. He looked at the map, lit up with lights showing the positions of the Hornets. Circles extended out in various colors indicating estimated range, distance, etc. "How close to the nearest land?" he asked, noting they were still over open ocean. "I don't give a damn if it's a rock the size of a parking space. What about ships, a rowboat, a flock of seagulls... *anything*? Tell me everything that's down there, and tell me NOW!"

The satellites zoomed in. Scans of the area showed no land, no ships, nothing.

"It could be EAMI," a lone technician from the far side of the room said, so quietly that Rathmore thought the woman might have sneezed.

"Excuse me, did you have something to say?" Murik asked her.

"I know it will not be a popular hypothesis," the woman said, slowly walking over toward Murik and Rathmore.

"What won't be?" Rathmore asked, upset by a distraction during this emergency.

"EAMI," she repeated. "Eysen Anomaly Matter Interference, it's—"

"I know what it is," Rathmore barked. "And you're damned right it won't be popular. You expect me to believe that the Sphere somehow made a plane disappear right in front of the satellites, six trained pilots, God, and everyone?" He scoffed and turned back to the satellites scanning the ocean. "Show me the last images we have of the Gulfstream heading into the cloud."

The woman looked at Murik. "I'm in here for a reason," she said.

"I know," Murik replied. He knew her from an earlier cross-collaboration conference he'd attended concerning the Gaines case. She was the NSA's, and therefore the US government's, leading expert on the Eysen-Sphere.

"Even when we believed the Sphere had been destroyed," she began, opening a projection view from her INU, "we knew Booker Lipton had obtained substantial amounts of information and technology from the object."

Murik nodded. He knew that. "I'm very familiar with the EAMI theory."

"Then don't you see that this is a dramatic example of just that?"

"But the Sphere is not on that plane."

"How do you know that?" she asked.

"If it was, then why did they get discovered at the airport? Why wouldn't EAMI have saved them much earlier?"

"Well, we don't know the limitations of EAMI."

"Fine, but what about the fact that Gaines was in Hawaii the day before? He would have had the Sphere with him. In fact, we have a witness who saw Gaines and the Sphere in Hawaii, so Asher didn't have it. The Sphere is not on that plane."

"We don't know the range of EAMI," she countered.

"We don't know *anything* about EAMI," Rathmore snapped, rejoining the conversation. "EAMI is all made-up conjecture and fanciful tales to explain Booker's latest technology and how we've failed to get inside his organization, discover his secrets, blah, blah, blah."

Rathmore's face contorted as if he'd just stepped on a large nail.

"EAMI is to placate those members of Congress who fund us and want to know just how Gaines and Asher got away so many times the first go-round," he continued. "It may work with Congress, but not in the real world!" He walked back to the other side of the room. "Imagine what the Senate Select Committee on Intelligence is going to say this time! We had Asher at the damned airport, and now she's dead again."

"I doubt she's dead," Murik said.

"She might as well be."

"If it *is* EAMI, Asher's status and answering to Congress are going to be the least of our worries," the woman said, so quietly that only Murik heard her. He immediately went to the communications screen to raise the sniffling Professor Yamane again.

forty-four

Savina was impressed with how fast Booker had responded, considering everything that was going on, but not really surprised. *He did personally try to hire me, and he must know the Foundation is trying to get his Sphere*, she thought. *I wonder if he realizes that we also have one?*

She pulled into the secure office park and stopped at the gate to present her identification. Two officers with automatic rifles efficiently circled and inspected her car, including the underside. After they had also looked into her trunk and waved some type of electronic monitoring wands over the vehicle, they waved her through.

That's a lot of security when Booker isn't even here in person, she thought as she found a parking space. Her assistant had conveyed the message that Booker would speak to her, but only across a secure, scrambled video line. With everyone who wanted to get to the man, especially now that Gaines was known to be alive, it made sense he would only have this kind of communication at a facility he owned.

She waited in a soft chair, glad the place was on her way home. Savina was uncharacteristically tired. Normally her metabolism kept her in high-gear and able to work fifteen-hour days, but the decision to circumvent the Judge had weighed on her heavily.

Savina sat for at least ten minutes in the overly-air-conditioned room, collecting her thoughts. She wasn't exactly betraying the Judge or the Foundation. She still

believed in the mission, and even that the Phoenix
Initiative was necessary, but there were two Spheres, and
Booker had spent billions of dollars, perhaps tens of
billions, and employed hundreds of the world's best
minds, who had been mining the secrets of the Sphere for
seven years. They were clearly ahead, and there was so
much to know and too much at stake.

Now, based upon what had happened to her, she
could no longer view the Sphere as simply the most
advanced "computer" ever created. Savina was desperate
to better understand the Sphere and the power it possessed
before launching the world-altering Phoenix Initiative.

The screen finally came to life, but instead of Booker
Lipton, she found herself staring at the smiling face of the
Judge.

"Savina, what are you doing here?" he asked in
friendly surprise.

She jumped up out of her seat. "I-I was, um," she
stuttered, recovering quickly. "A colleague set up a
meeting concerning the gravitational waves and it's
something I'm exploring with the Sphere."

"Well, I suppose that is *mostly* true," the Judge said,
still smiling.

It was mostly true, but either way, Savina realized
with a sinking feeling that she had walked into a trap.
"Judge, I didn't think —"

"No, you didn't," he cut her off sharply. "Oh, the
irony. Perhaps the smartest woman in the world, and she
did not think."

"I never thought you would allow me to meet with
Booker."

"Yes, you were correct about that. Do you know who
Booker Lipton is? He is the goddamned anti-Christ!" The
Judge glared at her. "I have spent *years* trying to save the
world from him. And he is so close . . . so *very, very* close,
to being able to destroy it all."

"What if he's trying to save it, but in a different way
than you are?"

"The Foundation has explored every conceivable solution to what the world is facing. The Phoenix Initiative is the only viable option. It *will* work."

"But the Sphere? What if it doesn't allow us to just see across time, what if we can use it to *change* time?"

"That's what I'm trying to do. We're trying to change the future before it destroys us all."

"No, not like that." Savina paced up to the giant screen, unconsciously trying to make her controversial point stronger. "If we could go back and manipulate something that happened in the past and change it, then we could possibly prevent the plague completely."

The Judge knew Savina to be a practical scientist, free from any beliefs not backed by strict observable facts, but as a leading-edge physicist, she also worked with theories. "I assume this is a theory."

"Only because I do not possess all the necessary data," Savina conceded. "But it is real, and that's why I need to talk with Booker. His people have to know about this. He's got the two top experts on gravitational waves on his payroll."

"So what does that mean?"

"Come on, Judge, it's a small community of physicists. I can put together a roster for you of who he's got working on UQP, but I suspect you already have that list." She smiled. "Look at the names in a pattern based on their expertise and you'll see what Booker is after, or what he already has."

"And what is that?"

"Time travel."

The Judge balked. "It's not possible."

"Of course it is. The proof is all around us. We've done it with particles. What about photons, light, the age of the universe, inflation, I could go on."

"That is quite different than actually doing something constructive, something that can result in change or anything concrete, for that matter," the Judge said.

"If it isn't possible to manipulate time, then how does the Sphere tell us what's going to happen? You may not realize it, but you've already built the Phoenix Initiative and put the entire fate of civilization at risk, all based on time travel."

"You're correct," the Judge admitted. "I don't know. That's why I have *you* working on the Sphere." He wanted to believe her, he *needed* to trust her, but she'd tried to get to Booker. She could ruin everything, yet the Sphere was critical, and no one on the Foundation's team knew as much as she did. "Why didn't you ask me before running off to Booker?"

"What would you have said?"

"You should have asked."

"Are you going to let me talk to him?"

"What if I let you talk to Gaines instead?"

"Gaines?" she asked, surprised. "Do you know where he is?"

"I expect he'll be in your lab by this time tomorrow," the Judge replied. "So you see, there was no need to go behind my back, no need to try to talk with Booker, who probably knows less about the actual object than I do."

Savina nodded quietly, suddenly unsure of her fate. She knew the Judge could use his power ruthlessly, but she had never known anything but kindness from him. "Then I guess I should spend the next twenty-four hours making sure we're ready for Gaines."

"Yes, that sounds like a wise course," the Judge said, staring sternly. "And Savina? I'm sure you'll not be bothered by the Foundation Security officers who will now be escorting you around the clock."

Savina swallowed hard. "I understand."

forty-five

Rip had trouble coping with what he saw, but he knew it was important to ignore his emotions—the detachment of a scientist—and figure it out. He'd seen countless things in the Sphere over the years, including the Earth in many stages of its long evolution, with and without humans, ancient Egyptians and South American civilizations using flying machines thousands of years before the Wright Brothers, but this time, when he saw it devoid of people, there was something else present. Ruins.

Even for a skilled archaeologist, it was difficult to ascertain just what the man-made remnants among the vast forested and open ranges of Earth were, but they were there. Metal and concrete, faded colors and patterns that did not belong in nature. As species of recognizable animals roamed, the traces of a past human civilization were still present, even abundant, but Rip's trained mind estimated it had been perhaps ten thousand years since the end.

The end? What happened? Rip tore his gaze from the air-tour of the human-less world and found Crying Man's eyes. "Is this what happened to the Cosegans? Or…" he hesitated, not sure he wanted the answer, "is this what happens to *us*?"

Rip felt Crying Man's wordless response and had to remind himself to breathe. "It is the same." He voiced the words he sensed, looking to Crying Man for clarification or confirmation. "What does that mean?"

"It is the same . . . without help."
"Help," Rip repeated.
Crying Man nodded.

–O–

Rip sat alone in the skyroom, silently contemplating what Crying Man had said and what he'd seen in the Sphere. *What if it was us that ended?*

He knew what lay ahead. Humans could easily destroy themselves in any number of ways. The Divinations had predicted three that were already visible on the horizon: a global pandemic, climate destabilization, World War III, or any combination thereof. Crying Man had disappeared again after conveying the word "help" into Rip's mind one more time.

Yes, please help me save Cira and stop the coming plague, the world-ending war, all of it, Rip thought. *How did the Cosegans craft such an interface? How does it know what I'm thinking? The artificial intelligence is mindboggling. No wonder Stephen Hawking, Bill Gates, Elon Musk, and others, have been warning against AI for so many years. It's so far beyond our human mind's capacity, or at least what we've been able to develop or tap into up until this point.*

Gale believed they could do more. So did Booker and his whole Inner Movement, but to a scientist like Rip, that all seemed like pure fantasy. Yet the Cosegans . . . they had done something, something that combined it all.

How?

Just as he was going back to the Sphere to try to search for ways to help Cira, instead of those long-sought answers, he heard a plane. It was a foreign sound on El Perdido. Booker had used every modern and Cosegan trick and technology to cloak the island. It was virtually invisible to satellites, planes, and ships, so either Gale had made it, or he was about to be attacked.

From his vantage point, the highest on the island, he watched the Gulfstream descend and touch down on the paved runway. Even before the plane stopped, a message came into his INU.

"Aren't you going to meet my plane?" Gale asked.

Rip raced downstairs and jumped into one of the many rugged golf carts they used for most of their jaunts around the island. By the time he reached her, she was already on her way in one of her own that was kept parked near the end of the runway.

Her driver, the AX agent who'd gotten her onto the Gulfstream, stopped. Rip parked and jumped out of his cart. Gale met him halfway and they melted into a long, desperate embrace.

"Cira," Gale said as she smothered herself into him. "Cira."

"I know," Rip responded, shaking, the sudden reconnection to his family exposing the rawness of his helplessness and pain at Cira's situation.

"I tried to stay with her. Booker wouldn't let me." She began to cry. "Kruse drugged me, They kidnapped me from our baby!"

Rip had suspected something like that, but never imagined they'd actually drugged her. Anger rose with his adrenaline.

"They said if I stayed, I might have been killed," Gale said through sobs. "They don't understand that I'd rather be dead than leave her alone."

"We'll get her," Rip said, as if the words were a weapon. "I promise you that."

The power of his conviction momentarily steadied her. Gale pulled back and looked at him. The tears in her eyes magnified the blue of them, like turquoise lagoons on a sunny day. "How?" she asked.

"Come on." He took her hand and led her into his cart. Rip did a u-turn and sped back to the main house. While Gale showered and changed, he asked the chef to prepare Gale's favorite macrobiotic dinner. Rip went to the skyroom to wait for Gale, and it was there, in that moment alone, that he realized what he must do.

forty-six

Rathmore and Murik, surrounded by the hi-tech maps and real-time video monitors of the NSA situation room, were deep in discussion concerning the possible whereabouts of the Gulfstream and whether King's unit could have played a role in the plane's disappearance.

A technician suddenly interrupted them. "We've picked up some chatter," the woman said. "The little girl, Gaines' daughter, may still be at the hospital in Fiji."

"How close is a team?" Rathmore asked.

"Close."

"Let's go! Move on that hospital. Own it, own it!" Rathmore chanted. "I don't give a damn if we blind or maim that girl so long as we have a breathing, talking little angel to use to flush out her God-forsaken, loving parents."

The noise in the room grew. A SEAL team with CIA and NSA operatives was prepped to go. Intelligence came flooding in as partial focus was shifted to Fiji. They learned of the Foundation's armed occupation of the hospital and quickly discovered what floor Cira was on based upon the number of soldiers concentrated there. The operation would be complicated by the presence of the Foundation's people and local police, but they were no match for a SEAL team and a surprise attack. The bigger issue was collateral damage to the hundreds of patients in the hospital, in addition to doctors, nurses, and other staff.

"The order is this," Rathmore said, raising his voice to be heard across the room. "Get the girl, alive. Everything, and everyone else, is second."

A few technicians and operatives gave him questioning looks.

"Everyone be reminded this is a Scorch and Burn operation!" Rathmore yelled. "Eat them up!"

"Sir," another technician interrupted him. "We just got word. The Chinese and Russians have engaged each other on the border near North Korea."

Rathmore looked at Murik, stunned. "How in the hell is *this* possible?" Rathmore asked, switching one of the big screens to satellite coverage of the region around the apparent Chinese and Russian conflict.

"I'll be a son of . . . " Rathmore stared at the images disbelievingly. "Those crazies are shooting at each other."

"Looks like a real war," Murik said, dumbfounded. "CIA didn't see this coming."

"Neither did the NSA, or the Pentagon," Rathmore said. "But somebody did . . . Yamane! Where is that dammed nutty professor?" he asked Murik before turning back to the subordinate who gave him the news. "What started it?"

"Apparently a flare-up over disputed territory amounting to 580,000 square miles of land that Russia's snatched from China over the past hundred and fifty years."

"And *today*, this comes up? *Today*!" Rathmore was dizzy with the scenarios crisscrossing his brain. The vanishing Gulfstream, Gaines' daughter still in Fiji, held by the Aylantik Foundation, a war between major powers in Asia predicted by . . . "Get that damned professor on the screen *now*!"

"I've been trying to track down Yamane since the plane disappeared," Murik admitted. "It's as if he's vanished."

"People. Don't. *Vanish*," Rathmore said in a controlled rage, emphasizing each syllable. "Planes and people *don't* vanish. They're out there somewhere, and we have the resources of the Untied States of America at our disposal. Bring it to bear! Do it!"

−O−

While they were waiting for agents in Hawaii to track down the sniffling professor and get him back in front of a camera link, they continued to prepare for the retrieval mission in Fiji. Even if the sniffling professor hadn't predicted the outbreak of war between the two powerful nations, the situation would have been a major distraction.

"World stability is a far more fragile conundrum than people care to admit," Murik said, feeling confused and overwhelmed and failing to see the humor in the situation. "On any given day, the final war can begin."

Even Rathmore, stressed, frustrated, and barking commands like a crazed fan in a sports stadium, willing his team back on top, was concerned by the Russia-China drama. Any political science major could tell them this was not like a skirmish in the Middle East. A war between these mighty giants would shake the Earth like nothing had since the fall of the Nazis. More than that, Rathmore was stunned and awed by the prospect that someone had seen this coming *in the Sphere.*

Rathmore, one of the NSA's top pitbulls, had rarely felt true fear in his life. The first was when he watched his father beat his mother, the second when his wife was destroyed by cancer, and now, this. All he could think of was a mirror smashing into his face, reflecting the fear, showing him his weakness, destroying his power. *Damn that Sphere!*

The giant screens circling the room switched from satellite scenes of the crisis in Asia to views of Fiji, and still others swept across views of the vast Pacific where the Gulfstream had vanished. Steady streams of data came across the twenty-six mid-sized monitors, which hung under the giant ones. Hundreds of conceivable scenarios rolled through the massive computer programs designed to anticipate every possible outcome. A new Korean war, hostilities bleeding over to include Taiwan, Japan, satellites targeted in space, even nuclear war.

It was a terrifying development. Rathmore paced, waiting for Professor Yamane, waiting for the SEAL team to get the kid, waiting for some sign of the Gulfstream, waiting for contact from King, who had suddenly gone silent. He didn't know exactly how, but his gut told him that the little girl wasn't just the key to finding the Sphere, but the Sphere was the key to containing the war in Asia.

"Everything depends on our getting that kid!" he said, tasting the bitter residue of tension on his lips. "Where the hell is Professor Yamane?"

"Sir," a young analysis began, "Honolulu PD has just confirmed . . . The professor you're looking for, Professor Yamane, is dead."

forty-seven

Taz's Foundation superiors were waiting for an update. Stellard had been clear — get Dabnowski back on board. Already having Gaines' daughter in hand, and adding one of the top UQP/Sphere scientists would put the Foundation in the lead in the race for the future.

Tugging nervously at the gold ring on his thumb, Taz didn't know what to do. He knew he was sitting on the greatest discovery in human history. *What can it do? What are the implications to the future? The past? Do they know? The NSA? The Foundation?* He also knew that Dabnowski's life was in danger, as was his.

"Wow," Taz breathed. "I'm sorry I was such a jerk earlier. I didn't know . . . I'm not the brightest guy in the world."

The admission amused and impressed Dabnowski. "Maybe at least you finally get it. You may not grasp it, obviously you'll never be capable of that, but you *get it.*" Dabnowski looked over his shoulder, scanned the trees, then cast a quick look up at the sky.

"Who else knows?" Taz asked, now fully on board with Dabnowski's nervousness and unable to deny the assessment of his ability to comprehend scientific knowledge.

"There are five of us who authored the paper, two more have an idea. And then there's the NSA."

"The NSA knows?"

"They know everything," Dabnowski said, his tone suggesting it would be silly to imagine otherwise. "How come no one wants to believe we live in an Orwellian world? In fact, it's way beyond *1984*. They have technology that even Orwell couldn't dream of, and if they get the Sphere, they'll be able to know what you're going to think *before* you even think it."

Taz nodded and clenched his fists, the heavy rings pressing painfully into his fingers, the largest, a gold broken heart he'd had made after the only woman he really ever loved walked out on him. Taz knew better than Dabnowski that privacy had choked its last few tortured breaths in the years following the September 11th terrorist attacks. Ever since, it had been an ever increasingly fast nosedive down the slippery slope.

"What about Gaines?"

"Gaines is an interesting man," Dabnowski said. "He's not a physicist, he's an archaeologist. It's odd the Sphere found him because it's not an artifact, it's a universe. As brilliant as he is though, he's not really equipped to study it."

"You said the Sphere found him. Don't you mean the other way around?"

"If you ever get to see the Sphere, you'll realize that Gaines was chosen to find it."

"What does that even mean?" Taz asked. Caught up in Dabnowski's paranoia, he never stopped watching the shadows. "He found it sealed in a cliff. Solid rock. The Sphere is eleven million years old, right?"

"Close enough."

"So who decided Gaines should find it?"

"The ones who built it. The Cosegans."

Taz didn't want to question Dabnowski further. He knew this nerd had ten times the smarts he did, but it wasn't for fear of looking stupid again.

Taz did not *want* the answer. He couldn't handle Dabnowski saying that somebody eleven *million* years ago knew all of this was going to happen, knew about Gaines, and had left the Sphere for him encased in stone. Taz couldn't even handle the possibility of time travel. He'd read a few novels about the subject, seen the movie *Back to the Future*, so he could play along with that, but advanced civilizations, millions of years earlier, dabbling in the current world? He couldn't go there.

"What are you going to do?" Dabnowski asked after a long minute of silence.

"Where are the other four authors of the report?"

"I'm not sure. Two of them are likely at the Observatories. The other ones might be at the university."

"Has the NSA detained any of the UQP scientists?"

"There are over a thousand of us," Dabnowski said, as if that number protected them from arrest. "We're talking about the brightest scientists in the world."

"We're talking about the NSA," Taz countered.

Dabnowski nodded knowingly as he looked up the beach at a man heading in their direction.

"It's only a matter of time before they get Gale Asher and then Gaines," Taz said. "And then they'll want a lid on this. Everyone with knowledge of the Sphere will be arrested. The NSA won't care if there are ten thousand of you. Count on it." Taz stared directly at the physicist. "But that's more than I can worry about at the moment. Let's concentrate on getting you and the other four authors away from here."

"Here?"

"Off the island."

forty-eight

Gale relayed the horrible saga she'd endured to Rip, beginning with the call from Harmer informing her that Cira had been injured and taken to the hospital. Each detail ratcheted up the couple's already strained emotions. The warm breeze carrying the fragrance of flowers and tropical fruits and the gentle sound of the turquoise waters lapping the shore belied the tension contained in her story. Rip listened silently, stunned by the plane crash into the Pacific, shaking his head at the decision to board a commercial airliner, and riveted by her account of Kruse getting them off that plane and onto the Gulfstream.

"But they must have followed you, right?" Rip asked. "How did you escape Hawaii? How did they even let you take off?" he wondered, looking up into the sky, expecting a squadron of fighters to spray the beach with machinegun fire.

"I don't know," Gale said, "but you know Booker is decades ahead in technology because of what we've discovered in the Sphere, what he's stolen from the Cosegans."

Rip didn't want to get into that debate again, not now. Although he was not in the mood to defend Booker after hearing of the deceptions he'd used on them in the past day and a half, he also couldn't deny that, at the moment, his family was still alive. They had all survived, except maybe the two people most directly involved with their protection, Kruse and Harmer.

Rip filled her in on what he knew, then shared the painful revelation that Cira was now in the hands of the Foundation.

"Get. Booker. On. The. Line," Gale demanded.

A minute later Huang's face filled the monitor from Rip's INU. Gale adored their collaborator, and was grateful to see him.

"Blue Eyes," Huang said, beaming. "Thank the stars you made it."

"No doubt I owe much of that to your abilities at cloaking planes and islands," she said.

"The NSA has an entire team devoted to uncovering what they call EAMI, but if they knew how far we'd come with Eysen Anomaly and the promise it holds, they would put the *entire* agency on it," Huang said, cocky with the triumphant victory of Gale's escape.

She nodded sadly, but couldn't help smiling at him. "But Cira . . . "

"I know, the sun is less bright," he said, a reference to her name's origin. "It's dangerous right now, but the Foundation is steady. They won't be careless with her, it's just that the others might. We have to get her."

"We haven't been able to raise Booker," Rip said.

"I'll try to bypass his queue," Huang replied.

Rip sent Huang an encrypted message while they waited. Huang relayed a simple ping as confirmation he'd received it and Rip knew his request would be followed to the letter.

A short time later, Booker came across on audio only. "Gale, I'm glad you made it."

"We can talk about that some other time, Booker," Gale gritted out, as though each word caused her physical pain. "You get my daughter or you're going to be anything but glad I survived."

"Gale, please don't threaten me. I know we've had our differences, but—"

"You have no idea what a threat is if you think I've even *begun* to threaten you!" Gale shouted back. "You've backed us into a corner, dropped us on this damned remote island, and left us with only one way to save our daughter."

"Which is?"

"You know what it is," Gale snapped. "And we're prepared to carry it out."

Normally Booker would have reacted to a threat in a very different manner, but he understood how she felt. "I'm all over it," Booker said.

"What's the plan?" Rip asked coldly.

"We're going in for a rescue in a matter of minutes." Booker went on to explain the false deal with the Foundation and the fact that the NSA was about to bring a SEAL team in to capture Cira. They needed to know the risks. There was no other choice now. "I'll be back in touch shortly."

"No!" Gale shouted. "Keep us on the line!"

But Booker was gone.

Rip thought of the message he'd sent Huang. If Cira was not returned safely to Rip and Gale, and if something were to happen to any of the three of them, then Huang was supposed to give the exact coordinates of El Perdido, along with a list of the key scientists who had contributed the most to the research, to Dixon Barbeau. Rip could still stop the order, and he wasn't sure it was the right thing to do, but he believed that Barbeau was the only other person who understood the stakes, and who also had the connections to get to the Sphere before the NSA or the Foundation. Still, it felt too much like retribution to Rip.

"This is not about revenge," Gale said. "Booker has had us and the Sphere for seven years. If we wind up losing Cira, then . . . "

"Crying Man promised me he would protect her," Rip interjected.

Gale looked at Rip with a silent stunned expression. "Crying Man? You've seen him? You *talked* to him?"

Rip explained everything that had happened in the past few days, starting in Hawaii. "All along, the Sphere, the very thing we were trying to save, has been the very thing that could save us."

"Us as in our family, or us as in the human race?" Gale asked.

"Both."

"Who else knows what happened in Hawaii?"

"A handful of the scientists," Rip said. "You remember Dabnowski? He and four others presented a paper to the brain trust." The brain trust was comprised of the top twelve scientists in UQP. "We're so close to a breakthrough. We actually found a command language, but it was beyond my skills. I have the data on my INU, but I don't really fully understand it."

"They've raided the university, Gale said. "The AX agent on the plane told me. They've started rounding up *all* the scientists and are grilling them. They won't talk, will they?"

"Some of them will. They're scientists, not terrorists. They know nothing about resisting interrogation methods, and the CIA is very good at getting people to talk."

Gale nodded, her expression conveying fear and anger. "How can Crying Man protect Cira?" she asked.

"Crying Man, or something, allowed your plane to land here undetected."

"That was Booker. The same way he keeps this island hidden, some program fed into the satellites. His company manufactures most of them," Gale reminded him. "If Booker wasn't certain that we could have landed invisibly, he wouldn't have let the pilot get within a hundred miles of El Prison."

"But he got that technology from the Eysen."

"He's taken much from the Eysen," Gale reminded him.

"Booker told me that the NSA has an entire team studying what he's been able to do. They have a theory called EAMI, Eysen Anomaly Matter Interference. They use it to explain stuff that is beyond scientific knowledge or current technology. It's a way to put together enough pieces of the puzzle that the government scientists can reverse-engineer some of what he's done."

"Or use it to find him," Gale added. "How has *he* been able to stay hidden, yet they found *us* in Fiji?"

"You know how," Rip said, grabbing her hand and finding her eyes. "Cira. It was all an accident."

"There is no such thing as accidents!" Glare protested. "Oh, Rip, our baby is all alone! She's suffering . . . alone." Gale stood up. "Damn that Booker. He had them drug me, and—"

"He may not have gone about it the right way, but we both know you'd be in custody now if he hadn't and Cira would *still* be alone."

"Are you on his side?"

"It's the truth, Gale. You know it is."

"Truth? The only truth I know is that Booker's about to bring a full-scale war into that hospital. Our little girl will be surrounded by explosions, guns, and death."

"Why are you so against Booker? He's kept us safe for seven years, allowed us the time to explore the Eysen. You knew having a baby could expose us. Whatever mistakes he's made, we're still here, and you're always telling me how powerful forgiveness is . . . Forgive Booker!"

Gale nodded, wiping tears. "I'll forgive anything once we have Cira back."

"Crying Man said he'd protect her."

"Where is Crying Man?"

forty-nine

Savina arrived at the lab seconds before her Foundation security escort. She also now assumed there was a transponder somewhere in her vehicle.

None of this is necessary, she thought. *I'm committed to the study of the Sphere. I'm committed to saving the future of our species, and that means I'm committed to the Foundation, to the Phoenix Initiative.*

The assistant she'd given the note to looked up at her with a desperate and apologetic expression. Savina had begged the Judge to allow him to stay. "Neither one of us was doing anything against the Foundation," she'd told the Judge. "We were trying to broaden our understanding of the Sphere."

The Judge may not have agreed, but the assistant had just been following Savina's orders, and, with all his experience, he could not easily be replaced. Booker's near monopoly on top talent meant the Judge sometimes had to be less exacting than he'd like.

Savina told both assistants what had happened, beginning with informing them that their conversations were being monitored. During the next few hours, she carefully dropped codes into their casual comments while working. The code, based on equation, was something that only someone with a strong knowledge of physics would pick up on and understand. She managed to convey her intention to bypass Booker and to contact Gaines directly through his Sphere.

"They're connected. There is a way," she told them as part of the coded instructions. "Let's find it."

Savina opened up every area of the Sphere she'd gained any control over during her years of research. Each time, she carefully repeated the steps, as closely as possible, that they'd taken prior to the earlier incident when the Sphere had swallowed them.

There's a way in, Savina thought, her pulse quickening. She wasn't just after Gaines and the other Sphere, modifying the future from the past, or even "time travel." Savina needed to know what was beyond all human knowledge, and she could sense that, and more, was only a breath away.

−O−

While the Judge seemed unaware that a SEAL team was about to raid Cira's hospital in Fiji, Booker took the news as just another logistic to contend with. Orders were changed, diversions increased, and Huang besieged Washington with a roaring cyber attack of technology. Booker remained confident, but knew his team had to get in first or they would lose.

"Is Cira prepared to move?" Booker asked when the Judge came on the line.

"Yes."

"The Bascom Palmer Eye Institute's protocols were followed?" Booker asked. "Because if she winds up permanently blind—"

"We've done what we could."

"Okay." Booker knew he couldn't ask for anything more. It would be risky, no matter what.

"And Gaines, you have him standing by?"

"He's still an hour away, but he's moving."

"Excellent," the Judge said, still wanting to push for the Sphere instead of just Gaines. However, the deal was better than it appeared. In one swoop, he denied the American government the trading power of having Gale and Rip's daughter, he took Rip and all his knowledge away from Booker, and he gained all that expertise to be shared with Savina and the Foundation's team. He also still had time, and other options, to get to Booker's Sphere, and Gaines would be the key.

He allowed himself a slight smile at his own degree of cleverness. With each minute, the fulfillment of his grand vision was coming closer to reality.

The two powerful enemies arranged the final details. Booker's people would bring Rip to an address in Nayarit, a coastal area of Mexico. At the same time, the Judge had assured Cira would be delivered to one of Booker's waiting boats in Suva Harbor, about a ten-minute ambulance ride from the hospital.

Once the call with Booker ended, the Judge quickly joined a previously scheduled encrypted video conference of the committee overseeing the Phoenix Initiative. After explaining the deal that would bring Gaines into their control, the Judge switched topics.

"It is an incredible understatement to describe our extreme solution to the coming troubles in the world as controversial," he reminded them while twisting wires into place and soldering the connectors on a circuit board, the inner workings of a small robotic finger. "Because of that, I've set up every aspect of the Phoenix Initiative to include double-blind backups. That is to say, we have to be certain that if any key participants change their minds, we'll have others in line to immediately take their place."

Unbeknownst to Savina, the Judge had a second group of researchers, led by a bright physicist working on her off-hours. The Sphere was too important to ever let it sit idle. From the beginning, he'd kept "Sphere expeditions" going twenty-four hours a day. It wasn't that the Judge didn't trust Savina, it was that he didn't trust *anyone*.

"The B-team has been pursuing its own routes into the Sphere, and they have found the first evidence that the Phoenix Initiative will be a success." He let his statement sink in before he showed them images. "This information is too sensitive to send to you directly," he said, enjoying the looks on the four men and two women on the committee as they saw a future led by the Aylantik Foundation. The Judge smiled. "You'll notice it isn't an awful or scary world."

"It looks incredible," one of them said.

"Paradise," another put in.

"When is this?" a woman asked.

"About fifty years from now," the Judge replied.

"Wow."

"As I have always said, bold action is the only way to save humanity," the Judge espoused, wrapping up the meeting and carefully putting the circuit board away. "If we do our job correctly, the Phoenix Initiative will never be discovered, but if it is, some may call us evil, and we'll certainly be misunderstood. One day though, history will see us as its greatest heroes."

They all agreed. Sometimes one must destroy everything in order to save it.

fifty

Rathmore stood in the dimly lit NSA situation room surrounded by massive monitors providing real-time images and data of the numerous crises swirling around the hunt for the Sphere. He stared disbelievingly at the young analyst who'd delivered the news that Professor Yamane was dead. "How? When?"

"Hawaii PD found his body behind a coffee shop across from the university campus forty minutes ago," the analyst said. "No sign of foul play. Officer on the scene said it looks like a heart attack."

"I'll bet it does," Rathmore scoffed. "How did they identify the body?"

"Wallet was in his pocket, driver's license, credit cards, everything. Apparently the dean has been called to make a positive ID, but that hasn't happened yet. No next of kin on the island."

"I want every scientist who may have worked on anything having to do with the Sphere arrested, although don't call it that. Refer to it as protective custody," Rathmore said. "Do it now. We're going to get this train back on track. Choo-choo, people, choo-choo!"

"Are you sure it's wise to start arresting Nobel laureates?" Murik asked.

"I've got a dead professor, a vanished plane, and a blind kid hiding in a hospital," Rathmore said. "I don't know what the hell is wise. I'm not even sure what's real anymore, but I do believe those scientists have the answers to all of this, and I intend to find out."

"I'd like to hear the plan," Murik said, "before your choo-choo turns into a train wreck."

After the devastating news of Professor Yamane's death and the disappearance of Asher's plane, they still had one lead, and it was safely tucked down the hall—Dixon Barbeau. If anyone knew how Gaines and Asher had escaped and could find the duo, it was the ex-FBI agent who'd tracked them from the start and then let them go.

"Barbeau is my plan."

"Barbeau's been in custody," Murik said, puzzled. "How is he going to help us find the plane, the Sphere, or Professor Yamane's killer?"

"You know as well as I do that seven years ago Barbeau let them walk. We don't really have a clue as to what he's been doing since. Whatever it is, it's a big secret, and he's too damn cocky. My bet is he's working for Booker Lipton. Speaking of which, any word from King?"

"His office says he's caught in the Russia-China situation," a technician replied. "The Unit's been rerouted to Asia."

"I'll bet," Rathmore sneered.

"What are you going to do?" Murik asked, tapping commands into his INU.

"Find that leech hole," he barked at his team, then turned back to Murik. "This is a damned Scorch and Burn! I'm going to give Barbeau one last chance to cooperate, and if he doesn't, he's going to find out first hand about how well we've perfected our enhanced interrogation methods."

"Sir, an update on the Russia-China conflict," another technician interrupted. "The Chinese and Russian air forces are now engaging one another in the Sea of Japan. In addition, breaches of airspace have been increasing. The Chinese are moving missiles, and there has been a major bombing in the Russian border city of Vladivostok."

Rathmore looked to Murik. "This is yours for the next hour. Send for me if we find Asher's plane."

"You do know the SEAL team is about to move on the hospital?" Murik reminded him.

"We're going in with overwhelming force. It's a Dark-Star unit. They never fail. They're going after a blind, sedated, six-year-old girl," Rathmore said. "Do you think you can handle that?"

"Hey, Claude, I'm CIA. That's what we do," Murik shot back. "I just thought you might want to micromanage because that's what the NSA does."

"I'm glad you think this is all so damned funny," Rathmore said, pausing at the entrance of the situation room. "Just make sure we round up every last scientist, because I promise you that if we don't, every single one of them is going to wind up dead or vanished." The door closed behind him.

Murik, happy to be free of Rathmore's heavy and tense approach to every situation, contacted his boss. After the call, he looked to prioritize the assignments. Although an outsider to the all-NSA staff, Murik was well-liked, and much more popular than Rathmore.

He consulted with the talent in the room as he handed out directives. The situation room and the converging events seemed to be brimming over with one crisis after another, each requiring crucial decisions. Perhaps the biggest question was how they were all connected. With Rathmore gone, Murik could use the NSA resources to focus on an aspect of the situation he had not shared with his gruff NSA counterpart.

The CIA was assisting the FBI in working a very disturbing case involving the recent disappearance of dangerous viruses from Centers for Disease Control and World Health Organization labs. For obvious reasons, it was being kept from the public, but Murik had other reasons for wanting to keep it from Rathmore. Murik did an unauthorized air-link of his INU to an NSA server. The illegal maneuver took about twenty seconds, and could have been completed only by a highly trained agent.

Murik juggled the updates and continued to watch the ever-changing monitors. The viruses, the escalating Russia and China war in Asia, the SEAL team about to take the hospital in Fiji, the continuing fruitless search for the disappearing plane, overseeing the rounding-up of Booker's UQP scientists in Hawaii, and monitoring the investigation into the death of Professor Yamane. As the events churned inside the NSA situation room, two pieces of information came in that Murik knew could make the difference in the fate of Gaines and his Eysen-Sphere.

Murik now had sole discretion as to how to handle the developments. He looked at the clock. He didn't know how long he had until Rathmore returned, but it could be at any time.

He contacted his boss and ordered a strike on a little known island that was owned by a private company, which was owned by a small corporation, which was a subsidiary of another company, which was controlled by a known associate of Booker Lipton. The island was in the flight range, and on one of the projected paths of the Gulfstream which had been carrying Gale Asher.

Then he directed agents under his command to isolate a key group of the UQP scientists from the master list. The scientists were the core Sphere researchers. Murik wanted them as far away as he could get them from the mass NSA roundup. Rathmore had repeatedly stated how much was at stake with locating the Sphere, but really, he had no idea.

fifty-one

Rathmore hurried down the corridors and moved through several security zones until he reached the holding area. There, as instructed, was a bottle of Gentleman Jack Whisky, Barbeau's favorite, or one of them. Rathmore cradled the bottle, along with a crystal glass, borrowed from some unknown source inside the NSA headquarters, and entered the interrogation room, where he found Barbeau sound asleep.

"Barbeau, waaake uuuup," he sang. "Time to go to school . . . or would you rather PAR-TEEEEE?" he asked, clicking the glass against the bottle.

Barbeau forced his eyes open and found the unwelcome sight of two things he detested: alcohol and Rathmore. The former had already destroyed his life, and the latter seemed intent on doing it all over again.

"What do you want, Rathmore?" Barbeau asked, as if a subordinate had interrupted his vacation. "Can't you see I'm trying to sleep? Which I must say is damned difficult under these awful fluorescents."

"I brought you a nightcap," Rathmore said, smiling as he swirled the amber liquid around inside the clear bottle of rare Tennessee whiskey. "Just a quick taste, what do you say?" Rathmore brightened his tone, as if offering ice cream to a toddler.

"Tempting," Barbeau replied, "but even when I did drink, I had two rules: never drink alone, and never drink with loser pieces-of-garbage." He glared at Rathmore, then in the tense silence, Barbeau slowly smiled and winked. "So even if you leave, and I wish you would, I still wouldn't drink that piss water."

"Oh, you'll drink," Rathmore said, his eyes burning through Barbeau. "You'll drink even if I have to get you strapped to this damned table and force an IV into your arm."

"Do it then," Barbeau didn't care. He assumed he'd be either dead or free within hours anyway, and it was beyond him to determine which it would be.

Rathmore stared at him while slowly twisting the top on the bottle until the black seal broke. He removed the cap and inhaled the powerful scent of aged alcohol. Then he tilted the bottle to Barbeau. "Just a sniff? That wouldn't hurt anything. Just smell how good this is."

Barbeau glanced indifferently at both the bottle and the man offering it, wondering if Rathmore really believed he was God, or if that had just become part of his shtick.

"I'm going to tell you a little story," Rathmore said, setting the bottle on the table directly in front of Barbeau. "What if I told you that Booker Lipton put Gale Asher onto a commercial airliner in Fiji, which landed a few hours ago in Honolulu, and from there she boarded a private jet, a Gulfstream registered to a media company most likely controlled by Booker?"

"So?"

"Let me back up a minute." Rathmore then told Barbeau about Cira and the fake plane crash into the ocean. "Sound familiar?"

"No."

"Really?" Rathmore sneered. "It should. *You* helped them fake their deaths before with an aircraft crash."

"Their helicopter blew up."

"The point is that it was a farce, and you were in on it."

Barbeau shook his head.

"Well, we followed the Gulfstream," Rathmore continued. "We had F/A-18 Hornets all over it, satellite tracking, everything . . . " He stopped talking when he saw Barbeau begin to smile. "What's so funny?"

"You lost her. You were hoping she would lead you to Gaines so you let her slip away, all cocky and sure, and then boom, she disappeared on you." Barbeau laughed loudly. "Why, hell, if that isn't a cause for a drink." He picked up the Gentleman Jack, inspected it, and took a long whiff. "Hmm, stronger than I recalled." Still holding the bottle, he smiled broadly at Rathmore and chuckled again. "Where was she headed?"

"West coast," Rathmore said begrudgingly. "Last projections pointed to San Diego, Arizona, maybe even into northern Mexico."

Barbeau nodded.

"Why did you help them?" Rathmore asked, really wanting to say, "Where the hell are they?" He was certain that Barbeau knew, or at least had a very good idea. He also knew that Barbeau didn't like him, and that he'd have to work around that and whatever motives Barbeau had for helping them in the first place if he had any hope of getting the ex-FBI agent to drop a clue.

"I didn't help them, but perhaps you should be asking why *Booker* helps them."

"He's greedy. The Sphere is a profit machine that keeps him decades ahead of his competitors."

Barbeau shook his head, remembering how he used to think the same way. "Do you believe our government is corrupt?"

"There's corruption in every government. You can't escape it. Corruption is built into the system."

"What if it keeps growing?"

Rathmore shrugged.

"What if it grows out of control? What if it becomes larger than the system?"

"What's this got to do with Gaines?" Rathmore asked impatiently.

"How come you can't pick up Booker?"

"Booker is too big to get, you know that."

"Too big to fail, too big to get, too big to stop?" Barbeau chanted.

"What are you talking about?" he asked, amused that Barbeau was rubbing his fingers over the smooth glass whiskey bottle, almost caressing it.

"The Sphere is too big to stop. It's not something to hand over to HITE. It could swallow up our whole existence."

Rathmore hid his shock that Barbeau knew about HITE. Only those with the absolute highest security clearances were made aware of the ultra-secret intelligence division.

"'Swallow up our whole existence?' Maybe you sniffed a little too much of that whiskey," Rathmore said.

Barbeau nodded. "Maybe, but you're so worried about where Gale Asher is that you fail to realize I just answered every question you've ever asked me."

"What? How?"

"I'm not going to do your job for you, Rathmore. Go play the tapes over a few times and see if you can figure it out."

"Where the hell do you get off being so smug? Do you *realize* how much trouble you're in? A washed-up federal agent, a dry drunk, soon to be convicted of treason, and you're acting all high and mighty as if you're superior. Superior to what? You screwed up your marriage and couldn't even get being a father right."

Barbeau hardly flinched, but he managed to douse Rathmore with most of the Gentleman Jack before a guard got into the room and helped subdue him. Barbeau laughed as they cuffed him. "Good time to go ask your boss for that promotion," Barbeau said, laughing harder. "Do you think he'll believe that *you* haven't been drinking?"

"I'm going to enjoy watching you fry," Rathmore spat.

"Fry? I'll be out of here before you can get the paperwork filled out," Barbeau taunted. "The thing is, Rathmore, because you're with the NSA, you think that you're on the top of the food chain. You think no one can touch you. But you're in a dog fight between F-35s and T-50s and all you have is a wrinkled paper airplane, not to mention you haven't even noticed the starships closing in." Barbeau felt a headache coming on, but let the fury of the moment carry him through.

"I'll see you on death row," Rathmore said, trying to blot the whiskey from his face as he stormed from the room.

"You fool," Barbeau shouted to the door, as it bolted closed. "You don't even realize *we're all already* on death row!"

fifty-two

Booker took a deep breath. He'd conducted a long list of operations over the years, ranging from delicate to blatant, nuanced to forceful. Some had been trivial in that they involved only money, and a few had been what he referred to as "fate of the world" missions, but rescuing Cira was more than all of them. Everything. The sweet little girl could be blind for life, or she could die, but beyond those risks, this undertaking marked the final stage of the end.

However it turned out, the Foundation and Booker would be locked in a daily battle as the countdown ticked off what days remained until the Phoenix Initiative sliced into humanity.

"Everything," Booker whispered to the photos adorning the wall of people he loved who had yet to be born. "*Everything.*"

Booker checked in with Huang, who would be, as usual, running various technical interference schemes meant to thwart the advantages of their enemies. EAMI was a powerful tool, but far less reliable and practical than certain "old-fashioned" maneuvers such as hacking into INU networks, utilizing satellite backdoors, and creating electronic diversions. Huang was a master of all those methods.

BLAX, the elite division within Booker's private AX army, would handle the operation. The ultra-trained commandoes known as "BLAXERs" and their BLAX-commander had already read the orders on their Eysen-

INUs. This would be his final contact before the action erupted. He communicated across Booker-owned satellites.

"We are nine minutes from strike."

The BLAX-commander and Booker could both see the progress of the incoming American Dark-Star team. It was a total dark ops scene, raid-ready CIA and NSA operatives trained and armed in the most sophisticated tactics and weapons joined to one of the Navy's three best SEAL units. Together, they were twenty-one men known covertly as "Dark-Star."

The BLAXERs totaled forty-nine, but Dark-Star was only part of their problem. Between the Fiji police presence and Foundation soldiers, there would be another forty opponents, and although they could go into the girl's hospital room window, the only way to safely take the patient out of the building was through the crowded corridors and entrances teaming with adversaries. Mission Impossible.

The BLAX-commander had wanted to wait for another BLAXER team, but time had run out. The Dark-Stars would be a terrible addition to the nightmare. Booker knew many of his men would not make it out of Fiji alive, but this was it. Everything.

"Are the charges all confirmed and ready?" Booker asked.

"Affirmative."

Booker looked at the timer. Seven minutes. "I've got one last chance to slow Dark-Star."

The BLAX-commander knew the delay, if successful, would only buy the BLAXERs another minute or two, but that could make all the difference. "Six minutes."

All cameras in the hospital would go down as soon as they killed the power and backup generators. They scanned the current status of every potential threat once again, debating whether to keep the power on for two reasons: one, it would give them vital views and logistical data during the strike, and two, it would save the lives of several dozen innocent patients who would certainly die without ventilators and other power-dependent life-saving equipment.

In the end, however, they deemed the power too risky to leave on. None of the Foundation soldiers or police would have night vision capability.

At three minutes out, with their final orders and plans made, Booker cut communications with the BLAX-commander. There would be no way to stop the strike now.

"Everything," Booker repeated quietly. A moment later, he smiled as he received verification that one of his aerospace engineers had been able to successfully alter the feed from the satellite that Dark-Star relied upon for tactical field data. Like most spy satellites, it was manufactured by one of Booker's companies. The NSA would be able to realign and shift to an alternate satellite, but it would hold their landing time back at least ninety critical seconds.

His team would have almost three minutes inside the hospital before Dark-Star arrived. It could be all they needed. BLAXERs wouldn't be able to evacuate the girl in that short amount of time, but they might be able get her close to the ground level. The plan called for a back door, lower-level exit, because Dark-Star would have the helipad and two roof levels occupied.

Booker watched the feeds coming in from the hospital security cameras and checked the time. The final thirty seconds felt like an hour. He could only hope the doctors had been able to follow the Bascom Palmer Eye Institute's protocols. He hadn't allowed himself to think about how the Judge would react to his betrayal, but he knew this move could easily lead to a new kind of war.

A war of Spheres.

fifty-three

Savina's assistant explained, in code, that he'd been forced to betray her to the Judge, but he did manage to get word to his friend who was still working on her message to Booker. She believed her assistant, and now wondered that if they did get through to Booker, whether she should still meet him, or if that would even be possible now that the Judge had her under constant guard. Savina decided she'd deal with it in the unlikely event that she ever heard from Booker.

In the meantime, the search for a passage to the other Sphere required every bit of her attention. A link, a scrap, a hint, any shred of data, all they needed was a direction which could lead them to Rip's Sphere. In the beginning, when they didn't know any other way, "freeform," just going where the Eysen led them, had been the way to discovery. It was still used the majority of the time, leading them to constantly new areas.

Because the Sphere reacted to whoever was present, and even more strongly to the person holding it, they would often change their configuration and direct their thoughts into a certain section, question, or idea. Savina had been preoccupied for most of the past year trying to determine how the Sphere managed to read their thoughts eleven million years after its creation.

"How does it know what I'm thinking today?" one of her assistants posed their oft-repeated question.

"The AI program is incredible," Savina said as the views from the Sphere sliced across the current world. "It knows what we're looking for. Why won't it show us?"

It wasn't exactly a new frustration. For as long as they'd been working with the Sphere, most of the time it would read their thoughts, tease in that direction, go close, but not straight to what they wanted, as if it knew best what they needed or were ready for. Perhaps Savina and her assistants were forgetting to add something to the equation, something they didn't understand, or didn't know they'd forgotten.

"It's the same piece of the puzzle we've been missing from the beginning," one of the assistants said.

"No, I think this time is different. Usually it wants us to give it more, like we're not taking the final step, but in this case, it's the one that's withholding, as if it doesn't want us to find Gaines. Like the Sphere is protecting him."

The two assistants shared a glance. They knew Savina sometimes treated the Sphere as a living thing, and she'd been increasingly blurring the lines between science and speculation even before the "swallowing," as they called the episode when the Sphere had engulfed the lab and cast them all floating in the ether. Since then, Savina seemed to be dipping into the territory of the Inner Movement wing of Booker's UQP world, where quantum physics met metaphysics.

"What do you want us to do?" she whispered, her lips almost touching the smooth surface of the Sphere, her hands caressing it like a lover. "Show me, please."

The Sphere suddenly sprayed light into the room, whirling patterns of a thousand disco balls. In seconds, they were floating in another realm, swimming in light and particles and shards of reality. Teardrop-sized worlds spinning, scenes magnified from the heads of exploding pins, dreams dancing within the blink of an eye, whispers amplified from merging passages of time. It was as if they were climbing through a kaleidoscope. At the same time, they had the sense they were somehow still in the lab, as they each maintained the same distance from one another.

Savina laughed. "I'm free! Do you feel it? Do you feel the freedom?"

The assistants could not deny what they felt, although one of them would later say, "It seemed more like a glimpse into the infinite universe."

"Gaines, are you there? Ripley Gaines, can you hear me?" Savina said, barely above her normal conversational tone. "Whoa!" Savina suddenly shouted. "Did you see that?"

"Who was that? Could that have been Gaines?" one of the assistants asked.

"No way," Savina shot back. "That . . . I think that was a Cosegan."

No one spoke for a moment. The man they'd seen, from the shoulders up, had a somber expression, and wore what appeared to be a collarless, white linen top.

"Did you *hear* him?"

"No," one of them said.

"Did he speak?" the other asked.

"Not with words, not a voice . . . " Savina said, awed. "But he conveyed a message. He expressed feelings. He changed the molecules in my mind." She looked around the still spinning room as if hoping to catch another glimpse of him in the dancing light, the rippling, illuminated shadows. "The Spheres were not random artifacts. They didn't survive by accident, they were *planted* for us. For Gaines and . . . me."

The room calmed. "What are you talking about?" an assistant asked.

"They told me, *showed* me . . . the Cosegans left *nine* Spheres with the intent that specific people would find them . . . They *knew* who would find each Sphere."

"Eleven *million* years ago?" one of them exclaimed.

At the same time, the other assistant asked, "Wait, *nine*? Where are the other seven Spheres?"

During the swallowings, the monitoring equipment, including the device that relayed the audio from the lab to the Judge, failed, but as the white noise and static cleared, he distinctly heard, "Where are the other seven Spheres?"

The Judge leaned back in a large leather desk chair and covered his face with his hands. "Impossible," he moaned. The Judge had long suspected there might be a total of three, and old Church documents hinted there might have been a fourth, but nine?

He phoned Savina immediately.

By the time she felt the vibration of her iPhone, the lab had fully reassembled, as if nothing had happened. *As if we hadn't been swimming in the light of stars and heard a message sent across time*, she thought. Savina noticed the Judge's number and answered.

"What just happened there?" he said, not bothering with a "Hello".

Savina, not surprised he knew, made an instant decision to play it straight and told him everything.

"So you just had a feeling there were originally nine Spheres?"

"He told me."

"The imaginary man?"

"Look, Judge, I am not going to argue about this. I'm telling you what happened. If you don't believe me, tell me this; do *you* believe in the future we've seen in the Sphere?"

"Where are the other Spheres? Have they survived?"

"I don't know," Savina said, annoyed she had not been granted the time to process what she'd just been through. "We're going back in and I'll let you know what we find."

"Savina, you know how close we are to the Phoenix launch," the Judge said. "If there are more Spheres out there—"

"I know, Judge. I know! We'll find them!"

fifty-four

Rathmore quickly showered and changed into a spare set of clothes from his office closet. While walking back to the situation room, he imagined all the ways he would get back at Barbeau. The first was to see Barbeau subjected to the kind of questioning that came with lots of physical contact and pain.

"That guy is worse than the criminals he's protecting because he was trained and sworn to protect," Rathmore muttered to himself.

Murik couldn't help but laugh at the story of Barbeau and the whiskey. "Gotta be careful who you choose to drink with," he said. "Seriously though, you should go back there right now and kick his ass." He chuckled, taking another bite from a sandwich. "I've got things under control here."

"Do you?" Rathmore asked, perusing the big screens. Russia and China seemed to be at about the same level as when he'd left. The plane was still nowhere on any tracking or satellite feeds. The SEALs, however, were just landing, and Rathmore anticipated some good news for a change.

"We're looking good in Fiji," Murik said.

"How are the arrests going in Hawaii?"

"Just getting under way."

Rathmore pointed back to the hospital. "What are they doing?" he asked, motioning to a group of Foundation soldiers pointing skyward. "It looks like they're expecting us. Are they?" He shot a glance at his team of leech trackers.

"Data on Fiji is flowing."

"Damn it! How are they getting the data out?" Rathmore shouted. "Find those holes, now!"

"Expecting us, or someone else?" Murik said, alarmed. "Who is that?" He stood up, abandoning his sandwich. "Zoom in there." He indicated a spot in the sky above the hospital. "That's not us," he said sharply.

Rathmore checked the time. "We should have already been there. Where are we? Who's that?"

"Sir, the Dark-Star team had a communication glitch with the satellite," a technician said. "They lost some time, but it's all good now."

"All good?" Rathmore asked. "Then who in the hell is *that*? A downed satellite, another crew incoming... a hundred dollars says Booker is going for the kid."

"Damn," Murik said.

"What else do we have nearby?" Rathmore shouted. "Get something in on this. How far out are we?" And then silently, tensely, under his breath, he offered the ultimate solution. "We have to kill Booker Lipton."

Murik glanced at one of the smaller screens, which showed two of the core UQP physicists being picked up by agents in Hawaii. In spite of the turmoil in Fiji, Murik allowed a slight smile. He knew the agents personally, and hoped that before the mess in Fiji was cleaned up they would have all twelve of the scientists who were most intimately involved with the Sphere. He glanced back at Rathmore, still completely engrossed in Fiji, and suppressed his smile. *Fiji is not a welcome development, but it does make a nice diversion,* he thought.

"Could this all be a diversion?" Rathmore asked.

Murik had a sick feeling Rathmore was onto him. "What?" the CIA agent asked, giving nothing away.

"Russia. China. The entire US government is completely focused on the Russian-Chinese border, the Sea of Japan, the South China Sea . . . Everyone except us. Well, even us to a point," Rathmore corrected himself. "Could Booker be powerful enough to arrange that?"

Murik sighed in relief and picked up his half-eaten sandwich. "Booker has more than a trillion dollars. He's a country unto himself. I'd say there's an excellent chance he's involved in the conflict. I mean look at this." Murik motioned to a large screen filled with BLAXERs landing at the hospital.

Rathmore nodded and called Tolis King, the head of the NSA's Veiled Ops. After updating his boss and assigning an analyst the job of connecting Booker to the conflict in Asia, Rathmore looked back at the monitor filled with empty ocean, the one next to it showing empty sky.

"Give me everything we have on EAMI," he said to the woman who had initially raised the possibility that Eysen Anomaly Matter Interference could have been used. "Show me every theory on how Booker could make a plane evaporate. Gale Asher didn't vanish. She's either still flying on one of those original courses, or she's landed in a place where we can find her. Booker can't make a runway disappear."

"Actually," the woman said, "he might be able to do more than that. I think he could make an entire island invisible."

fifty-five

Taz stood on the upper deck of a super yacht belonging to one of the top Foundation billionaires. His cropped hair didn't move in the gentle breeze, but his hand tightened around a plastic bottle of water, the sun glinting off his gold rings.

Somewhere inside the luxurious, three-hundred-foot floating palace, Dabnowski and the other four scientists, who had authored the papers describing the Cosegan time travel method, were huddled around large monitors. The five brilliant men worked feverishly on their INUs, which were linked via satellite to both the university, and Mauna Kea Observatory networks. It was a race to access and download all the data they needed before the NSA successfully locked the systems down.

The yacht, aptly named *Bright Future*, was cruising toward international waters. Among its many amenities were military-grade anti-aircraft and anti-missile defense systems, as well as concealed large caliber guns designed to defend against attack. Taz had no illusions that those features, and the twelve Foundation soldiers onboard, could withstand a CIA or a SEAL strike force. Still, he felt better being off the island. The *Bright Future* also carried two helicopters, as well as a mini-sub that could evacuate eight people.

Finally, a call from Stellard came through.

"Did you hear from Wattington?" Taz asked.

"Yes," Stellard replied. "There is a SEAL team about to hit the hospital."

"Get her out of there!"

"I just gave the order, but there won't be time."

"Damn!"

"We have the scientists," Stellard reminded him. "Even if we don't get Gaines or his Sphere, we'll have the power to fight back if they manage to change things." His words trailed off into mumblings that Taz couldn't understand.

"It's more complicated than that," Taz said. "According to Dabnowski, Time-shifting is incredibly complex and risky."

"I imagine time travel would have to be."

"It isn't really time travel though, it's time manipulation. That's the trick. It's not like in the movies where I would go back to some date in 1984 and kill someone or whatever. We're talking about rearranging subatomic particles in some basically invisible pattern which then has a ripple effect across the cosmos. Across time."

"But we have the geniuses to do it . . . to change time, no matter what you want to call it," Stellard said.

"As long as they don't mess things up, we might save the human race, but if one atom is out of place, we may never exist. No one would ever know we were even here."

—O—

Gale and Rip stood in the skyroom, reviewing the findings from Hawaii while the Sphere projected in every direction. Rip looked at Gale. "We may have just discovered the key to stopping the Aylantic Foundation, but will we have the time to use it?"

"And do we have enough?" Gale asked. "Or is there still work needed with the scientists? The NSA is going to have the university and the observatories cleansed by this time tomorrow, and all the scientists will be on their way to Washington, or wherever secret places the government maintains for their worst deeds."

"It's going to be crazy close," Rip said. "Somehow we'll have to get to the observatories. We can't change time without the help of space."

Gale was wondering if they could use the time-shift technique to save Cira before the accident. Rip could almost see her mind working.

"Gale, even if time-shift works, it isn't so precise, at least our understanding and ability to utilize it aren't, that we'd be able to adjust things before the playground."

"I know," she admitted.

"Even getting to the point where we can utilize time-shifting to stop the Foundation is a long shot," Rip said. He pointed to spots in space that the Sphere was showing where they could start. "Manipulating the future by rearranging particles in the past is a scary prospect, one I'm not anxious to do without some guidance."

"Crying Man?" Gale asked.

Rip nodded.

"Where is he? Could he somehow be with Cira?"

"He's a computer program," Rip said slowly.

"You don't really believe that."

"Gale, he's been dead for eleven million years. I'll admit the AI work is breathtaking, and that the power of the Sphere to project into and affect the surrounding environment is staggering, but he's a design element of the Sphere's user interface, and we're six thousand miles from Fiji."

"If he's not real, then how is he going to protect her?"

"If I understood that, I would know how to answer the five Cosega mysteries and stop the Death Divinations . . . but somehow I simply *know* Crying Man will protect her."

"*How?*" Gale shouted. "How do you know?"

"Because he told me!"

—O—

In the midst of managing the strike in Fiji, Booker ordered two more actions. The NSA was rounding up his UQP team, and that meant AX and BLAXER units would need to engage with US government agents, and possibly even the US military, in Hawaii.

At the same time, with the preparations for the Phoenix Initiative intensifying every day and the launch date less than three months away, it was urgent that Booker seize their greatest asset. Thanks to Savina reaching out, he now knew her exact location. Huang was already busy trying to break the formidable electronic defenses utilized by the Foundation to monitor and protect their most vital research facility.

Booker took his eyes off the drama in Fiji just long enough to send every available BLAXER in the vicinity of northern California on the most critical mission of his war against the Foundation. His final instructions to the woman leading the mission were, "Get the Foundation's Sphere and their top physicist. The physicist is even more important than the Sphere, so if it comes down to a choice between them, make sure you bring Savina."

fifty-six

From the skies above Fiji, BLAXERs rained down with propulsion-assisted packs, hitting their targets within inches. At the same moment, in a precision-timed maneuver, two advanced military BLAXER helicopters landed in the parking lot. The forty-nine men stormed the hospital in a blistering assault.

Booker had ordered the use of pulse shots, penetrating pellets coated with an activated serum which caused instant paralysis. Another advantage, aside from limiting casualties, was that the shots dropped the opponent instantly, and therefore removed the threat of an injured combatant still doing damage. The pellets could be lethal if they hit the wrong area, such as the eyes or mouth, or if the pelleted person had certain other health issues, or was on specific medications, but most would recover within twenty-four hours.

Doctors, nurses, and other staff dove for cover. A few patients caught in the corridors were inadvertently shot. Somehow, a small fire started in one of the nurse's stations. There seemed to be more police than their intel had shown. The sound of automatic gunfire echoed down the corridors, mixing with a deafening chorus of screams, alarms, and military commands.

The BLAX-commander led one of the seven units, each made up of seven "Specialists." The police and Foundation soldiers put up a surprisingly strong fight. Unlike the BLAXERS ammunition, the incoming rounds from the police and Foundation soldiers were live and deadly. Six BLAXERs were lost on the ground level, three more killed on the roof, and five on the floors in between.

Booker watched, wishing he'd had more personnel in the fight. Dozens of simulations had shown it was going to be a hard victory, but they'd already lost more than twice as many BLAXERs as expected at this point. Dark-Star, now less than two minutes out, would bring "hell, fire, and death." BLAXERs, engaged in a standoff on the heavily defended floor which housed Cira, had to move.

"Get the girl and get off that floor," Booker yelled, but the BLAX-commander could not hear.

The BLAXERs each wore full body armor, but the Foundation soldiers were picking them off, nailing headshots as if using magic bullets. Booker had tried to apply Eysen-Sphere technology to military hardware and arms, but it had not been easy. It seemed the Cosegans had no physical weapons, but in the modern era of war and violence, with a little imagination, he had found applications that could help his private army.

However, watching the accuracy with which the opposing soldiers shot, he wondered if the Foundation had made better use of the Sphere's secrets, or perhaps theirs had different resources.

"How the hell are they getting those shots?"

He didn't understand why the electricity was still on either. Something must have gone wrong. The cameras didn't cover a crucial part of the basement where an unknown group of Foundation soldiers were located. The Unit put up an incredible fight and forced the BLAXERs to use portable exploding plastics, or PEPS. Ten more BLAXERS died getting to the secured hospital utilities area.

Forty-five seconds until Dark-Star. Already the BLAXERs numbers had been nearly halved. Booker wasn't sure they had enough left to withstand the elite forces. He watched, on a larger screen, as satellite images showed three incoming and highly armed choppers. Two touched down on the two roofs, a third landed on the lower helipad. Booker checked the distance to the BLAXERs' waiting helicopters.

This could end in a dogfight in the air, Booker thought. *That is if we get lucky enough to have anyone left to escape the building.*

As the Dark-Star fighters entered, all electricity in the building was shut down. Blackness instantly strangled the hospital, turning it into a cave. The Dark-Star men immediately donned NVGs, night vision goggles, and stormed forward. BLAXERs engaged them at every entrance. Pockets of Foundation soldiers and police who had not yet been neutralized by the BLAXERs also returned fire, but in the gloom, without NVGs, they were completely blind, stumbling over bleeding and lifeless bodies, dodging a dizzy tangle of bullets, choking smoke, and clipped orders.

With the shield of darkness, Booker's people made progress on Cira's floor and were now only one room away. There was a chance they could still survive this, but Booker could only gauge their progress in abstract estimates and by following random piercing lights emitting from various equipment hanging off the BLAXERs. He grew frustrated that the lights were still off, but not because he couldn't see them. The electricity had been a key part of the plan, and was set to be one of their best weapons.

Suddenly, the building lit up like a sports stadium at night. The BLAXERS, expecting it, had already removed their NVGs a second before. The Dark-Stars, caught by surprise, froze as their NVGs bloomed out, going completely greenish-white, leaving them lost and without vision. Dark-Stars staggered momentarily into ambushes. They tore off their NVGs, but a few seconds later the place went completely black again. In the confusion, the BLAXERs took out a third of the Dark-Stars.

They repeated the "light show" several more times with a seemingly random count that only Booker's men knew. In the process, BLAXERs managed take Cira's room.

A helmet mounted camera showed Booker the most important child in the world. Each BLAXER had memorized the Bascom Palmer Eye Institute's protocols, and one of them used precious seconds to determine if they'd been followed.

"I'm no doctor," he said to another BLAXER, readying the bed to move, "but as best I can tell, they have her all set to go."

"Let's do it," the other said, figuring that blind or not, if they were going to get her out alive, they were already out of time.

The light shows continued, effectively rendering the Dark-Stars NVGs useless. They brought down five more on the way to the ground floor, timing their elevator ride with the intermittent blackouts.

The lobby was a toxic turmoil of fumes and fires. Enough light came from the flames that survivors from all three sides could see enough to fight effectively. BLAXERs and Dark-Stars wore gas masks, as the air was further poisoned by canisters of tear gas introduced by the police, and some sort of sleeping gas by the Dark-Stars. The final Foundation soldiers fell, and in a combination of luck and strategy, the last six able-bodied BLAXERs burst into the night air and darted as fast as they could push Cira's bed toward their waiting chopper. Three more were picked off by pursuing Dark-Stars before they made it into the air.

Booker had been right. The Dark-Stars immediately sent an Apache attack helicopter after the BLAXER's chopper.

fifty-seven

The Judge discovered it wasn't just the SEAL team coming in after Cira. It didn't take long to figure out that the third force present in the Fiji hospital belonged to Booker. He put in a call, surprised when Booker actually took it.

"You think you can just betray the Foundation?" the Judge demanded.

"If the Foundation could protect the girl you'd agreed to trade for Gaines, I wouldn't have needed to send in my forces. Gaines is safe. You need to learn how to protect your assets."

"I don't believe you!"

"I don't give a damn what you believe," Booker replied. "If you can't live up to your deals, don't blame me."

"We'll see about that," the Judge said, ending the call. He immediately contacted Stellard. "Do not let them take that girl out of the hospital alive."

"Just to be clear, you want her terminated?" Stellard asked.

"Kill her!"

—O—

The Judge then contacted Taz aboard the *Bright Future*. Normally, he wouldn't have spoken directly to an operative, but everything was flipped around. Because of the developments with Dabnowski, Taz was handling Hawaii while Stellard oversaw the battle in Fiji.

"Is it real, what they've written in these papers?" the Judge asked tersely.

"These are all Nobel laureates, the best in the world. They all believe it's possible."

The Judge smiled for the first time that day. He didn't know for sure if their Sphere had the same "DNA" map of the universe, which they'd need, to find the precise points where it would be possible to manipulate time, but he assumed it was in there somewhere, and that Savina could find it.

He ordered more people to Hawaii. Keeping the *Bright Future* safe was critical if the Phoenix Initiative was to preempt the apocalyptic prophecies of the Sphere. The initial idea for Phoenix had come to him one night while sitting up with his two-year-old son, who was not sleeping well.

His wife had read about a method to help kids sleep called "wake to sleep." Waking him prior to his normal nightly waking time would somehow break the pattern and allow him to sleep peacefully through the remainder of the night.

The Phoenix Initiative took the wake to sleep principle to a radical extreme. By engineering a controllable plague, the Aylantik Foundation could choose what portion of the population died, and when they would die. Wake to sleep, just like Phoenix, was about controlling the crisis. After the Foundation-created plague, the survivors would go peacefully into the night.

Out of the ashes, a single government could be created to rule the survivors. With Earth as a single nation, and the massive reduction in population, the Phoenix Initiative took care of the Death Divinations — climate change reversed, no war, and all of humanity would not be lost. The chosen would survive.

The Judge knew most would see it as dangerous, even evil. "When we're talking about the end of all human life on the planet, it doesn't matter if we have to kill a few billion to save the rest of us," he'd told the secret committee who had approved the Phoenix Initiative. "There is no other choice."

The fact that they would profit and end up ruling the new world, although certainly not their objectives, was merely a pleasant perk.

fifty-eight

The Eysen-Sphere fell dark, taking all the surrounding light with it. Their INUs, the sun, everything was black.

"What's happening?" Gale whispered fearfully. "Are we under attack?"

Rip moved to where he thought one of the windows was and felt the warm glass, but he could not see it. He returned to the Sphere and picked it up.

"Are we dead?" Gale asked. "Maybe they bombed us and we died instantly."

"I don't think so," Rip responded. "It's the Eysen . . . Crying Man, are you there?"

"Help," Rip heard a strained, raspy voice reply.

"Did you hear that?" he asked Gale excitedly.

"Someone said, 'Help,'" she said.

"He must be helping Cira."

"But where did the light go?"

Suddenly, the Sphere lit up in Rip's hands. The glow grew so powerful that it left his grip and levitated between them.

The Cosega Sequence began and projected all around them. As soon as it completed, they were in a Cosegan city of light. Beautiful pillars stretched into the sky. Translucent blues next to purples, glowing greens, and golden yellows created shapes, structures, buildings of epic proportions.

The darkness fell apart as the powerful lights melded into a world of magic. Shards of light fell like drops of rain from the tallest of heights, as if splintering off the tops of the buildings. Crisscrossed, laser-like beams in a thousand colors created walls of wildly complex edifices. Behind them were the largest structures of all, what appeared to be colossal monuments, constructed entirely of shifting, shimmering light.

"Look!" Gale said.

Rip followed her stare and saw Crying Man emerging from a twisting, luminescent tunnel radiating red behind him, transforming to purple, and finally violet in front of him. There in his arms, like two worlds colliding, was Cira. As he grew closer, Gale ran to them, Rip close behind.

Crying Man's face conveyed a stunning sadness, tears running down his cheeks. Rip felt *déjà vu* from the first time they'd ever seen him back in Asheville, North Carolina seven years earlier.

"Rip. Is Cira . . . Is she dead?"

Rip looked from his daughter's limp body to Crying Man's desperately sad face.

"Help," Crying Man said. They actually saw his lips move as he said the word. He extended Cira to Gale without ever taking his eyes off Rip. Just as Gale was about to take her daughter, the entire scene shifted. In an instant, the Cosegan City, along with Crying Man and Cira, was gone. Suddenly it was just the skyroom. They were still on El Perdido.

"Where's Cira?" Gale screamed.   Then she felt something in her hands. "Rip... It's Earth." She held up Cira's little cloth cat. "But it can't be . . . I left Earth with Cira at the hospital."

"You couldn't have," Rip said. "It's probably been in your pocket all this time."

"No," Gale insisted, her voice trailing to a whisper. "Crying Man brought it."

−O−

The California office complex that housed the Foundation's secret research facilities was understated and purposely mundane in appearance. However, it housed the Foundation's single most valuable asset, and its security reflected that. Booker expected nothing less when he sent more than three hundred heavily armed BLAXERs into what would turn out to be one of the most dangerous missions ever undertaken by his private army.

Booker was counting on the same thing that had saved him repeatedly over the last few years—Cosegan technology. While Gale and Rip and his team of more than one thousand great minds worked to find the secrets within the Sphere, which could preserve the future, Booker knew that money and technology would also be needed if they were going to win the war to save humanity. He had a team of almost one hundred people extracting data from the Eysen research to find ways of creating better weapons and smarter tech that he could use to beat his enemies. Now he was going to put it to the test yet again, this time to get the biggest prize of all. Another Sphere.

Huang rubbed his fingers as if warming up for a concert. Although he also extensively utilized voice and virtual commands, he still preferred traditional keyboards and regularly wore them out. From his darkened room, lit only by dozens of monitors, the forty-year-old, who looked closer to twenty, wreaked havoc around the globe for anyone opposing Booker's interests.

He knew the stakes were higher today than they'd ever been for anything he'd done before. *The very future of humanity depends on saving Cira and capturing Savina.* He took a deep breath, closed his eyes briefly in a kind of instant meditation, and then whispered to the swirling colors on the screens surrounding him, "Time to work."

−O−

Savina was pushing the limits of her knowledge as she zipped around the views of the universe being projected out of the Sphere. "We're all just dead stars looking back at ourselves." She whispered the famous quote loudly enough that one of her assistants quickly looked up from the INU that tracked and processed the Sphere's displays.

That was when they heard the first explosion.

fifty-nine

In Fiji, the BLAXER chopper was equipped with a sonic-obliteration weapon, which Booker's engineers had devised from Sphere technology. The Cosegans did a lot with sound waves, even constructing buildings from them. One of Booker's favorite discoveries in the Sphere had been the Cosegans' use of a sonic propulsion system. "Sound as fuel," he'd said upon learning of the amazing practice. "What great things we'll do with this."

It hadn't been his intent to use it first as a weapon. However, times were difficult, and necessity dictated the applications of destiny more than any noble wisdom would allow.

With their pursuers destroyed, the BLAXERs utilized a cloaking device and flew below radar, heading toward the tiny Pacific island of Samoa, their transfer point. Cira would be loaded into a small jet and flown to El Perdido, where the top doctor from Bascom Palmer Eye Institute was also headed.

Rathmore and Murik were in shock. A Dark-Star unit had never failed a mission, and this one had suffered one hundred percent casualties. According to initial reports, of the twenty-one Dark-Stars believed to be dead, only seven actually were, thanks to the BLAXERs non-lethal ammunition. Who had perished had either been caught in the helicopter obliteration, or downed by Foundation fire.

In reviewing the same reports, Booker was convinced that the Foundation had used some kind of smart-ammunition. Rathmore didn't have the luxury or information to consider such things. He was handling an angry call from King.

−O−

Moments after the light city faded and the skyroom on El Perdido returned to normal, Gale's INU lit up with a call from Booker. She gave the voice command to answer it in speaker mode.

"I'm happy to report that Cira is safe, and is on her way to you as we speak."

Gale couldn't get any words out.

"She's okay?" Rip asked. "Really?"

"Yes," Booker answered, obviously enjoying the chance to deliver the good news. "She's aboard one of my helicopters and will soon be on a jet. ETA to El Perdido, four and a half hours. I've also got a top doctor from the Bascom Palmer Eye Institute en route. He should be there about the same time."

"Her eyes?" Gale barely managed to ask.

"She was packed up as safely as possible," Booker said. "We won't know for sure until the doctor examines her. Think good thoughts."

Gale nodded, closed her eyes, and remembered her little girl in Crying Man's arms. "Thank you," she said out loud.

"You're welcome," Booker responded. Although she had meant her gratitude for Crying Man, she was happy to share it with Booker. In spite of everything, she knew he had never stopped trying to save their daughter.

"Thank you, Booker," she repeated.

−O−

Aboard the *Bright Future*, Taz took the news of losing Cira badly. "I should have moved the girl the minute we found her," he said to Stellard.

"We can't waste time with regrets," Stellard replied. "We have the masterminds behind the time-shift theory. That may be the most important thing to come out of all of this."

"We need to get them out of the reach of our enemies."

"No one knows where you are," Stellard assured Taz.

But both men were worried. Even then, the US government, utilizing CIA, FBI, NSA, and military personnel, was in a race against Booker's people and Foundation agents, all sides trying to round up the remaining UQP scientists in Hawaii. While it was true they didn't yet know the five authors of the time-shift theory were missing, it would not take long, and both the US government, and Booker, had the resources to find them quickly.

Unfortunately, Hawaii was one of the most isolated population centers on Earth. The *Bright Future*, now in international waters, would take six more days to reach California. By then, one of their adversaries would find them, and even with the yacht's many defenses, they were up against far greater forces. Stellard voiced what neither of them wanted to admit.

"The only way to escape Hawaii is to go back to Hawaii."

sixty

A government scientist appeared on one of the screens and tried to explain to Rathmore how Eysen Anomaly Matter Interference worked.

"Could EAMI make a whole Island vanish?"

"Not actually *physically* disappear," the scientist explained. "But to our planes, ships, satellites, as well as radar and other monitoring equipment, it would be invisible."

"Then why can't the pilots see it from the air, with their own eyes?" Rathmore asked impatiently.

"There are any numbers of ways that someone of means—"

"Like Booker Lipton?"

"Yes," the scientist continued. "Someone exactly like Booker Lipton. He could utilize smart fabrics and cover an island, or a plane, with materials that instantly and digitally blend with the environment around them. Or, and it may be more likely in this case, he might be using 3D projection technology so that from the air the pilots would only see ocean."

Rathmore nodded. He'd been aware that the US military had been experimenting and using the same type of technology since 2000 to conceal aircraft and confuse enemies. It seemed incredible that it could hide an entire island, big enough to accommodate a runway capable of allowing the Gulfstream to land, but he knew it was possible. Anything seemed possible these days.

"So how do we beat it?" Murik asked.

The scientist shook his head. "Put a thousand boats in the water and hope one of them runs into it."

"In the Pacific Ocean?" Rathmore said. "Too damned big."

"Go ask Barbeau," Murik said. "Make him tell you everything he knows."

Rathmore scoffed. He'd showered and changed, and even though a couple of hours had passed, he still smelled faintly of whiskey.

"Ask him for a list of Booker's islands in the Pacific. Tell him if he helps us find Asher and Gaines, we'll drop all charges. He'll be a free man." Murik knew firsthand that Booker had more than one island. A covert raid of Cervantes Island had punctuated that point. There could be numerous other Booker-owned landmasses in Asher's flight path.

"Barbeau won't buy it."

"Then promise him a presidential pardon," Murik said. "We've lost the plane, the kid, we've got a dead professor, and I'm not sure how many of Booker's other UQP brains we're going to be able to round up. Russia and China are forcing us to reallocate resources. We're kind of losing this one."

"We can't lose this," Rathmore said. "*This* is *the* one. It's the future we're talking about."

"Then get Barbeau to cooperate," Murik replied. "I'll handle things here."

Rathmore nodded and headed for the door.

"Oh, and Claude?" Murik called after Rathmore. "Better wear a raincoat this time."

Rathmore flipped him off and stormed out. His already brittle mood had deteriorated drastically after Cira's rescue. He found himself looking forward to pummeling Barbeau again.

That bastard knows where they are, he thought as he navigated the maze of corridors leading to the detention and interrogation area. *He's another government employee on Booker Lipton's payroll.*

When Rathmore reached the holding room, he found no guard on duty and no Barbeau. It took him almost fifteen minutes to ascertain that the former FBI agent had been released.

"On whose authority?" Rathmore demanded when a colleague finally broke the news.

"It's classified."

"Classified? Are you kidding me? I'm on an SAB case. Do you even *know* what those letters stand for? Scorch and Burn! Full authority to do anything, and my key witness gets yanked out from under me . . . I'm going in to see the Director right now!"

"The Director is at the White House," the man said. "Haven't you heard? Russia and China are making a mess in Asia?"

"It's just a damned diversion," Rathmore shot back. "Screw this then. Is King in the building?"

"I think so, but the unit is en route to China, so his hands are full. Barbeau is gone, and no one can help you get him back. Forget it. Find another way."

Rathmore didn't want to forget Barbeau, and he needed an excuse to see King anyway. If he was the leech, Rathmore had to know now.

It took another twenty minutes before he could get in to see King. The meeting left him even more shocked. King claimed not to know where the order came from, or at least wasn't willing to say anything more than it was apparently a MONSTER with a "red card," which trumped every other order and priority. The incredibly rare "cards" had to be signed by the President of the United States.

"Call the President!" Rathmore demanded.

"I just got off the phone with the White House. That's why you were kept waiting. They verified the red card."

"Why was it issued? Who requested it?"

"They aren't saying."

"We're the NSA," Rathmore whined angrily. "If they can't tell us, who can they tell?"

King shook his head.

"Why wasn't I notified?" Rathmore asked.

"*I* wasn't even notified," King said, stretching a rubber band between his hands.

"What's your best guess? Why did they spring Barbeau?"

"He knows something."

"Damn right. He knows where Gaines and the Sphere are."

"CIA is in on this with us. What other agency would be pursuing Gaines? Who has more clout than we do?"

"FBI?"

"No way."

"That's where he's from, but how does the FBI rate higher than NSA or CIA on this case? This is national security times a million."

"Maybe that's your answer," King said. "We can't risk failure. The stakes are too high, so they have *everyone* on it."

"Then why aren't we working together?" Rathmore asked.

King raised an eyebrow. "This is the US government we're talking about. They don't know *how* to work together."

Rathmore shook his head. "Murik is CIA. Maybe he'll have an idea who could have done this. I've got to get back to the situation room. But before I go, one last question?"

King looked up, annoyed. The monitors in the room filled with maps and live images of the Chinese border and his unit getting closer.

"We've detected a leech," Rathmore said. "We're losing data at every turn. Booker Lipton knows before we do what we're about to do."

"How do you know it's Booker?"

"Who else?"

"Do you want a list?" King snapped. "Do you think Booker is the only other person who wants the Sphere?"

"No, but—"

"Have you isolated *anything*? Run overlays of knowledge and dissemination?"

Rathmore nodded.

"And?"

"They point to you."

King stared at Rathmore silently for a moment, his expression changing from blank shock to amusement to outrage. When King finally spoke his words were slow and steady, but filled with venomous force.

"Get. The. Hell. *Out*. Of. My. Office."

—O—

Murik was as surprised as Rathmore had been to learn about the release. However, Rathmore didn't tell him about confronting King. He was still trying to process that nightmare.

"Who would pull Barbeau?" Murik asked, popping a chewing gum bubble. "Who could even get that done?"

"Booker has the juice." Rathmore said. "No one else."

"He's on the other side. We're fighting him," Murik said, chugging an energy drink. His little corner of the NSA situation room was a mess.

"Washington doesn't have enemies, only opportunities," Rathmore said, irritably looking over at the candy wrappers, empty chip bags, and a fast food bag covered with grease spots. "You know the government will make a deal with the devil if it will get them their objective-of-the-week."

"Okay, so it's Booker. Maybe. Why would he burn his influence to free Barbeau? Loyalty? I mean, he did save Gaines and Asher, but that's an incredible play by Booker in the middle of all this to use up a presidential-level favor."

"It's not about loyalty. Barbeau knows where they are, and we were going to get it out of him."

"Too late now," Murik said.

"We don't have Barbeau, we don't have Asher, we don't have the kid, we don't even have the goddamned sniffling professor. We don't have anything! Can this day get any worse?"

"A message for you, sir," a staffer interrupted.

"What's this?" Rathmore asked as he opened the envelope, read the note inside, and then reread it. He looked at Murik as if he'd just been stabbed. "Unbelievable. It's from Barbeau!"

"What?"

"Where did this come from?" Rathmore demanded.

"A private courier service delivered it," the man said. "It came through security."

Rathmore waved the man off, then read Barbeau's note out loud.

"You're looking in the wrong direction. The threat to national security is not Booker, it's the Aylantik Foundation."

Rathmore's face contorted as if he were reading the note for the first time.

"Who does he think I am? Am I wearing clown makeup? Why would he ever imagine that I'd believe this?"

sixty-one

Booker's BLAXERS had expected a tough fight as they charged into the Foundation's sprawling research complex. Still, the full force of the resistance was staggering. Lasers, triple reinforced-lock-downs, and teams of heavily armed soldiers, trained and ready. The Foundation had prepared and drilled for years, waiting for what they knew to be inevitable, that one day someone would come for the Sphere.

The woman leading the BLAXERS, a former Mossad agent, showed no mercy, unleashing a bloody and dangerous barrage of high-tech weapons and smart bombs. Booker's people were the best trained and equipped special ops soldiers in the world. They were also the highest paid, had an extremely low casualty rate, and were loyal and experienced.

The sound of alarm sirens pierced the air as Savina grabbed the Sphere, and placed it in the foam-padded aluminum case that had been used to originally transport it to the lab. According to long rehearsed procedures, she was to secure it in the "impenetrable" floor safe.

Instead, she gripped the handle tightly, stared at her assistants, and wondered if they were going to try to stop her. Neither moved.

"Shouldn't we try to get out?" one of them finally shouted above the noise.

Savina's INU lit up. She saw that it was the Judge and ignored it.

"We're safer here," Savina yelled.

"Whoever it is wants the Sphere," the other assistant shouted louder into the noise. "They'll kill us and take it."

"They want us, too," Savina yelled, strapping her INU to her side case.

"Well, I don't want them," the assistant yelled.

"Me either," the other one agreed.

"If you go out there, you'll get killed in the cross fire!"

One of them ran for the door. "It's locked! We can't get out!"

"It must have locked down when the attack started," the other said.

It didn't take long before they heard some type of ram hitting the other side of the thick steel door. "Stand clear!" came a muffled command. The three scientists ran to a far back corner of Savina's office and huddled together.

The door blew and the BLAXERs came in heavy. Six black-clad soldiers, along with their female leader, all with laser-sighted automatic weapons, began searching the lab.

"We're not here to hurt you, but if you come out voluntarily, your odds of survival are much higher," the BLAX-commander shouted as she shot out the speaker emitting the awful siren. It could still be heard from the hall, but at a fraction of the decibels. "We don't have much time."

Savina stood up, raised the case containing the Sphere over her head, and marched from the office to the lab. "I am surrendering," she said, wondering how this had happened and whom the invaders worked for. The assistants tried to stop her, but it was too late.

"Are you Savina?" the BLAX-commander asked.

"Yes," she answered, not sure if she'd get shot.

"And in the case, that's the Sphere?"

"Yes."

"Open it," the woman ordered.

Savina did as she was told. The BLAX-commander smiled as she confirmed the contents. At the same time, some of her soldiers found the assistants in the office.

"Scientists?" the BLAX-commander asked.

"Yes," Savina answered for them.

"You all come with us," the woman demanded, closing the case.

"No," the assistants both protested.

"Fine," she nodded toward one of the soldiers, who quickly handcuffed the men to lab fixtures. "Let's move!" she shouted.

The BLAXERs and Savina ran into the hallway. Savina looked back, worried about her assistants, but she was pushed along. The BLAX-commander led the way, holding tightly to the Sphere case.

Around the next corner of the adjoining hallway, they encountered Foundation soldiers. It cost them eight minutes and two BLAXERs to punch through. Fifty feet later, thick black smoke choked the passage. The BLAXERs donned masks and somebody roughly pulled one over Savina's face. The chemical smoke burned at Savina's exposed skin as they ran into the oily air. Blind and confused, Savina held onto to a BLAXER, praying she wouldn't trip. After an endless few minutes in the poison blackness, they finally burst out into open.

Across a courtyard and one last firefight. Another BLAXER down. Some kind of percussion bomb wiped out at least seven Foundation fighters. Barely forty seconds passed before she was tossed into a helicopter. No one pursued. No one was left.

Savina, fighting fear, caught one last glimpse of the complex as flames shot out of the roof in several sections. She hoped her assistants would be able to escape or survive until the fire department reached them. Then she recalled the sprinklers. They'd be going off by now.

The BLAX-commander radioed Booker. Savina heard the report through her headphones. "We have the love letter and Juliet. Twenty-one Romeos heading home."

Savina understood the message. Love letter was code for the Sphere, she was Juliet, and obviously twenty-one of Booker's soldiers had survived. Savina guessed that scores of the Foundation's forces had been lost, some she'd known for years. She wouldn't learn until later that one hundred and eighty-two BLAXERs had died getting her and the Sphere.

Savina looked across at the silver case holding the Sphere and wondered if she would soon get to see Rip's version of the magic orb. One thing she knew for sure was that she was finally going to get that meeting with Booker, but now, would it be worth the cost? Her body trembled.

The cost, she thought. *This is just the start, a small beginning, but nonetheless, the beginning of the end. Billions live . . . or billions die.*

sixty-two

Reacting to the spectacular loss of the Sphere and Savina, the Judge convened a videoconference of the Phoenix Committee. He explained, in general terms, that due to Booker Lipton's aggression, the loss of a chance to get Gaines and the other Sphere, and now, with the Foundation Sphere in the hands of their enemy, they faced the possibility of Booker being able to successfully block the Phoenix launch.

The decision was to either put the Phoenix Initiative on hold, or to move the date up as far as possible. The Judge, who controlled one of the world's largest pharmaceutical conglomerates, and another committee member, a CEO and major shareholder of a multinational agrochemical and agricultural biotechnology corporation, agreed they could be "ready enough," within thirty days.

"So it's a matter of deployment and control," the Judge said, turning to the head of the biggest food distributor and the operator of the hospital system, which ran more than seven hundred healthcare facilities.

Both assured them they could be ready in a month. The final decision on whether to change the Phoenix launch date would be made when the Judge spoke with his government contacts, but as the meeting adjourned, everyone expected that the Phoenix Initiative would begin within four weeks, ushering in the greatest change in human history. It didn't come without risks, but they had super computers running the latest Eysen technology, which had explored a trillion scenarios. They'd been preparing for years, and the computer simulations showed they could manage it, predicting a ninety-two-point-four percent chance of success.

"Removing more than half the world's population and uniting the survivors under one government is not an easy task," the Judge told the CEO of the agrochemical corporation on a private call. "If it were simple to exterminate billions of people, someone would have already done it."

−O−

Rathmore looked at the note from Barbeau again, then quietly initiated a tsunami against the Foundation. In NSA-terms, a tsunami meant covering a target with a total and sudden surge of agency attention. By this time tomorrow, he would know every time the word "foundation" was spoken anywhere in the world, how many members it had, their blood type, complete medical histories, sexual preferences, what food they ate, and every single one of them would have all of their digital communications reviewed and summarized by real-life NSA analysis. Their movements and patterns would be followed and studied, every aspect of their companies scrutinized and cross-analyzed.

"Someone got Barbeau out," Rathmore said to Murik. "That took enormous power, so maybe I'll play his game. Chasing Booker hasn't been working out too well."

"Are you sure?" Murik asked. "Seems like you're falling into Barbeau's web."

"Maybe, but what if he's right?"

Murik nodded. "I guess we have to follow every lead, but at a time when government resources are spread thin, this seems like a dangerous gamble."

The CIA agent then excused himself. In the hall, he sent a coded message from his INU to Stellard.

−O−

Some time later, security aggressively apprehended Murik while he was trying to leave the building. The note might not have led immediately to his arrest, if Barbeau's message hadn't also included information detailing Murik's connection to the Foundation. Murik knew every second the Foundation had in advance of an NSA tsunami could make the difference between success and failure. He'd had to chance it.

Rathmore, stunned by the betrayal, savored the moment when he found Murik detained in the same holding room where he'd questioned Barbeau.

"Tsk, tsk, tsk," he said, shaking his head. "I never liked you and your sophomoric attitude, but I'll admit I never figured you for the leech. The CIA has so many holes. That's why we at the NSA have taken the lead."

"I have nothing to say."

"Really? Don't be silly, Murik, or should I call you by your code name, Wattington?" He walked over and slapped his former partner in the face. "We're finally making some progress and you're not going to slow things down now."

Murik appeared to have recovered from the slap, as if it hadn't happened, but his hands, chained to a bar under the table, were clenched. "Mind getting me a bottle of whiskey?"

"Still a comedian," Rathmore replied with a fake smile. "You're not going to get rescued like Barbeau, so we'll see how loud you laugh on your way to the gas chamber."

"You don't scare me, Rathmore," Murik said with a chuckle. "You slapped me. Where'd you learn your interrogation methods? Are you going to pull my hair next?"

Rathmore yanked Murik's head backwards by his hair and punched him in the eye. "Good idea, pulling hair. What else does the CIA teach you?" Rathmore asked as he slammed Murik's head back to the table.

Murik managed a smile. "Nothing."

"Nothing?" Rathmore echoed, as if astonished. "Oh, I've found a lot out in the past couple of hours. You might want to talk while there's still some value to your cooperation."

Murik nodded. "Prove it. Tell me what you've got, and maybe I'll fill in the blanks."

"Okay," Rathmore sneered. "I've got nothing to lose. You're not going anywhere. I've discovered enough that I believe our government, in fact, no government anywhere in the world, is actually operating in the best interest of their citizens. They're really working for the Foundation."

"It's not like that."

"Oh yeah? Then tell me what it's like."

"Tell me how you caught me."

"It turns out that the US Attorney General, who you'll recall was the FBI Director during Barbeau's pursuit of Gaines seven years ago, was the one with all the juice. He got Barbeau out, and he also told me that you were a Foundation spy. I didn't believe it, but just in case, I had your INU mirrored. Miner, the man I believe they call the Judge, whom you tried to send a message to, never received your warning."

"And you think you can beat the Foundation?" Murik scoffed. "They own this government."

"Not all of it."

"Most of it," Murik said. "If you want, you can partake in the gold."

"Partake in the gold?" Rathmore scowled. "What are we, pirates?"

"They'll pay you ten million just as a signing bonus."

"Do you think it's really wise to throw money around like that? Because your corrupt friends might need all their funds for legal fees."

"Rathmore, you don't have a clue what's really going on," Murik said. "This isn't about corruption. It's not about who's *actually* running ours, or any other government. It's about the *future*."

"We'll see about that."

"Do you like the state of the world?" Murik asked. "Because I don't. Wars, hatred, divisiveness, terrorism . . . and it's going to change. Powerful people are making sure of that. And you have to pick sides."

"I already have. I side with the United States of America."

"Naïve talk from a senior NSA official. The United States hasn't really existed for decades. Corporations run the world now. The future is either going to be decided by Booker Lipton, or the Foundation, and if you know anything at all about Booker, you'll choose the Foundation."

"Why don't you tell me all about the Foundation?" Rathmore said, smiling. "Explain their great plans for the future. Convince me."

"No. I'm not saying anything more. You think Barbeau got out of here fast? Watch how long it takes until someone shows up with a red card for me."

"Want to bet?" Rathmore asked. "You won't even be here if a red card shows up."

"You think the Foundation can't find me? You think the NSA hasn't been infiltrated?"

"I guess we're going to find out."

"Don't you see? By going after the Foundation, you're giving the entire world, actually, giving the *future*, to Booker Lipton. Is that what you want?"

"Unlike you, Murik, I don't pretend that I can control the future."

"Here's my last bit of advice for you," Murik said, staring hard at his former colleague. "Think about it and join with the Foundation before it's too late."

"Anything else?" Rathmore asked dryly.

Murik smiled. "Yeah. I'd *really* like that whiskey."

sixty-three

Savina was exhausted and stressed after the battle at the Foundation labs, several transfers from helicopter to plane to car, then to another plane, another car, another helicopter, and finally to a secret underground building buried beneath a mountain in Mexico. The woman who'd commanded the BLAXERs raid on the lab had stayed with Savina the entire time. Now, she escorted her down a long, wide corridor that was filled with such beautiful "daylight" that Savina could scarcely believe they were fifty feet below the forest floor.

After showering and changing into fresh, perfectly fitting clothes that were waiting in her private room, Savina rejoined the BLAX-commander in a common waiting area where, finally, she was turned over to another woman.

The new woman, dressed as if she'd just returned from a mountain hike, led her back to an elevator, down a long hall, and past an indoor waterfall, which cascaded at least thirty feet. A glass room, with a stunning view of the falls, was visible up ahead, where she saw Booker Lipton waiting. He stood next to the silver case which had held the Foundation's Sphere.

"Savina, thank you for coming," Booker greeted, smiling. He steepled his hands and bowed slightly. "And for bringing such a lovely gift."

"I didn't know I had a choice," Savina said, looking up at the high ceiling, which seemed to be a hole cut into the heavens. An incredibly dazzling section of the universe captivated her. It couldn't be real, but it appeared so authentic that she gasped.

"I believe you asked for this meeting," Booker continued, enjoying her reaction to his creation.

She nodded, thought of saying she hadn't asked for her lab to be destroyed or all those people to be killed, but it was too late for that.

"Why haven't you opened it?" she asked, motioning to the silver case. "Don't you want to see your prize?"

"I thought you might do the honors, tell me what you've discovered in there."

Savina could see the strength of the man before her. His dark eyes concealed a depth of knowledge, his charming smile adding to the powerful confidence he exuded, but she knew he wanted to stop the Phoenix Initiative. To her, at least before her discoveries of the past few days, Phoenix had seemed like the only hope for the future of the species. But now, maybe in the multiverse, maybe with the wrinkle of time-shifting, with the contact of the Cosegans, there just might be another way.

"Have you ever considered the possibility of the multiverse?" she asked.

"Yes, I have. In fact, I've lived my life in a constant state of considering the possibility of everything."

"Can I show you something?" she asked, trying to reconcile the public image of Booker with the rumors she'd heard about him, UQP, and the Inner Movement.

"Of course," he said, turning his palm to the silver case. "It's your show."

While they waited for the Cosega Sequence to complete, Savina began with the basics. "It wasn't that long ago that people were certain that the Earth was flat, but it is round. People were also positive that the heavens revolved around the Earth, that humanity was the center of the universe, that the Sun, the other stars, and planets, circled us. Those theories also proved wrong," Savina said, pointing up to the stunning stars filling the ceiling. "Once we knew of nothing beyond our solar system, yet we now know Earth is part of a solar system which is one of millions in a galaxy, and that galaxy, in turn, is one of billions in the universe. These ideas were once laughed at and controversial, but each one of them is now accepted as fact. All those things that were once just crazy theories all turned out to be true."

"Yes," Booker said, nodding, waiting for her revelation.

"The multiverse is real," Savina blurted. "It's being studied at MIT, Cambridge, Cal Tech, Oxford, Harvard."

"And the University of Hawaii," Booker added, smiling, "I know. You don't have to convince me. I've looked into the Sphere. I've seen remarkable things far beyond my understanding, even past the point of reasonable description. Some people think the Inner Movement is some New Age cult, but it is nothing like that. IM is more about physics than psychics. The Inner Movement is after dreams, answers, what is possible, and what we have lost or forgotten across time. I have no doubt the multiverse is a part of that."

"Then what are your reservations?"

"You're aware of my little UQP project?"

"I'd hardly call more than a thousand of the brightest scientists in the world a '*little*' project."

"Yes, but consider all the things we humans have wasted our time on. Do you realize we color our food to make it prettier? We make things that are disposable. All the waste, the plastic, fossil fuels, weapons . . . " He stared off into the distance for a moment. "Anyway, it seems like a very tiny project compared to what it should be."

"What have *you* discovered?" Savina asked.

"So many things which we can discuss at length, but first I have a question. It's the same thing we've been asking since that hot, humid day in Virginia when the Eysen-Sphere and other artifacts were first unearthed. Who left them there, and why?"

She nodded.

"If these were stagnant, benign, pieces of pottery or bone, gold idols or bronze tools, that would be one thing," Booker continued. "But the Spheres are the seeds of civilization. No," he corrected, "they're much more. They're the memory of all of existence."

"At least in this universe," Savina said.

"Yes, but why?" Booker asked. "Why does such a thing exist? Why was it left there? And why did we find it?"

"And why was there more than one? How many were there? I have reason to believe there were nine, possibly more."

Booker's eyes brightened at the confirmation of his research. "I also have a theory that Jesus had one, and many other great thinkers across the ages. One can look back in human history and see great people or great achievements that seem so out of step with their times, it's as if they knew something—"

"Or had seen something," Savina finished, "that others of their day had not."

"Right. Were the Pyramids constructed so perfectly because of ingenuity that radically exceeded the capabilities of the day or, did they have help?"

Savina smirked. "Some think it was aliens."

"Maybe it was," Booker said, "but not in how they think. Perhaps an Eysen-Sphere was present in ancient Egypt. It's so advanced, even now, that to us it seems like an *alien* artifact. What if they only saw occasional glimpses?"

"Rip has had full access to an Eysen-Sphere for seven years, and during all that time, working constantly on decoding and dissecting it, how much of what he's discovered have I found in the years I've been working on this one?" Savina asked. "They contain the infinite. I'm willing to bet we've crossed very little common ground."

"Rip has a theory that the Spheres are able to personalize themselves to the viewer."

"It is possible that they read DNA."

"Without a blood or tissue sample?"

"We do touch them you know," Savina said, looking down at her hands. "Their technology is light-years beyond ours. They could do it."

"But why would they? And who are they?"

"We may never know."

"We *have* to know," Booker said, sounding almost desperate. "Don't you understand? We have to know because that is what will save us!"

"Save us from what?"

"Don't tell me you've worked with the Foundation for the past four years and you don't know what I'm talking about."

"I do," she said quietly. "You mean save us from ourselves."

"The Foundation is wrong in how they're going about it, and they're doing it for the wrong reasons."

"To save humanity is wrong?"

"To enrich the elites even further? That's what's wrong."

"What do you mean? *Somebody* has to fund it. The world can't just save itself. And you have little room to talk about enriching yourself."

"Savina, they're using what they know of the future as an excuse. Sure, they want to save humanity because *they* don't want to die, and they want their children, grandchildren, et cetera to survive. They want a legacy. They want heirs."

"This isn't about money," she said, appalled.

"Yes, it is. The coming crisis may come either way, but the results *can* be controlled, and they want to make sure it goes their way. That they end up ruling and profiting forever."

She controlled her temper and did what she always did at times of uncertainty. She thought. The defensiveness she felt might be justified, or it might be coming from guilt, from knowing she might have been helping the wrong side. Whereas Booker had an awful reputation, she intuitively trusted him, and where the Foundation had an illustrious reputation of generosity, her intuition told her there was a lot she didn't know, and maybe her world was a little backwards.

"What do you mean exactly?" Savina asked. "Do you have proof?"

"I know what our Sphere showed."

"Which is?"

"That they're going to engineer the plague to eliminate whom they want, and to make sure they alone sell the cure. The Phoenix Initiative."

Booker expected her to be shocked, but instead she replied calmly.

"The Foundation is engineering a plague in order to stop a larger outbreak that could wipe us all out, and they're making sure that we have the cure available. What would you have them do, let the plague wipe us out before we have a cure? Many will die, of course, but we can't avoid that. The Phoenix Initiative is the best chance we have. With it, we'll save as many as we can."

"Billions will die!"

"If the Foundation does not act," she snapped.

"No, billions die *because* of the Foundation. They're seeking to control the population by outbreak and vaccine, a cycle of dependency on the pharmaceutical and agrochemical industries."

"I don't believe that."

"Do you believe the Sphere?"

"Of course."

"Then you will believe it," Booker said as he pressed a button. A ten-foot section of the wall next to them lit with images. A few seconds later, she found herself staring at Rip Gaines.

sixty-four

The Judge didn't yet know that Wattington, aka Murik, the Foundation's best inside source in the government's search for Gaines, had been compromised. Plenty of Foundation agents had infiltrated the CIA, NSA, FBI, Defense Department, Justice Department, Homeland Security, just about anywhere money could buy influence, which was everywhere, but Murik had been at the top of the Sphere situation.

Moving up the launch of the Phoenix Initiative would be much easier if they could find one of the other seven Spheres Savina had mentioned, but that seemed unlikely, even if any of them still existed. Whoever had one would obviously guard it and keep it secret, but he suspected they were still buried somewhere. The idea of seven more was so new and mind-boggling that he really didn't know *what* he thought.

The Foundation had already put its considerable resources to work in an effort to locate the two Spheres in Booker's possession. The Judge gave the order to seek and destroy any location that could be used to hide Gaines, Savina, and the Spheres. Going forward, he would operate under the assumption that the launch would proceed without the Spheres.

"I don't like heading blindly into the most dangerous period in human history, but the plans were completed based on years of data pulled from the Sphere," the Judge had told the committee. "The sooner we move, the less chance we have that some variable will change."

The Judge also knew that as long as he had the five scientists who authored the time-shift paper, he could prevent Booker's UQP team from manipulating something in the past to derail Phoenix.

He'd just sent several teams to Hawaii in order to assist Taz's return to the island. A large operation had also been secretly put into place to fly the five important scientists to a hidden Foundation facility in Central America, where Savina's two assistants, who had been rescued from the fire at the lab, would be waiting.

−O−

Ever since he'd let Gale and Rip escape seven years earlier, Barbeau had been heading a powerful DIRT unit, the deep covert group of trustworthy agents within the Bureau known only to the former FBI director, who was now the US Attorney General. DIRT's mission, to uncover corruption inside the NSA, CIA, FBI, and other government agencies, had yielded hundreds of bad agents and officials.

However, the Attorney General had decided on a bold strategy: rather than expose it and risk destroying the very fabric of the government, DIRT continued to track and monitor its targets, waiting for an opportunity to cut out the biggest source of the corruption, namely the Foundation. DIRT had also discovered much of Booker's infiltration into many agencies, but for unknown reasons, the Attorney General had determined this to be less of a threat.

Answering only to the Attorney General and having access to MONSTERs, Barbeau exercised significant power, which he applied with subtle subterfuge. He'd learned early on that the Foundation and Booker were locked in a battle over the Spheres and, ultimately, the future, yet the insanity of the Foundation's Phoenix Initiative remained murky to Barbeau. Because of the Foundation's blatant and widespread abuse and bribery, disguised as contributions, grants, contract awards, and other various ploys, it was easier to target, so he had no problem with his boss's directives to follow every Foundation lead.

For years, Barbeau had believed the Foundation's actions were based mostly on corporate greed. Recently, however, as more information surfaced about the Phoenix Initiative, he began to piece together the absolute terror of their true motives. Barbeau assumed the Attorney General saw Booker's empire, although also frequently on the wrong side of the law, as a necessary counterbalance to the Foundation. Booker's well known "by any means necessary" mantra meant he bribed, stole, "removed" threats, and did whatever else he deemed appropriate to achieve his goals.

But Barbeau's once-firm belief in a black and white – right and wrong, good versus evil - world had fallen into many shades of gray, like ashes blowing in the wind. The complexities of the crisis were well beyond him, and in order to have as few of his excruciating, relentless headaches as possible, he wanted to keep it that way.

When the news of Gaines' surfacing reached the back rooms of the intelligence community, Barbeau's DIRT team had picked up the information. With fresh data, as reports poured in and the drama flushed out all sides, the horrific details of the Foundation's ultimate plan were confirmed. Once Barbeau learned the truth and intent of the secret Phoenix Initiative, a scheme he could barely believe was real, his head pounded constantly and he had hardly slept. The Attorney General ordered all resources available to close in on the Foundation.

The Attorney General knew the government, over-burdened by massive corruption, could not fight off the Foundation alone. It would be like a brain surgeon operating on himself. Several times over the last few years he'd done things that would help and favor Booker's side of the epic battle, not out of loyalty to Booker, but as a way to keep a balance of power. Now that assistance was critical to potentially save billions of lives.

After intercepting a transmission from Stellard, DIRT had learned of the ship of scientists in international waters in the Pacific. Barbeau got a MONSTER to clear the way for US Navy intervention. SEALs boarded the *Bright Future* and, after a brief firefight during which they overwhelmed Foundation agents and rescued the five authors, Barbeau quietly arranged to release the scientists to Booker's people in Hawaii.

Taz, now in custody, was already undergoing a rigorous interrogation. DIRT agents were searching for Stellard, and expected to arrest him within hours. They didn't have enough to indict the Judge yet, but Barbeau had other ideas.

During an encrypted conversation with the Attorney General, Barbeau asked for authorization to take more drastic measures. The conversation had been short.

"That would be too difficult in the current climate," the Attorney General had said. "For us, anyway. Why don't you broach the subject with Booker directly?"

Barbeau agreed, and that would be his first step, but he assumed Booker would have already done it if he could. Barbeau decided that should Booker decline, he'd enlist several top DIRT agents into his plan to assassinate the Judge, even without the Attorney General's blessing.

Under Booker's direction, Huang had been feeding Barbeau and DIRT information for years, but Barbeau had never fully understood the extent of the Foundation threat. Now, however, he knew time was short. He dialed a secret number and waited for several minutes while the call was routed in a ping-pong pattern around the globe. Huang smiled when he saw the incoming communication was from the man he'd helped to free, and someone he knew would be a big help in the continuing fight against the Foundation.

—O—

Harmer, after a rough interrogation session, which included shock "therapy," had been freed by Booker's operatives in Hawaii. Her liberation had come at a cost— two BLAXERs and four Foundation agents had died. They got her onto a waiting plane with the five scientists where she collapsed into the seat, a nurse tending to her injuries. Also on board was Professor Yamane, whose death had been falsely reported by Honolulu Police. Barring any interference, their plane would land on El Perdido in a few hours. In spite of Harmer's repeated attempts, none of Booker's people seemed able to confirm Cira's status.

sixty-five

"It's you!" Rip gasped upon seeing Savina across the large INU projection. Booker, excited about the two of them working on the Spheres together, had arranged the video conference to start the process he saw as critical to stopping the Foundation's Phoenix Initiative.

Savina seemed surprised to be recognized, but only in the event itself. The fact that he knew what she looked like actually reassured her. "Professor Gaines, a pleasure to finally meet you, and so nice that you're not dead."

"Who are you?" he asked, still in a daze, as if not believing she was real. "And do you really have a Sphere? Has it survived?"

"Yes," she said with a smile, moving so he could see the other Sphere.

"Where did you get it?" he asked.

Booker was going to break in and suggest they compare notes about their Eysen-Spheres at another time, but he realized the importance of the two brilliant scientists—also the only two people on the planet who'd extensively studied the Spheres—to find their own common point of discovery with each other.

"The Foundation."

"The Foundation has a Sphere? No!" Rip groaned, as if he'd been shot. "How long have they had it?"

"I've been working on it for four years," Savina said. "But I assure you, it is no matter of concern."

"*Concern?*" Rip barked. "You're right. Concern is far too mild a term. The Foundation having a Sphere is a matter of Armageddon!"

"I was hoping you two would agree to work together," Booker interjected.

"Together?" Rip was shocked. "Booker, she's with the *Foundation.*"

"Not anymore," he said, looking at Savina.

"Is she your prisoner?" Rip asked.

Savina raised her eyebrows to Booker as if to echo Rip's question.

"She is free to go, but I'm going to have to insist on keeping the Foundation Sphere," Booker said. "I collect them, you know." He gave her a quick wink and a half-smile.

"I'm not leaving without the Sphere," Savina replied.

"Excellent," Booker said. "She has agreed to stay. Should I fly her out? Aren't you desperate to see what happens when we get two Spheres side-by-side?"

"Absolutely," Rip said.

"Of course," Savina concurred.

"But her loyalties are with the Foundation," Rip protested.

"Rip, if that were true, do you think I would allow her to visit El Perdido?" Booker ventured.

"How about it?" Rip asked, looking directly at Savina. "Are you finished with the dark side? Will you disavow the Foundation?"

"Rip, she may not be ready to make that decision yet," Booker warned, "but I have every confidence that you'll convince her within hours of her arrival." He ended his statement with a nod to Rip, which clearly meant, "*This is how it is. Trust me.*"

Rip took a deep breath and nodded back. "I guess we'll see you soon."

"I look forward to it," Savina replied.

"She'll be there in three hours." Booker signed off and then suggested Savina try to get some sleep on the plane.

The woman who had taken her to Booker's private office appeared with a small duffle bag. She led Savina to a helipad concealed in a large open cavern and explained that there were clothes and toiletries in the bag. There would be food and water available on the plane.

As the helicopter flew out of the cave, Savina reached for the beautiful array of sushi and realized she hadn't said goodbye to Booker. But sitting next to her was the silver case with the Sphere, so Savina knew she'd see him again.

sixty-six

Gale and Rip walked out onto the skyroom balcony overlooking the Pacific. Rip told her, with uncharacteristically grand gestures and lavish descriptions, of floating in the blackness and seeing the woman with the other Eysen-Sphere. "It was Savina."

"She's with the Foundation," Gale said. "She's the enemy. We've been fighting her, without realizing it, for years."

"I know."

"And what did the Foundation learn from their Sphere? Are we lost? Have they won?"

"We're about to have both Spheres, and I suppose we're going to learn what they learned," Rip said. "It's difficult to imagine someone having so much knowledge of the Sphere that she could use it to reach me, yet not being affected by it. Not understanding the malicious intent of the Foundation."

"We were never able to find the other Sphere," Gale mused. "What else has Savina discovered that we haven't?"

Rip slowly shook his head, staring into the distance. "The possibilities of the two Spheres, of another field of research . . . it's thrilling to imagine."

"Look," Gale said, pointing at a plane.

Even though they were expecting Cira, an approaching plane still made them nervous. It turned out to be the doctor and a nurse from the eye institute. The team went right to work preparing for Cira's arrival. Staff had already readied Cira's old first-floor room, and now with equipment brought by the doctor, they converted it into a full-fledged hospital room.

−O−

The next plane was the one they'd been waiting for. Huang had messaged them giving them fifteen minutes to prepare for Cira's arrival. Gale, Rip, and the medical team stood at the end of the runway. Although they'd been warned that Cira would still be sedated, Gale kept thinking that she would run from the plane yelling "Mommy, Mommy!"

That didn't happen, yet the sight of her daughter, safely returned, left her crying. Regret for all the time their daughter had been alone, in danger, and how close they had come to losing her, kept the tears flowing.

When Cira was safely in her darkened room, the doctor began his examination. "There is only so much I can tell at this point," he said, "but our protocols were followed, and she suffered no apparent damage during her travels."

Hope.

Two hours later, she woke up. "Mommy?"

"Oh, Cira, I'm right here. Mommy is right here."

"Mommy, it's dark. I can't see."

"Your eyes were hurt, sweetie. Do you remember?"

"The playground."

"Yes, yes. That's right."

"I'm sorry."

"Oh, no, sweetie. It's not your fault."

"When can I see again?"

"Soon, sweetie. You'll see again soon. The doctor did some tests, and he needs to look at your eyes now that you're awake. I need you to be a brave girl and do what the doctor says, okay?"

"Okay, Mommy."

Gale's elation turned to overwhelming gratitude and sorrow for Harmer and Kruse for sacrificing so much to save her and Cira. *This moment wouldn't be possible if not for their heroic efforts,* she thought. *Booker somehow managed the impossible.*

She said a silent thank you to each one of them, including Booker, but it was the thought of Kruse that made her cry. *You lost everything, so that I wouldn't have to. Please forgive me, Kruse.*

Rip came in while the doctor was taking the bandages off. He didn't want to excite Cira until the doctor was through, so he remained quiet.

A few minutes later, the doctor finished and asked to speak to Gale and Rip out in the hall.

Gale looked at the doctor, alarmed, and then to Rip. "I don't want to leave her yet," she said. Rip walked out with the doctor.

"She's going to see," the doctor said in hushed tones, "but there will be significant vision loss in her left eye."

"How much?" Rip asked sadly, looking back into the room.

"Hard to say, but I don't think she'll regain much use of that eye. It's the one which sustained the most trauma. There'll be visible scarring, and once she's older you might consider cosmetic surgery."

Rip nodded.

"Mommy, when will Daddy be home?" Rip heard Cira ask from inside the room.

"I'm right here, baby," Rip said, nodding to the doctor and rushing into the room. He took her hand. "How's my little girl?"

"I got hurt, Daddy."

"You sure did."

"Did the doctor say I'm going to be all better?"

Rip glanced back at Gale as she went out to talk to the doctor.

"You're going to be more than that, Cira," Rip said, squeezing her hand. *She's alive*, he thought. *We saved her. My daughter is going to grow up!*

– O –

Rathmore suddenly began receiving data from an unnamed source about the Foundation. Huang had many channels and aliases at his disposal. At the same time, the NSA director and King were locked in a power struggle. The director somehow came out on top and took him off the Gaines case. "Too many failures" was the reason given, but Rathmore suspected something else. In either case, the Foundation was a meatier assignment, and one that he thought might lead him back to Gaines, or at least to Booker.

Stellard was arrested in Thailand after an email tip appeared in Barbeau's inbox. The sender showed as anonymous. It had been difficult for Huang to trace Stellard, but simple for him to make his email to Barbeau untraceable. Some of what Huang did for Booker looked easy, but years of work often came down to precisely timed, complex moves that might involve dozens of operatives, EAMI, and help from the Inner Movement.

Dozens of the dirtiest Foundation agents whom DIRT had been watching for years were brought in. For the first time in his life, the Judge was suddenly on the defensive. Ultimately, his wealth and power would protect him, but his grand plan would be slowed, at least enough to give his opponents time to stop Phoenix, especially for Gale and Rip. If they were able to try the time-shifting theories, every moment counted.

Later, the scientists arrived on El Perdido. An unexpected guest, arriving on the same plane, staggered in and walked quietly to Cira's bed. With tears in her eyes, Harmer, aged at least ten years it seemed, bent down and softly kissed the little girl. "I'm so sorry about everything."

Gale immediately jumped up and hugged Harmer. "Rip told me everything you went through to save our daughter. Thank you. Thank you for protecting Cira. I'll never forget it. Cira will be so happy to see you when she wakes up."

"*See* me?" Harmer asked.

Gale nodded, smiling widely.

Harmer let out a joyful laugh. "We did it." She turned back to look at Cira. "I hope she'll forgive me. In the confusion of the raid on the hospital, I wasn't able to save her little cat. As they dragged me out of the room, the last thing I saw was the cat laying on the floor."

Gale pulled the blanket back and revealed the cat, resting next to Cira's hand.

"How did that get here?"

"Crying Man."

sixty-seven

The meeting, less awkward than expected, stirred much excitement amongst Gale, Rip, and Savina for the possibilities of the Spheres. Savina might have been working for the other side, but she was a brilliant physicist, who seemingly knew as much about the Sphere as they did.

After the initial introductions, Rip pointed to the silver case. "Is that it? The other Sphere?"

She nodded, smiling, as if she'd brought a present.

Gale and Rip had already decided not to go to the El Perdido lab, but instead to view both Spheres in the skyroom. They drove there in a single golf cart, but Gale had stopped off in Cira's room.

As Savina stepped into the skyroom, she set down the silver case and went straight for Rip's Sphere. "It's the same," she said.

"May I see yours?" Rip asked, motioning toward the case.

"Yes, yes. I can't wait to see what they do next to each other."

Rip carried the case to the table that already held his Sphere. He carefully opened it and stared disbelievingly for a moment. Then he lifted it out and held it, absorbed in awe. The reality of a second Sphere seemed to confirm that the Cosegans were more than just an ancient civilization.

"They did this," he whispered to himself. "They had to know we would find them, but why?"

"They made nine of them," Savina said.

"Nine?" Rip asked, brought out of his spell. "*Nine*! My God, I thought there were only three. Are they . . . did they survive?"

"I don't know. During what I call a 'swallowing', the information was put into my head. Imagine if we had all nine."

"Why nine?" Terrified and elated at the same time, Rip could not slow his racing mind. *Why would they have made nine? How hard had they been to construct? Who else had found them? Where were they? Did they all need to be used together to ultimately unlock their secrets? Nine! Why nine?*

"Why any?" Savina replied.

Rip nodded. The burning question had consumed so much of his life, but he repeated quietly, "Why *nine*?"

"Shall we?" Savina asked when she saw Gale enter the room.

"Do you have a chip?"

She nodded and pulled it from her pocket.

They set the Spheres next to each other and Savina and Rip touched the sides of their respective Spheres to illuminate them. They were amazed from the moment the orbs lit up and ran identical sequences. Once they completed the run, the Spheres remained in a standard state.

"What, no fireworks? Gale asked, joining them.

"I did think there might be a cumulative amplification," Savina agreed.

Rip was also disappointed. He explained to Savina the Five Cosega Mysteries and asked if she could answer any of them:

1. *What is the Sphere?*
2. *Who were the Cosegans?*
3. *Where did they come from?*
4. *Why did they leave the Sphere?*
5. *What happened to them?*

"Although I didn't call them that, I've been looking for answers to those same questions, but most of my time has been spent trying to understand the physics of this thing. How could they do this? Contain all this energy in this small object?"

"Any-sized object," Gale said.

"Exactly," Savina agreed.

They spent the rest of the day comparing the experiences they'd had, and what each had learned over the years. During their deliberations, Gale and Rip continuously took turns visiting Cira, but she mostly slept. Harmer had also stationed herself in a comfortable chair next to Cira's bed.

Savina shared the detailed information about the "swallowings" and Rip told her of floating in the blackness. However, it was the Crying Man who fascinated Savina most. She believed he was the man she had seen the day before.

"It was the first time I'd ever seen a person within the Sphere," Savina explained.

Gale and Rip were quite surprised to learn that. "How did you manage to find your way around without a guide?"

"Simple," Savina replied. "I followed the laws of physics. Not that the Cosegans are subject to the same laws we are, but they seem to have known all of ours and more. Between that and my knowledge of the universe, I could figure out a lot." She looked at them and shrugged. "Saying that would be like someone coming from another planet and claiming to have explored Earth after they'd only spent a few minutes in a child's sandbox."

"Yeah," Gale said. "After seven years, we're still in the sandbox too."

"Oh, we might be on the beach," Rip said, "but we're not even close to where we should be." He went on to explain the Divinations, and that they had spent most of their time with the Sphere trying to use it to find a way to change the future.

"That's kind of what we've been doing at the Foundation," Savina admitted.

"But part of what we've been trying to stop is the Foundation's idiotic Phoenix Initiative."

"The Phoenix Initiative may sound crazy to you, but it is designed to save the human race."

"By *killing* half of them?" Gale asked.

"Better than losing *all* of them," Savina snapped.

"But haven't you seen the results in your Sphere?" Rip asked. "It's disastrous. It's the end."

"That's not what we've seen."

"Well, maybe you haven't been deep enough," Gale said. "How far out have you looked?"

"Phoenix replaces the coming uncontrollable plague with ours, one designed to be controllable. The aftermath is a utopian world instead of a brutal end of humanity," Savina said. "Haven't you seen the gasping end?"

"Your so-called utopian world is short-lived, and leads to a horrific war," Rip said. "Let me show you what's really going to happen." He manipulated the light and forms projecting from his Sphere.

Fifteen minutes later, Savina shook her head and stammered. "I... I don't understand how they can be so different." Before Rip or Gale could comment, she continued. "Unless... unless it's the Copenhagen Interpretation."

"That nothing is real until we observe it?" Rip asked.

Savina was impressed. "Yes. How do you know of it?"

"It's one of the basics of Booker's Universal Quantum Physics."

"Of course, UQP has borrowed so much from Quantum Mechanics," Savina said.

"And the rest from metaphysics," Gale added. "Booker is the major backer behind the Inner Movement."

"I know," Savina said. "A lot of people think he's crazy. But then a lot of people thought Niels Bohr was crazy, even Einstein."

"Bohr?" Gale asked.

"He first proposed that nothing is real until we observe it," Savina explained. "And although he and Einstein actually got along well, they famously opposed each other on this epic point."

"Who was right?"

"Most say Bohr, but even after all these decades, we still don't know for sure. But if Bohr was right, it would seem to invalidate Booker's idea that Einstein might have had a Sphere, or at least looked into one."

"Maybe not, as we were saying earlier," Rip began. "The Sphere is incomprehensibly vast. He couldn't have seen everything, solved all the equations, so anything is possible."

"That also makes my point," Savina said. "Quantum Physics tells us that there is no such thing as reality, only the potential of reality."

"Meaning?" Gale asked.

"Reality depends on the observer. So what your Sphere showed you about the future is not what mine showed me."

Rip regarded her carefully. "More than one possible future," he murmured. "That has certainly been a central theme to the work of Clastier, and specifically the Cosegans."

"So which is right?" Gale asked.

"The one that we see," Savina said. "So let's make sure we're seeing the same thing from now on."

Suddenly, the two Spheres glowed as if on fire, and from within the flames jumbles of mathematical equations appeared in an endless stream. The brightness of the scene, nearly blinding in its intensity, left them gasping for a few moments until their senses adjusted, or the frequency of the display changed, or time slowed down, they had no idea. Then the Spheres merged, or rather, became part of a sea of nine glowing orbs, which fractured into millions of smaller Spheres. Inside each of those millions, even more were visible. Rip tried to focus on just one, but it only enlarged and even more spheres appeared from within that one until he became lost in the flood.

It's infinite, he thought. They swirled and blurred as if all the stars in the universe had merged into one single spot, the Sphere. Then he realized what it was showing him . . . the multiverse. Somehow the Sphere was able to display what was almost impossible even to conceive. *Somehow*, he thought, *the Cosegans found a way to capture the multiverse.*

"They mapped it," he said out loud. "How did they know?"

"Because," Savina answered, already ahead of his thoughts, "the Cosegans have traveled the multiverse. They know the secrets."

sixty-eight

Soon the two Spheres returned to their pre-merging state. However, each seemed faster, brighter, more powerful. For the next forty-eight hours, unaware if it was night or day, Gale, Rip, and Savina worked constantly on the two Spheres, showing each other where they'd been and the progress that had been made. Theories were discussed and experiments undertaken. With the possibility that more Spheres existed, the chance that the Foundation would react aggressively due to the loss of Savina and her Sphere, coupled with the optimism of being able to pool their resources, they felt a jointly renewed sense of urgency to find answers to the five mysteries and to try to bend the future into something survivable, maybe even something good.

Savina explained the multiverse findings and what she'd discovered about time-shifts. Rip showed her the papers the five scientists, all of whom she knew by reputation, had written on the time-shifts.

"So it is possible. I knew it!" she exclaimed after reading their work. "What if the Cosegans mastered all of this?"

"What?" Rip asked.

"The *multiverse*," Savina said, as if nothing could be more obvious. "What if they found a way to travel between universes?"

"How could they do that?" Gale asked. "Is that even theoretically possible?"

The question of the physics was an issue Savina had studied at MIT. It came down to the possibilities of which laws would govern — the ones from the universe that contained the Milky Way galaxy and current human existence on Earth, or the neighboring universe.

"Of course it's possible."

"But how do you know that?" Rip asked, wanting to hear her explanation in scientific terms.

"Because *anything* is possible. Even traveling across millions of light years. There is always a way. They could be talking to us from there now."

"So are you suggesting that eleven million Earth years," Gale began, "isn't that long in another universe?"

"Anything is possible given enough time," Rip said, grasping her concept. "And time is a funny thing."

"Eternal inflation," Savina said. "Dark energy pushing away everything at an ever-accelerating rate. The entire world of physics is ever demonstrating the infinite. What are smaller than neutrons and protons? Quarks. And smaller than quarks? Strings, and they form everything, depending on how they vibrate, including extra dimensions."

"The Spheres are somehow produced in that way?" Gale asked, not sure she understood her own question. She still didn't know how her plane had been made to vanish.

"Each Sphere shows the observer what they see. Mine shows the multiverse, time-shifts and physics. Rip's showed him Clastier, ancient cultures, and brought those Divinations to life. Clastier and Malachy's Spheres showed the flaws and fraud of the Church. When the UQP scientists viewed it, they found time-shift and an understanding of our universe."

"But they've all shown prophetic visions of the future," Gale insisted.

"Because time is the common denominator to all of us," Rip said. "Everyone wants to know what's coming, and a Sphere easily shows us the meaninglessness of time."

Ironically, it was then that the five authors of the time-shift theory, along with the sniffling professor, knocked on the skyroom's door. For the next twenty-four hours they argued, envisioned, and debated the possibilities of actually conducting a time-shift experiment and whether or not the multiverse existed.

"Eternal inflation, Dark Energy, string theory, they all point to the existence of the multiverse," Savina said, "but the Spheres prove it."

"Then where are the Cosegans?" Dabnowski asked. "What happened to them?"

Before Rip could address the topic, his INU lit up with a call from Booker. Afterwards, Rip whispered to Gale and Savina, "The Foundation is moving up the launch of Phoenix. We may have only weeks to stop it."

"You know more about it than any of us," Gale said to Savina. "You must know a way to get to them in time."

Savina felt guilty about her prior work with the Foundation, which made her even more determined. She looked around the room at the incredible talent and brainpower, and at the two Spheres, which were continuously projecting one astonishing thing after another. "We'll solve it," she said. "We need to buy time."

"We need Crying Man," Gale said.

Savina's fascination with their stories of the Crying Man had led to much frustration, as they could not seem to raise him. They all agreed that if they could figure out how to accept the help he had been offering, they could find the answers and change the future.

"The Judge once told me that if the Sphere showed a different future without the plague, climate changes, and World War III, he would be happy to call off the Phoenix Initiative."

"And you believed him?" Gale asked.

"He's not a bad man," Savina replied. "You may think it's crazy to engineer a plague that will kill half the world's population, but you've seen the future. It's hellish, and possibly ends in human extinction. The Phoenix Initiative stops all three of the Death Divinations."

"It seems like throwing the baby out with the bathwater," Gale said. "There must be a better way."

"What is it?" Savina asked.

"Crying Man, a representative from the most advanced civilization the world has ever known, has offered to help us," Gale said. "That is the better way."

"What if Savina is wrong?" Rip asked. "What if he isn't real? We don't know that he isn't an elaborate AI program."

"He's *real*," Gale insisted.

"But how do we know?" Rip asked.

"Because our little girl is asleep downstairs," Gale said. "Cira's alive because he said he would keep her safe, and she'll see again because he *did* keep her safe."

sixty-nine

Gale, Rip, and Savina, along with the six other scientists, worked late into the night. Everyone was on edge that the NSA might find them and barge in at any moment. With the report that the Foundation was working to unleash Phoenix as soon as possible, there was a strange mix of tension, pressure, elation, and awe as they pushed into the depths of the Spheres.

The next morning, while working through a breakfast prepared by Booker's staff, Savina suddenly pulled Rip and Gale aside.

"What if," Savina began in an excited but hushed voice, "Crying Man is not saying 'help' as an offer *to* you, but rather he is *asking* for *your* help?"

"Asking *us* for help? It's Artificial Intelligence. He's not really inside the Sphere," Rip said.

"I know what you think," Savina said. "But pretend everything I said is right, that he could still be alive in some realm, and is trying to talk to us. What if he *is* real? Not *inside* the Sphere, but communicating *through* it."

The other scientists all stopped their conversations and listened to what had become a heated debate.

"Communicating from where?"

"From the time of the Cosegans."

"He is talking to us, or at least interacting with us," Gale said. "I mean, wait until he stands in front of us. You'll see. I love Crying Man. He's . . . he's *changed* us . . .

you know how you feel when you see him. The man has mastered love."

"But he died eleven million years ago," Rip interrupted. "We're just experiencing his avatar."

"What if the Cosegans are not in the past?" Savina suggested. "What if they are in the future?"

"How could that be?" Rip asked.

"Time is not a line, it is a single instant," Dabnowski said, joining in the discussion. "Think of it as an infinite loop."

"The sign for infinity, the sideways figure eight," another time-shift author added. "No beginning, no end, just always in motion."

"So the Cosegans are behind us *and* ahead of us," Savina said.

"That would mean Crying Man is . . . " Rip started.

"Still alive," Savina finished.

"Then he really is communicating with us, as a person, in real time," Gale breathed. Her blue eyes filled with unshed tears at the realization.

"Yes." Rip nodded slowly. "Oh, what if it's true . . . "

"And he needs our help," Savina said.

"If we save the Cosegans, we save ourselves," Rip said.

seventy

Gale and Rip went searching for the Crying Man within their Sphere. They pulled up all the data they had on every occasion he'd appeared and replicated the conditions. Savina also tried to find him using the same technique in conjuring the exact situation, the only time she'd caught a glimpse of him.

It was nearly ten p.m. when the heavens, thick with stars, changed to blue. Not the blue of the daytime, rather the deep indigo and electric shades Rip had seen in the Cosegan city of light. But the exact hue didn't really matter, it was the startling fact that the world around them had been so transformed, as if to warn of what Rip knew was about to happen—two worlds colliding.

As the outside air filtered blue and purple light, inside the atmosphere glowed white, and suddenly, standing next to the two Spheres, the Crying Man reached out his arms and turned his palms toward the ceiling.

Rip, as astonished as the rest of them, looked on. He had enough history with the "mythical figure" that he managed to ask the vital question. "Do you need *our* help?"

"Yes," Crying Man said.

Rip looked quickly around, trying to confirm that Crying Man's response had actually been audible. Gale nodded.

"How can we help?" Rip asked, trying to adjust to the fact that Crying Man was still alive.

Crying Man's gaze swept around to all those assembled. Fresh tears ran down his dark cheeks. "We waited so long for you to find us." He paused and looked directly at Rip. "We are dying."

Rip, ashamed that he'd never thought to ask if he could help the Cosegans before, took a few seconds to answer. "Why are you dying?"

"Because of this," he waved his arm as if indicating all of the current world. "You found us in your past, but *our* past is your future."

Rip looked at Savina.

"As you move steadily toward your own destruction, you are also destroying us."

Rip tried to put it all together. "The Cosegans' past is our future," he said. "You really are before the beginning."

Crying Man nodded. "We left nine Ohsahs, what you call Eysens or Spheres. We knew who would find them because we have the history. The Spheres were to be found at different intervals during the past five thousand years." He stopped, faded slightly. "It has been very difficult to get through to you across all time, and with your limited perceptions. And," he hesitated, "our ability to transcend that continues to weaken. I could not be here without the use of at least two Ohsahs."

"What happened to the others Spheres, er, Ohsahs?" Rip asked, thinking of the Egyptian pyramids, the Incas, the Mayans . . . could they all have had Spheres?

"They were used to advance your civilizations rather than to help ours," Crying Man said quietly, yet firmly.

Rip thought of the greed and selfishness of people. He wondered if anyone in the long history of the Spheres had acted differently from him. *What could have been?* Even trying with all of his being to save the future, he'd never thought of saving the past. *And I'm an archaeologist!*

"The Ohsahs are complex," Crying Man continued. "It is not easy for people to find their true meaning, but the Ohsahs were all that we could leave. They are not solid objects, as you think. Ohsahs are contained energy . . .

crafted from stars, just like you and me. They hold everything," Crying Man looked at Savina, "because they are *everything*."

"So you came from us," Gale said in a hushed tone. "That means we must have survived."

"You did once, or we would not have been, and had we never been, you would not have been," Crying Man said stoically.

"The past depends on the future," Rip said.

Crying Man nodded.

"Are you alive . . . somewhere?" Rip asked. "Or are you some sort of artificial intelligence program inside the Sphere?"

The scientists in the room waited in breathless anticipation of the answer to this all-important question. It would confirm or deny a hundred theories, and it might create an entirely new way to view time and space.

"I am alive."

"Eleven million years ago?" Rip asked, astonished. "*And* now?"

"Yes," Crying Man said.

The silence in the room seemed to echo a cosmic void as all held their breath, trying to force their brains to absorb this information.

"How is that possible?"

But he already knew the answer. Time is a funny thing.

"The understanding of time, in your era, is badly limited," Crying Man said. "But that is something you will work on. More important is the view of the future you have seen. It is something you can change, and you *must* change, because if you destroy your future, you not only destroy us, but you will erase all that has come before. You will never have been."

"Can't you help us?"

"The Spheres are our help," Crying Man said. "They are all we can do, but they should be enough. We have shown you *everything*."

"We may fail," Rip admitted.

Crying Man nodded. "A group of my people have left. They have been gone a very long time," Crying Man said, looking even sadder. "There was disagreement about how to save human life on Earth." He walked around the room, looking at each person as he spoke. "The group who left, we call them 'the Imazes'. They believed the answers were out there, in space."

As he said the word, the Spheres projected stars all around them so it felt as if they were standing on a small moon looking into the vastness of the universe.

"What happened to them?" Savina asked.

"Another group believed the answers were to be found in the physical world on Earth," Crying Man said, ignoring Savina's question. "Almost half of my people were Imazes, most of the thinkers, the ones with the greatest imaginations, and they all went away. The ones who remained, we worked on the Ohsahs project and lived a life of searching."

"For what?" Rip asked.

"Answers," Crying Man answered. "A way. For the Imazes. For you."

"Did you ever see the Imazes again?" Savina asked.

"Some returned every so often, durations equal to fifty of your years, and then it came to be longer periods."

"Where did they go?" Savina asked.

Crying Man nodded, as if he knew she had guessed.

"The multiverse," she said. "They went to different universes?"

"Yes."

"How?" one of the other scientists asked.

"You have not figured it out yet, but you will. You are on the right track with gravitational waves and time-shift points."

"Did the Imazes find a way?" Rip asked. "To save us?"

Crying Man shook his head. "Not yet."

"Have they encountered other intelligent life?" one of the scientists asked.

"You have been looking for others," Crying Man said. "You think beings from other planets have come, but it is my people, the Imazes, the ones you call *Cosegans*, who have been coming. They have returned throughout your history. They have helped you, trying to show you a different way, a way to change you, to *save* you."

"How could they come over millions of years?" Rip, ever the archaeologist, asked.

Crying Man looked at him with the tired patience of a parent watching a child trying to take his first steps. "Time . . . let go of what you think that means."

"So all the crazy theories of ancient aliens visiting Earth are true, except they weren't really aliens at all. They were actually us?"

Crying Man nodded. "Look at the sequence which starts the Spheres. It shows each major visit since the beginning. As the visits get further into the distance, the range is longer, and they return less. It started out millions of years ago with exact times. Eventually, it became specific dates, then a range of days, weeks, months, years, decades, and finally this one—sometime within a hundred years, but that's not the important part." Crying Man looked at Savina. "The Imazes are coming only one more time, between now and 2120. It is hard to know when, but it will be their last visit . . . ever."

"Why?"

"Because after that, it is over," Crying Man said. "No more chances."

A heavy hush fell over the room. Although they sat and stood among the stars, their faces were all clearly illuminated, and they exchanged glances ranging from confusion, to concern, to outright terror.

Rip finally spoke. "So humanity might have less than one hundred years left?"

"Or *far less* than that," Gale added.

Crying Man nodded. "People should stop looking at how the world is, and start looking at what it can become."

The Conversation

"I have a dream for the future," Booker began. "It's a place where we live together, not as members of different races, religions, or even nations, but as citizens of Earth, as creators of reality, an incredibly beautiful, harmonious, and dynamic reality."

"I've seen that place in the future of which you speak," Savina said. "But I've also seen the nightmare from which you run. Where will we wind up? It's a simple choice, or really many simple choices that we each make every day, with all of our decisions. Do we go toward the nightmare, or the dream?"

"In some ways, they're the same," Gale added. "The seeds of the dream have always been contained within the soul, and the nightmare has long been carried in the personality, the part of us that feels fear. So we experience both. There is no way to avoid it, but which one becomes real is something we can control."

"Because when we learn where we came from, we will discover where we're going," Rip suggested. "And we now know that in the stars, there is the limitless possibility for everything."

Epilogue

Rip, Gale, Savina, and the six scientists took the information given to them by Crying Man and used the two Spheres to adjust the current world. Early experiments with "tweaks" to the past using time-shifts were promising. They managed to keep a glimmer of the Cosegans' world alive, but Crying Man came less and less as he dealt with the growing crisis facing his people due to mistakes in our present time.

Booker, utilizing Cosegan technology and his private army, along with occasional help from DIRT, managed to keep the NSA, CIA, and other agencies away long enough that the Spheres could be used to work on the immediate urgent threats.

Rip and Savina made the report to Booker.

"We have at least temporarily averted the Death Divinations," Rip said.

"Climate destabilization, World War III, and most importantly, the horrific plague no longer shows in future forecasts," Savina added.

However, the Aylantik Foundation continued. The elite, steered by greed and fear, grew in power. Their Phoenix Initiative, although buried for now, still hung as a constant threat. The Foundation had the power to change the future at any time, and they would eventually use it.

"The future is a fragile place," Booker said.

But each moment of "time" that the Sphere team and Inner Movement bought meant they were a moment closer to when the Imazes would return to help one last time.

END OF BOOK FOUR

Eighty years after Cosega, the search is on for the Justar Journal. Discover THE LAST LIBRARIAN (book one of the Justar Journal) available now.

A Note from the Author

Thank you so much for reading my book!

Please help - If you enjoyed it, please consider leaving a quick review (even a few words) on Amazon.com. Reviews are the greatest way to help an author. And please, tell your friends!

I'd love to hear from you – Questions, comments, whatever. Email me at my website www.BrandtLegg.com. I'll definitely respond (within a few days).

Join my Inner Circle - If you want to be the first to hear about my new releases, advance reads, occasional news, and more, please join my Inner Circle at my website www.BrandtLegg.com

About the Author

Brandt Legg is a former child prodigy who turned a hobby into a multi-million-dollar empire. At eight, Legg's father died suddenly, plunging his family into poverty. Two years later, while suffering from crippling migraines, he started in business. National media dubbed him the "Teen Tycoon," but by the time he reached his twenties, the high-flying Legg became ensnarled in the financial whirlwind of the junk bond eighties, lost his entire fortune ... and ended up serving time in federal prison for financial improprieties. Legg emerged, chastened and wiser, one year later, and began anew in retail and real estate. In the more than two decades since, his life adventures have led him through magazine publishing, a newspaper column, photography, FM radio, CD production, and concert promotion. His books have excited hundreds of thousands of readers around the world (see below for a list of titles available). For more information, or to contact him, please visit his website www.BrandtLegg.com. He loves to hear from readers and always responds!

Books by Brandt Legg

Outview (Inner Movement, book 1)
Outin (Inner Movement, book 2)
Outmove (Inner Movement, book 3)
The Complete Inner Movement trilogy

Cosega Search (Cosega Sequence, book 1)
Cosega Storm (Cosega Sequence, book 2)
Cosega Shift (Cosega Sequence, book 3)
Cosega Sphere (Cosega Sequence, book 4)
The Cosega Sequence (books 1-3)

The Last Librarian (Justar Journal, book 1)
The Lost TreeRunner (Justar Journal, book 2)
The List Keepers (Justar Journal, book 3)
The Complete Justar Journal

Acknowledgements

Most of us have had years when everything changed; I've been fortunate enough to have had many of those years. I'm grateful for this interesting and ever-changing life, but this year has been different, beyond all the others. This year time stopped . . . and began again.

The Cosega Sequence was originally only supposed to be three books, but so many of you, a shocking number actually, contacted me asking for more. The requests flattered and ultimately challenged me. I could not refuse, so I deviated from my normal writing schedule, putting a planned series of political thrillers on hold. It was exciting to delve back into the Cosega world; I hope you find the same magic.

Once I made the decision to publish Sphere, I expected it to be ready in April. However, as I mentioned, this year has been unlike any other, and time is a funny thing. In either case, you are reading this now due to the help of some wonderful people. Roanne Legg, who reads first and toughest, and this year did it while doing everything else. Barbara Blair, who always tries not to be too easy on me, but usually is anyway. Bonnie Brown Koeln, my last reader who always leaves my work even better. And finally to Teakki, who patiently waited to find out more about not only Rip and Gale, but rather Frank, Joe, and Chet, until I finished writing each day.

CPSIA information can be obtained
at www.ICGtesting.com
Printed in the USA
FSOW02n1003310317
32567FS